Homeland, A Comedy

✯✯✯✯

by James Hufferd

HOMELAND, A COMEDY

Published by: Progressive Press,
PO Box 12834, Palm Desert, Calif. 92255,
www.ProgressivePress.com

Published May 5th, 2012
ISBN 1-61577-803-9, EAN 978-1-61577-803-4
74,000 words on 182 pages, 6 x 9 in.
Distribution: Lightning Source
List Price: $15.95

BISAC Subject Area Codes
FIC037000 FICTION / Political
HUM006000 HUMOR / Topic / Political
POL030000 POLITICAL SCIENCE / Government / National

... IN WHICH WE FIND OUT

WHAT HAPPENS TO OUR

HOMELAND

WHEN THEY OFFER TO

BUY THE U.S.A. OUTRIGHT —

AND OUR PRESIDENT

GOES ALONG FOR THE RIDE!

To Stephanie~

. . . . that it might not happen after all

Table of Contents

Chapter One – The Main Event

Atlanta, Georgia, August 13, 2032 (Friday)

It was all so simple. Yet, it just could be the biggest and most monumental opportunity ever. *So very simple. And yet...*

"You're proposing to *buy* the United States?"

Senator Peter Aloysius Gossens, the Republican nominee for president, had to put down his sweaty glass of mint lemonade. It was not at all what he expected from this meeting, which Herschel "Old Hen" Henry, his handler and chief pollster, had billed as "a casual little tête-à-tête." Now he regretted turning down the walnut-paneled conference room with its presidential-looking leather armchairs for the back veranda of his Peach Tree Street campaign headquarters. A man contemplating the fate of the "free" world couldn't be expected to think clearly in a plastic pool chair.

Edward Lambent of The Company cleared his throat. "Not in that straightforward a way, no." He leaned back in his lounger, showing his inimitable half-smile, lips curling, revealing just the gleaming tips of his eyeteeth. "Of course, we already own more of the country than anyone else could ever *dream* of. And, as you might know, what we *are* proposing to do is not even unprecedented. Remember, after all, that the new Federal Government assumed the unpayable debts of the early states. Remember that, Gossens? The *colonies* back then... in order to gain their support for the Constitution and form the United States back in 1787?"

Gossens raised an eyebrow. It was news to him.

"Now, almost two-hundred and fifty years later," Lambent continued, "all real accumulations of money transfer at the corporate level, the level of sovereignty these days. These days, we of the corporate world of course pay for and see to the majority of the constituent staffing of the government in both the legislative and executive branches. And they, of course, between them, staff the judicial branch as well. And we have, in fact, done that for quite a few years. Now, we simply want to control *officially*, and *predictably*, what we through our agents already do control as a matter of fact. Which is the governance of this controlling country."

Gossens still couldn't quite wrap his mind around Lambent's proposal. "You say, since you've *paid* for it already really?"

"Yes, oh well, yes. Please don't be so naïve, Senator Gossens. Surely you are aware that we of The Company are responsible for installing the last number of presidents as well as many of the key members of Congress."

Actually, he wasn't sure he was aware of any such thing. But he wasn't going to let Lambent know that. He, like most people, had only the dimmest knowledge of The Company, or as it was also known, Rassole Corporation, after the largest of its divisions. Gossens vaguely remembered a somewhat subdued NNN report on The Company (originally known as Rassole Corp.). Apparently, that entity had been quietly acquiring and forming linkages among companies until it had grown to become, in fact, the largest and most powerful conglomerate in the world.

"We back whoever is the most useful candidate for us," Lambent explained, "of whatever majority party – yours or, occasionally, the other. Since there's not enough difference to slide even a *hair* in between them."

Again, Lambent bared just the points of his eyeteeth in a smile that didn't appear at all friendly. Gossens involuntarily shuddered.

"There's actually very little doubt about who's really calling the shots, Senator Gossens. The political arena has its uses. Countries and governments count. But, the *corporate* level – meaning multi *trillion*-dollar finance and banks – is the level of sovereignty these days."

A funny thing was that the candidate wanted to protest that there was undoubtedly more to it than just the purchase of power by the most wealthy. But, he didn't quite know how to say it. Was old Hen aware of this new proposed deal?

"Don't misunderstand me, Mr. Gossens. You in politics and in government do serve an important function. The Company has not forgotten the superb service you've rendered us. It admirably serves *both* sides! But don't forget that there is a reason the government has absolutely nothing now to spend for services or health care or education, or upkeep on highways, bridges, space missions, safety, or anything else. That reason is, of course, *politics.* The government has been far too, shall we say, *accommodating* in its efforts to pacify individual constituencies.

"And now, it finds itself in a quagmire of debt. Why? Well, it goes back to Bush, Jr. and Mr. Obama. They spent more money than there even actually *was* and took an awful risk; that didn't pan out too well, you know. Not that Barack didn't *try* to retrieve the whole thing… he *did... valiantly!* Almost *violently*, *vehemently* even if you read the history books. And it worked, like a Band-Aid always does. The indebtedness had just become far too large, and it has literally snowballed since. This is exactly where we of The Company can step in now and be of assistance, to retrieve it *for good and all*. Happily, we are in a position to assume the vast, accumulated debt in which the country is drowning and, at very long last, completely *eliminate* it."

Lambent sat bolt upright, planting his expensive loafers on the terra cotta tiles. "Just think of it, Senator Gossens. In one fell swoop we can together *solve* the most devastating financial debacle this country has ever seen. And by 'we,' Senator, I mean we of The Company and *you*."

"Me?"

"Naturally, we'd retain control. But we need a point-man out front – someone capable of implementing our plans, all of which are 100% beneficial to the people of this great land. It's a tremendous honor, Senator Gossens, to be chosen as The Company's candidate at this point."

It *was* an honor, Gossens conceded. The Company was one of the most powerful entities in the world, if not *the* most powerful. But still, a bid to buy the United States of America? That was really outrageous! *Preposterous!*

Wasn't it, after all?

"I see you're still not convinced," Lambent said. "Allow me to be of assistance. You are no doubt aware of the headlines in every major newspaper these days."

Actually, he wasn't too much into all that doom and gloom. He didn't like reading the papers. He nodded to Lambent in a way that he hoped appeared thoughtful, concerned.

"Alas, the present total government freeze-up, its inability to restore the country's economic health or even operate on a subsistence level, is, deservingly, *the* subject right now. Why, we could bomb Switzerland, for instance, back to the Dark Ages and no one would bat an eye, so absorbed are they in blaming the government for failing to plump up their retirement funds. Let's get right to the point, Senator Gossens. You are not going to defeat Abe Gole unless you can solve the economic crisis – there's absolutely no way. Otherwise, he'll win in a walk."

Gossens' already florid cheeks flared crimson at this. "I know no such..."

"—Forgive me for my lack of discretion, Senator Gossens. Please remember that we want *you* in the office, in power. You have been carefully selected. The Company believes it is your ideas that are most in accord with our own, and that together, all of your – and our – ideas will prevail."

Lambent resumed a supine position on the pool lounger, but Gossens could see that every nerve and synapse in the man was taut, ready to fire.

He had no doubt that the stories about this unusual and somewhat terrifying man – having to do with his having studied and revived "the claw," an old '50s wrestling hold that permitted him to grasp someone's wrist and effortlessly throw it out of joint, in which condition it would remain until he himself released it – were true. It was just like the man to do something like that. It was also said that he could do much the same thing with the gear selector of any vehicle, rendering it inoperable, undrivable. And those were only a couple of the tales, which only got wilder, but were probably most of them true.

"Now, you haven't been subjected to the severe shakedown serious presidential candidates normally are… at least, not as yet," Lambent said evenly. "Mainly, because we see you as already one with us. But that remains to be seen, Senator. Currently, you have our full support, but should you begin to stray from what The Company deems best, circumstances could necessitate an adjustment. Which might not be at all pleasant for you, unfortunately." His blue eyes had never penetrated more piercingly.

Gossens trembled involuntarily just a bit, stunned by Lambent's hard-as-iron control and logic as much as any threat that he carried. Solve the unsolvable debt problem and rule – or lose! How could he disagree with that?

"In fact, Senator Gossens," Lambent went on, "we can transform *everything* by this total obligation-discharging transaction, bringing the country all at one great bound out of the debt mess it's gotten itself into over the years, back to an unprecedented, unburdened level of dynamism and health. Just think of the great part you'll be playing in history!"

Lambent really had a point. He, Gossens, was excited to see that he would be integral to the plan's success. The Company was nearly all-powerful, but they couldn't do it without ol' Pete Gossens, the "shambling cracker from Podunk," as his detractors had uncharitably styled him. He wished everyone who'd ever doubted him, who'd accused him of being a dim bulb, an ignoramus, a baboon in a suit, dumber than a dumb string-bean vegetable – including his daddy, God rest his soul – were around to see this! He *was* starting to appreciate the powerful simplicity of Lambent's plan. Plus, there was the matter of beating Abe Gole.

"And then, the government, *as reorganized*, of course," Lambent went on, "can once again begin to serve, more efficiently and inexpensively than ever before, the needs of our mutual clients, or what they have been called up to now, the *citizens*, the little people. The fiscal crisis will pass, freeing up the country's wealth and talents. And, rest assured, there's not a soul, from shore to shore, that won't be relieved at having the great burden that was considered impossible, *lifted*. Indeed, it will be an escape from the otherwise unsolvable trouble we all find ourselves in, and we of The Company regard it our absolute patriotic duty and responsibility to provide it, since we alone have the means."

"But, with my assistance," Gossens said.

"Of course."

"But then, *you'll* control the country?"

"But again, we already *do.* As you just agreed."

"And so, that's the idea you want me to carry to the country, for voter approval in this election?"

As appealing and logical as Lambert's proposal was, there were implications and hazards to consider.

"The idea of rescue, yes. As the gist of your platform, now that you've won the nomination. You... or, if not you, your *opponent* perhaps. If you win, the country will find itself completely unburdened by debt for the first time since 1837, that is, in very nearly two hundred years. Old Hickory Jackson would be proud. You will be the man out front this time, a national hero already at your inauguration. People will thank *us* for doing it, too, eventually, but first and foremost, *you!* And then we can get on to solving other problems and real challenges."

Struggling to gather his thoughts, Senator Gossens stared at the newly watered lawn behind his Peach Tree Street headquarters. He strode purposefully a short distance across the damp grass and pushed up a ridge of rust-red earth next to the cobblestone path with the shiny black toe of his boot. He hoped he was casting a contemplative, presidential figure. Personally, he was ready to sign on, and his running mate, Governor Ben Weck, would be no problem, as he was a supremely adaptable yes-man, but how could he frame it for the country? It was going to take a heap of brainpower and south Georgia charm to bring off.

Whatever it took, he *had* to succeed. The deal could turn him from a likely also-ran into the most dynamic and prepared president ever in history, credited with having solved at a stroke the biggest economic problem any nation had ever faced. Perhaps just as important, it could *redeem* the country from the absolutely intransigent bondage it had gotten itself into by getting mixed up with foreign, mainly East Asian, financial interests. Further, it did have a certain appeal for anyone who believed in business, which was America's business, if he could frame it that way. Democracy simply meant too many cooks spoiling the stew!

He bucked up and stared into Ed Lambent's steely-blue eyes. "OK," he said evenly, crossing back to the veranda. Lambent stood, and though he,

Gossens, towered over this man whose singular aspect struck him not as a personification of The Company but more like a column of compact, cold steel – conscious, knowing steel. This gargantuan, this mega-man Lambent seemed much larger than he actually was. Peter Gossens knew he would have to speak now before his sense of calm left him and his voice dwindled down to a whisper. "OK, Mr. Lambent," Gossens said. "You have yourself a deal." He offered his big hand and winced involuntarily at Lambent's vice-like, but velvety, grip.

"Wonderful, then," Lambent said. "We'll get back to you with a plan for integrating the idea into a common message and coordinating it operationally in the next few days."

Unused to speaking in what he had learned were "process terms," and pleased with his cool performance with the renowned Lambent, Peter Gossens shambled back into his headquarters. Just inside the door, Herschel Henry was waiting for him.

"A very brave and good choice, sir," said Henry.

When and why had old Hen been tipped off in advance on the substance of this meeting? Gossens wondered. Ah well, details, details!

"Hen, fasten your seat belt. We're going to have us a country to run."

"Fired up, ready to go, sir."

They strode through the kitchen to meet with the campaign staff.

Lambent departed graciously, alone with his driver, moving back toward downtown traffic in The Company's sky-blue Lexus, blending seamlessly into the blue calm of the afternoon.

Chapter Two – Launch of a Different Vessel

August 16, 2032

The Democratic presidential nominee, ex-Vice President and former Senator Abe Gole from southwest Virginia, who had been – due to a political family pedigree and a weak opponent – a rare member of the Senate from his party to be elected by the venerable Commonwealth, woke up alone at 6:00 a.m. in the big over-soft bed in the Presidential Suite of the Hyatt Imperial in Philadelphia to the pleasing baritone presentation of a news digest assembled specifically to awaken and at the same time inform him, prepared by a top-name reportorial firm, Alexis News.

As the familiar opening two bars of a modern symphony faded, candidate Gole heard Don Danton's stentorian voice say something that seemed to be straight out of the confused mists of the dreamland he had departed only seconds before: "Republican presidential nominee Peter Gossens has announced in a press release today that he will be touting in the next twelve hours a new main plank of the campaign platform he is to unveil officially at his party's convention opening tomorrow.

"He is proposing, if elected president, to endorse the offer reportedly made last Tuesday of the universal holding company, now known as the Rassole Corporation, the managerial division of the giant consortium known as The Company, to purchase outright all of the assets of the Government of the United States. If the offer is accepted, The Company will assume the daily operations of the country and immediately liquidate its debt, which has ballooned to $19.27 trillion in the latest official calculation. As is widely known, most of the national debt is held by the government-controlled markets of Eastern Asia, and its servicing in recent months has completely overwhelmed and disabled the U.S. government, preventing it from spending on anything else."

The inimical voice of Danton continued for some time to spell out the known details of the amazing offer and its apparent acceptance, including the fact that not a single elected official or spokesman from either party had yet been willing to comment on it for the record. Abe Gole's usually suave and astute, but now stunned political mind took in no more than the content of the first two sentences and disregarded the rest. Buy the country? They're going to buy the country? Could this possibly be real? That bumbling south Georgia cracker actually has the audacity to *sell the country*?

He held his breath for nearly a whole minute as he took the concept in and rolled it over in his mind. And suddenly he smiled. Let Gossens try and sell the country! Let him! The people of the United States would never ratify an end to the county's sovereignty – *never*. In fact, if the Republican chiefs had any sense whatsoever, they would bump Gossens from the ticket posthaste! He wouldn't be able to carry even a single state with such a platform as that.

Gole guffawed aloud as he rose from the bed. Let Gossens create his own destruction. Let him! His own path to the White house was now virtually insured. He smiled, even preened as he eyed his wide figure not-too-critically in the full-length mirror at bedside before stepping into a waiting steam shower. He wouldn't even have to say or do anything. Gossens had just greased the skids for the Dems' victory, right into the White House.

"*Yip-a-de-doo-dah!*" Gole sang as he lathered up.

So, to the daily chagrin of reporters and pundits alike, Gole never directly answered even one question regarding what was easily the single biggest campaign issue in a century, perhaps since the Great Depression. He didn't have to. He only had to show up from time to time and flash a winning presidential grin, and the presidency would be his.

His advisors and handlers saw the matter precisely as he did, not wanting, or, they thought, needing to risk a misstep. Gole and his wife, Jewell, began discussing, jokingly at first, what breed would be the most symbolic, of them, of the country – or was it *suitable* to think in such terms? – for the country's First Dog.

* * *

Republican candidate Gossens, meanwhile, felt equally assured of victory, and spent many leisurely hours on the veranda of his headquarters imagining the tasks that lay ahead of him. In light of the unprecedented transition of power that was about to happen, his upcoming duties were a little difficult to pin down, but he understood that his first responsibility would be to legitimize the legally changed governmental arrangement with the people and institutions of the country.

But what would the actual changes involve? Would they be so behind-the-scenes that an ordinary citizen would not even notice the difference, aside from the glorious benefit of freeing the economy from its enslavement to the onerous debt and obligation to East Asian creditors? There would still be a President and a Congress, after all, and all elected officials would continue to serve, at least through the duration of their terms. He had exacted that provision from The Company, through the intervention of Edward Lambert, who continued to act as intercessor between himself and the upper echelons of The Company, who apparently were too burdened with working out the details of the transaction to be bothered. After that, The Company would exercise *some* say, as he understood it – probably quite a bit, and *formally* now, instead of through less-direct control as before through financing and some influence on legislation – but exactly what that would entail was still to be hammered out. Lambent assured him that The Company would grant him any and all authority as long as their interests, which he assured Gossens were completely in accordance with his own, were being served.

Every now and again Gossens became slightly concerned about the enormous power The Company would wield, but it was nothing a few minutes of deep breathing (a benefit from the bit of Yoga he'd learned back in Waycross) followed by a weak gin and tonic couldn't assuage. Plus, Gossens told himself, there *was* such a thing as economic democracy, meaning that The Company would certainly not want to alienate its domestic customer base by introducing shocks, a course which would presumably be most imprudent business-wise. In the end, the most important thing was that he, Peter Aloysius Gossens, the soon-to-be-President-elect of the United States, had gotten the country moved permanently off its disastrous and enervating debt impalement, in absolutely the only way possible. From this point on the country would be bounding freely into greener pastures. And he would be the hero of it all, claiming enough political cred, capital, and arrows in his quiver to do, well, *anything*. Now, he could do anything!

The alternative was just squeaking by in the election (that is, if he could be elected at all, which, it hurt to admit, was doubtful), re-dividing the populace, and being – no, *remaining* – bound by grievous, enervating obligations to foreign and corporate financial backers. Taking that course would drain his power, narrow his possibilities, and crimp his, or any other conceivable president's, latitude. With The Company's offer, however, he would be able to *do* things. He would be able to quickly complete, for instance, the privatization of prisons, schools, highways, and airports, and the security and defense forces of the nation, all things on which The Company would have stood squarely behind him in any case.

One thing he wasn't 100% clear on was The Company's views on religion. He'd have to make a note to ask Lambent about that at their next meeting, because matters of faith were at the top of his agenda. He considered it his personal mission to go as far as possible toward demolishing the last remaining vestige of a wall between the religious establishment and governmental power, finally squeezing out doubters, nay-sayers, and spiritual dead-enders who dealt in mindless loud complaints and obstruction and cost too much money and energy to have endlessly to overcome. The country must be *positive* – a realm of *believers*, not of doubters!

"*One way ahead!*" he said aloud.

That was his campaign slogan. And in all ways, it fit. Those who had expected a mild-mannered, malleable and fuzzy Georgia peach in the White House were soon to be confronted with what his fraternity friends back at Athens had endearingly dubbed him: "the Bulldog." He intended to make The "Lambent Protocol," as he called it, go through if it was the last thing he did. It was the natural course; it just made sense in today's world. It followed. And the country would follow, too.

* * *

Still, a little extra precaution wouldn't hurt. And even though Gossens thought he had a slam-dunk plan, Lambent's firm assertion that he could not win without the backing of The Company rankled. After all, what did that stuffed shirt Abe Gole have that he didn't? To ensure that victory would indeed be his, he dispatched a super-secret three-man team to turn up any and all dirt on that sometimes unpredictable chucklehead Gole. A man that dull in appearance – that *geeky* – was bound to have bones practically dancing in his closet.

And *skeletons* there were, aplenty! It seems that as a young journalist, Abe Gole had penned a filthy novel entitled *The Husband-Elect*. Its amoral protagonist was interpreted by reviewers at the time as a thinly veiled stand-in for a rapacious younger Abe Gole himself. The actual book was said to have been a bit dry, but the word circulated was, nonetheless, that it detailed and gave vent to his appetites for depraved and creative liaisons with bevies of wayward femmes. And, perhaps somewhere in its 600-odd pages, it did. The tabloids picked up the story and ran with it, and within a week, half the nation considered Gole a sick pup. It didn't matter at all that the book was probably 100% fiction. In the wake of such sensational insinuations, he found it hard to defend himself.

More troublesome, or welcome to Gossens, because it was current, was Gole's increasingly-reported fraternization with the questionable group of liberal senators and congresspersons centered around Senator "Drinker" Topel. Apparently, he and the gregarious "Drinker" were becoming quite chummy. Gossens didn't know what they were up to, but he felt deep in his south Georgia bones that it had to be no good. At the moment, however, none of that mattered ; all that mattered was that Gole's name was linked inextricably to a left-wing extravagant lush.

And finally, November 2 came and the nation rocketed out of its long complacency and resignation to futility: a record of over two hundred million Americans (including the number of early-voting quasi-absentees, whose votes no one seemed to know quite what to do with) marched to the polls. Every poll, for days, indicated that the people of America were diametrically split, with Gossens retaining only the slimmest of leads.

Then, the very last-minute opinion polls showed Gole, the Democrat, creeping up and closing the gap with the Republican Gossens and finally eclipsing him by a single point. Predictions across the board shifted, prompting the pundits to declare that Americans would, in the final analysis, not barter away their sovereignty as a nation, even with their solvency and financial freedom at stake. The exit polls indicated that the question would be settled in favor of the status quo under the going-on-two-hundred-and-fifty-year-old federal Constitution.

But then the almost-Vice President Ben Weck – until then, unanimously considered no more than a nullity – had the presence of mind to demand a recount, and in a resounding turn of events not even Hollywood could have scripted, a computer glitch affecting the outcome in the states of Florida and South Dakota was discovered. The numbers were checked and rechecked, with the results finally showing that the Republican won the election, by 52 to 48 percent, carrying 30 states. Bells rang and tolled joyfully at one end of all the cities and towns, while a spattering of historically-literate souls in the America concentrated mainly in the other half of most of its towns and countryside slumped into a deep and endless ache of mourning and dread. For, what they had known and counted on all of their lives as the core of their country had slipped away beyond redemption in one single, gloomy day.

And the day following the announcement, the Dow closed under 17,000 for the first time in five years.

In the endless post-mortems conducted round the clock by all the media, it was concluded that given the Democrats' (in particular, candidate Gole's) refusal to take a position on the debt sale issue, its champion, Peter Gossens, in the end convinced enough wavering tax-payers to cast their votes for him. An NNN correspondent, Dena Rosen, summed up the election results thusly: "When charged with deciding which was the real, quintessential American document, the majority of the people have chosen the dollar, and consigned the Constitution to a museum."

Others endeavored to expound upon the consequences of the momentous trade-off that had been approved. What, exactly, would it *mean?* Even the opposition admitted that it meant, first and foremost, that the national debt was set to vanish as if by cannibal enzymes, halting abruptly the enormous, compulsive out-hemorrhaging of the nation's money supply. But beyond that, the vexing question of who was in charge began to rise at once. Would it mean civil war? Endless acrimony and bickering? Or unprecedented plenty and prosperity? People protesting and marching in the streets? Or quiet acquiescence with no real change? *Just what?* The country held its collective breath waiting to see would happen.

*   *   *

Whatever was to happen, The Company and Gossens had their work cut out for them. Circumstances impacting the situation of the nation in 2032 included:

The rise of Canada, concurrent with the fall of the Middle East. Here, President Gossens relied on his new favorite historian, Calvin College professor of history and C-Span-featured author Clifton Werz, for his best information. As Werz taught in his 2031 book *Present at the Re-creation*, by the 2030s America and the world had largely "*re-created*." Its long-time dependence on Middle Eastern oil was a thing of the past, as Middle Eastern oil was a thing of the past. America's attention had, accordingly, turned elsewhere. Now, America and many parts of Europe depended on Alberta tar sands oil and Rockies shale oil, both obtained at an astoundingly high production cost, to obtain their fix, as well as Arctic and Antarctic Ocean off-shore oil, bio-fuels, wind power, and the like, in that descending order.

The Canadian lobby was alleged by some, including Werz, to exercise way too much power in Washington for the representative front of a demographically smaller nation, neighbor or not. The Middle East, denatured by the dramatic withdrawal of western interest after the abrupt, sputtering end of its era of oil, now once again lived on overseas investments in its vast wind power, rug sale revenues, dates, figs, caviar, camel culture, hashish, and leather. Archaeological relics and international adventuring and sacred tourism also contributed to its respite at the margins. But, its main experience was neglect, now that its squalid revenues could no longer mount a threat to Israel.

The now generations-past age of terrorism, both genuinely and ingenuously attributed to Middle Eastern sources, was regarded in the Middle East itself as the sort of confused opium dream of a graying generation, ever since the mysteriously unindicted 9/11 suspect (or scapegoat) Osama bin Laden's bones turned up at least two decades earlier. The direction of hapless, weakened Iraq, depleted of its wealth, was still being kicked around like a soccer ball by different national would-be protectors in the region, and mostly ignored by the Americans and other westerners now, and absent from news reports, even though ever-abundant Afghan poppies were still rumored to more than pay the bonuses of western banking executives.

The threat from East-Asian Axis countries, China, Japan, and United Korea had become overreaching and imperialistic, according to Professor Werz's assessment, and President Gossens readily agreed. Their intentions were distrusted and guarded against by the modest Americans, right-thinking Europeans, and other erstwhile friendly allies of the American administration. American entrepreneurial interest in brokering Central Asian oil, which was still fueling the rising East Asian industrial powers, was keen, the Russians having become the leading rivals of the Americans as its foreign purveyors.

Regarding labor and production issues, the African lands, sporting horrific economic conditions, were once again, as in the long-distant past, regarded as a logical source of lucrative, tractable labor. The majority of non-skilled and lower-skilled service sector jobs were being filled by "new immigrants," provided by brokers and conducted from Africa in levies by special fleets. This brand new petty laboring class was being paid at a rate only a trifle under the cost of importing the produce and largely hand-spun textiles their work had begun to provide. The cities were becoming largely service hubs.

Meanwhile, virtually all remaining domestic manufacturing tasks were now performed by imported Japanese robots. Robots and outsourcing had rendered the long-troublesome urban working class all but non-existent, the survivors finding grudging refuge out on the labor-intensive micro-farms. Manufacturing employment involved, for the first time, less than one per cent of all human employment.

In the realm of public institutions: Work proceeded by the end of the year, in light of the fresh mandate delivered by the election, to transfer schools and prisons still under public management to fully-constituted private contractors, as the newly-elected government was preparing to channel a very sizable chunk of the huge revenues suddenly liberated from exclusively servicing the public national debt in their direction.

Meanwhile, the popular campaign led by many church leaders to shut down public libraries as decadent and transfer their holdings out was steadily gaining momentum. Their books, rated and accordingly availability-graded on the basis of "truth-value," were going into privately held collections availed through the sale of pricey family and individual memberships to those still determined to read. Plumb-quality books in private collections were sold to the book "commodifiers," as they were called. Church leaders were thus able to reduce access to knowledge strictly to the "responsible," those who would presumably not be unduly tainted by it, and in turn, people were able to obtain funds to pay their mortgages and purchase food.

The food supply. Displaced native-born workers were shunted increasingly toward and being re-trained to successfully operate private market gardens of 12 or 40 acres' extent, depending on their financial wherewithal, in the vast vacuous rural zone. The bulk of the former agricultural lands on which grain, beef, and other bulk food and fuel commodities had been grown were converted to accommodate mass imports of those commodities now more economically produced abroad, the cost of labor having become cheaper than either technology or the cost of importing for the small consumables. Working-age poorer residents of inner cities were bussed daily by new private, publicly-subsidized transport lines to participate as salaried day gardeners.

As ex-President Hobson from Michigan, who served in the 2020s, was famously quoted as saying (though perhaps inaccurately), "Once there were farmers and workers. Then, there was still the *idea* of farmers, but there weren't any farmers. Now, there won't be any workers." Interviewed a few weeks after the election, he had tellingly added, "There will be farmers again now, just a different kind." And he added, trying to be ironic, "But the only other thing is, we don't shoot them."

"And, there won't be voters," Abe Gole added to himself when he heard the interview.

And *they* were America's plurality. Again Gossens turned to a Calvin College professor, Dr. Heinholz, to keep him updated on religious matters, his own views being in accord with the stated motto of the college: "One World, One Christ, One Way!" Besides the dreaded Islam, the major perceived threat to Gossens's idea of Christendom in 2032 was the growing, simplistic "Branch Religion," which had crossed the Atlantic from England and was making inroads as, some thought, a more credible alternative. "Branchists" stopped just short of deifying King Arthur, whose tenets the new creed was said to personify. The followers of said Branchism believed that, just as in the instance of the storied Arthur, whenever anyone died, her or his being simply branched off into a newly minted copy of the full universe projected by the person's mind, such being, after all, nothing more than a mental construct in any case. One died in one's former universe and continued onto the next one, unaware that death had even occurred. Hard-core Christians inevitably slammed this new, brash theology with singular vehemence, because, if true, malefactors ("sinners") would never receive their just deserts. And the incoming government, accordingly, slammed it, too. As soon as Gossens took office he meant to outlaw the printing or proliferation of any Branchist materials, explicit or not, and restrict its extant literature to its current members.

And of course, the economy bore telling changes as well. Besides the obvious, overwhelming issue of the excruciating debt and its expiation, a current sensation with a growing few was an idea for an alternative world economy originated in a little book published privately two years before by Eduard Chelsington, a humble Manx shepherd, entitled *Bright Pebbles*. Mr.

Chelsington had gotten the idea, he said, while bedding down his flock one night on a pebbly beach near Stanley, the Isle of Man, and ruminating on the circumstance he was induced to consider by a C-TV documentary, *to wit* that most of the world's wealth was locked up in computerized balance sheets accessible only to a mere handful of otherwise practically worthless idle rich dolts, and backed by nothing tangible, while over a billion people were starving and endured miserable lives for lack of funds.

His prescription was elemental – indeed, simpler than that. He would have different-colored pebbles found abundantly in nature serve as money. The pebbles' qualifying characteristics would, of course, have to be standardized scientifically, with the relative instance of the different colors and sizes inventoried by a sampling and census. Rough and moderately-tinted rocks, broken chards, and boulders would not figure in, only smooth "True Pebbles" of a standard size range. Once the proper proportions were established and values were assigned, the bright opaque red and yellow, blue, green, black, beige, white, lavender, pink, brown, and orange examples certified as "True Pebbles" would be universally-accepted as legal tender, regardless of where they were found. Workers and pensioners everywhere would be paid in pebbles, and thus everyone would have tangible assets. And a certain equity would obtain among nations.

Henceforth, no one would ever need to starve if they could but look around them and find a few pebbles. And there would be no unemployment among the able-bodied. Banks would have warehouses full of bins of True Pebbles, and people could borrow until they managed to come up with sufficient funds themselves. People could conveniently carry enough of the common currency around in bags for their daily needs, and mail in packets to pay their bills.

Rich institutions and individuals would be given a limited period of time to convert their holdings into pebbles by offering incentives to the public to turn over some of what they had found. And, since certifiably True Pebbles, like everything else in nature, would be in more-or-less finite supply, newly-manufactured ones, with the issuing government's stamp affixed, would be re-seeded here and there periodically to assure continued availability to expand and refresh the money supply. An international treaty would limit emissions and, hence, gross inequity and inflation.

A society known as the World Bright Pebbles Federalists was already at work, through lobbying and petitions, to influence congresses, parliaments, and chambers of deputies around the globe to enact the initiative. Monmouth County, TN, and Tulare, CA, had already endorsed it as policy, though no national politicians had yet unequivocally endorsed it, and the chairman of the Fed had denounced it in no uncertain terms as "communistic." (Mr. Gossens, on one known occasion, indicated his agreement with the Fed chief on the matter, while Abe Gole withheld comment). The religiously-inclined, including the new President in their number, made nervous by the prospect of a social order shift, had a ready response that had already become a cliché: that people shouldn't go around scouring the ground for pebbles, but should, more practically, look to the sky for deliverance.

But PEBBLE POWER placards could be seen on the outskirts of some recent rallies, even though Eduard Chelsington was not a known figure personally, and had never consented to an interview outside his home parish, reportedly due to threats of violence.

Gossens, true to form, came through more vividly in an interview before taking office with the observation that "domination by the rich is natural and is not to be trifled with, because it's their money."

* * *

In December of 2032, a month after the election that, for all practical purposes, ended constitutional democracy, demonstrators began to fill the downtowns of major cities, primarily in the Northeast and on the West Coast, in response to rumors that large, less-populated parts of the distant interior (ironically, little-represented among the demonstrators), which were known to habitually absorb more federal funds than they provided in revenue, were to be cut off from direct representation and full citizenship under the new government.

Some reasoned that one effect of the buy-out (or "sell-out," as the critics of the action were calling it) must of necessity be a suspension of the ballyhooed American rights guarantees. And, if all or parts of distant states were to be effectively excluded from equal participation in the country, where would it stop? Would an ethnic test be imposed next? What of the rumored upcoming suspension of free speech, religious liberty, and the rest? What would become of the residents of the excluded zones? Would they still be considered "Americans" in the usual sense? What, for crying out loud, was the full story as to the cost of restoring economic options to the country? Would America still be America, or more so? Purer and less-hindered? Or, snuffed out?

On December 12, President Gossens took to the podium and the airwaves to explain and reassure the nation that, while remaining passive, was growing more apprehensive by the day. His staff had staged a mock-up of the Oval Office in the auditorium of the DeKalb Memorial Christian Soldiers Charter High School Academy deep in his home grounds expressly for the purpose.

"Friends and fellow-citizens," Gossens said in a noticeably husky, faintly-accented voice, "the conspiracy theories and rumors that have arisen and swirl around all of us are bunk. To attest: if they were true, do you think I could get Governor Weck, my Vice President you elected, from Montana, in the heart of the so-called 'slough-off' zone of the country, to go along? We have a phrase for such conspiracy buffs as those who are spreading such disinformation in south Georgia where I come from: 'Get real!' Meaning, it really isn't true. And, to assure you further, let me remind you that, even without said proviso, Ben Johnson Weck and I both love this country, and I would never allow such a thing to happen, to injure my own beloved country, you can be sure of that. You have my pledge. And, just as soon as those who claim to have leaks on good authority from my administration have divulged to me who the leakers are, we will out them and prosecute them. Because, no leaks or leakers compromising the national interest are ever going to be tolerated, no matter who they may represent or implicate. And you can rest assured that I will run down these particular leakers and throttle them!

"I am about to be your president, and you can rest assured that I will not permit your Constitution, which I have sworn to you to defend, preserve, and protect, to be compromised in any way whatsoever, so help me God. And that is my final word on it.

"As far as the principle of privatization that I believe in, of the schools and the prisons, there is just one reason for that: as we all know, government cannot do anything right. And, I will lead a government that will, according, strive to do less wrong than most. I will see to it that the aspects of our national life are discharged as effectively and efficiently as is possible, even though it hardly is with government, and that with the help of God. And, having said as much, I must roll up my sleeves and get back to work now to protect, preserve, and defend the American people, by God!" His words echoed and seemed to linger on for a moment in the rafters of the gymnasium.

The school choir's ethereal chorus of "The Battle Hymn of the Republic" in turn echoed off the walls, and the lights dimmed on the president-elect still standing ramrod straight at the podium, bearing a look of benevolent determination he'd practiced beforehand in the boys' bathroom. And then, the network's regular programming resumed after at least half a dozen commercials.

In the audience, the nine members of the newly recruited "Travel Team" (informally nicknamed "the Mouseketeers" by some in the establishment media) immediately began comparing notes they'd furiously taken during the president-elect's speech. The Travel Team was employed by the incoming administration's newly created News Without Opinions (NWO) board to feed the media its core stories. The Team consisted of nine of the best and brightest from across the country, their main qualifications being active membership in or leanings toward the Republican party and a perceived willingness to cater (or, as the President once said to his briefers, "crater") to the whims of authority. The President-elect himself, to be sure, had reviewed their dossiers and personally signed off on each of them.

The Travel Team could have been the cast of a sit-com. The most physically striking of their number was a blond belle of undisclosed age from the tiny town of Autry (nicknamed "Blinkenmissit"), Mississippi, accordingly named Sarah "Blink" Dawson. Sarah was innocuous-seeming, by consensus the sweetheart of the group, dear to all, though nobody's close friend, soft-spoken, a lady, mellow in tone, and the most uncerebral.

Fuba "Tex" Thorter, 26, stocky and 5'11," had become the group's unofficial leader. Haling from a sports-mad West Texas family with siblings named Bascaba and Golphe, he was part-Comanche with a smidgen of itinerant Jew blood and had short, brown Brillo-pad hair. He was somewhat taken to animal fetishes, derived from his tribal side, but an inbred sense of caution put him in good stead to advise and lead the little troupe, although a loner.

And then there was Melinda "Beantown" Thalanis, 24, from Beacon Hill, Boston, sometimes called "Iodine" by the others. She was high-strung, tall, fragile-looking, spindly-thin. Tending a little toward the hysterical and whistle-voiced, she could have easily been caricatured. But on the positive side, she was known as a more-than-good writer of copy, and served as a source of accurately remembered background detail, even quotes, for the others when their stories otherwise lacked substance.

Mackenzie "Macko" Wood was the plain Plains daughter of a black land grain farmer and a grade school teacher from Beebeetown, IA. Macko was multi-talented in that she wrote and occasionally pinch-hit as a fill-in broadcaster on the NNN national news, which she delivered as a compilation of small-town happenings. An enthusiastic "people-person," she inevitably bestowed upon her subjects plaudits that exceeded their real standing, though she did so with such a bright smile that no one seemed to care. Further, she was a superb classical flautist who played unannounced for an hour or more on occasion in the Team's secluded bunker.

Luden "Lucian" Bond, 31, a bit of a brainiac, but for all that a suave and decent fellow, was from Bronx, New York; Holly Bronson, a.k.a. "Woody," 28, matter-of-fact, clothes-y, another nature-lover, considered something of an airhead, and a bit older than the rest, was from El Segundo; and Adonis "Mr. Woo" Wong, 30, inscrutably "Oriental" at times, given to fits of spontaneous hilarity, on occasion more than his natural friend Luden Bond's equal in sheer intellect, hailed from Seattle.

The Travel Team routinely worked together for as many as fourteen hours a day, and naturally, friendships and working partnerships developed. And despite an explicit rule to the contrary, one romance, between Web Bootle, 29, an accomplished journalist from Tucson, and Camilie Auden, 30, sandy-haired, soft in demeanor, and a nature girl from Corvallis, Oregon, flowered forth from nearly the very first day. Their fellows, mostly accepting, looked the other way and ran interference when necessary.

The Travel Team was bound by explicit instructions always and only to report "positive news." If a plane crashed, they were duty-bound to report the number and the stories of the survivors, not the casualties. If a battle occurred, they were to report on the enemy's casualties, and only on our side's survivors, casualties on our side no longer being assets going forward. They were to report only on gains in the stock market and the companies who promulgated them, never on the losses, negativity being for losers. Besides, as the incoming President himself had told them during their initiation meeting, at which he'd conferred nicknames upon each of them in order to foster an atmosphere of bonhomie (or, as he put it, "bon-hominy."), people had enough on their minds already. They neither wanted nor needed to hear anything too in-depth.

The Travel Team settled into the Lady Bears' locker room, which had been converted into a makeshift newsroom. All nine of them, freshly out of intensive NWO training (which included more than a few all-nighters and, in one instance, confinement without food and water and enforced absolute silence), were gung-ho and ready to go. Their initial assignment – to positively spin their ultimate boss's first major speech as the nation's new President-elect – was a formidable one, but they were, one could say, unusually motivated to please. Besides their being portrayed as diehard Republicans who naturally wanted to support their preferred candidate, the NWO trustees had threatened immediate dismissal and the assurance that the young journalists would be flipping protein burgers for the rest of their earthly lives were they to publish a single unfavorable word about the new president or any of his policies. Plus, the Travel Team member who produced the most positive story of the first month would be awarded $5,000 and a dozen tickets to the national 2-Car racing championships, the nation's latest uber-rage. (It turned out that the winner – co-winners in their case – would be personally anchoring national coverage of the championship races). Within an hour, they had written the core storyline covering Gossens's "Reassurance Speech" for the evening's late editions, tomorrow's headlines, and the all-but-salivating morning talk shows, following Sarah "Blink" Dawson's inspired lead: "President-elect lays doubters to rest."

Chapter Three – A Reckoning

Over the next two weeks, the largest volume of wind-driven snow in more than a century drifted first over much of the Midwest and then across the East. By Christmas, the nation was digging out and, for those who were facing the loss of the conceptual lodestone that was the Constitution, the added insult of foul weather felt like digging out of a bad hangover or an irreversible nightmare. Slowly, plans only mentioned theoretically before began to come together in a flurry of court cases against what were seen as overwhelming shadow powers holding all the levers. The Company was sued as class action by the ACLU, the States of New Jersey and Hawaii, and the national Democratic Party for vote buying by purchasing the whole government, and the case was declared frivolous in the U.S. District Court of the Northern Virginia. Peter A. Gossens was sued for bargaining in bad faith, since he did not hold national office when he bargained with The Company, by the State of Vermont in the U.S. District Court of New England. In this case, it was ruled that a state did not have the standing to dispute a federal matter. And, there were other cases, none of which proceeded far enough to admit evidence. Genuine patriots who cleaved loyally to the tradition of an American constitutional state were finding themselves simply in despair, shaken off like fleas by a flea-harassed dog, as reducing the electorate to exclude some came each day to seem more and more likely, no efforts to deviate from the implemented plan originating from the ordinary citizenry at whatever level being entertained.

An attractive mirage of decency and stability for some lacking the erudite vision of a functional republic consisted of the President-elect, Peter Gossens, and his winsome family. There supporting him in the alluring picture were his stately strawberry-blond wife Sarah, their blond, late-teenage twins, Sylvia and Cynthia, who made up a rising country-gospel recording duet to mixed reviews, and their energetic preschool identical twin sons Tip and Tab. For the new flesh-and-blood First Family, December had become a blur of appearances, interviews, and coordinated, mostly non-substantive, statements for the press. President-elect Gossens was on the road the entire month, despite the weather, making cameo appearances before supporters at regional airports and in small-town armories and gymnasia, meeting and greeting major donors in dozens of locations and talking to actual advisors and planners on a fleeting, catch-as-catch-can basis.

On Wednesday, December 17, Gossens, desiring a little privacy, was escorted and driven by a lone Secret Service agent from the air terminal at Chattanooga, Tennessee, to a banquet in his honor sponsored by the Republican Party of Hamilton County in Cincinnati. The driver – not his usual driver, Maury, with whom he'd become cordial – was not a talker, and it was just as well. Gossens was unusually tired, so after ordering the driver to take back roads to avoid the crowds, he fell into a deep sleep.

He awoke with a jolt when the Benz limousine swerved and slipped on the snowy roads. Was this driver a fellow Southerner? His people were the salt of the earth, but they knew less than nothing about snow. They swerved again, and though Gossens appreciated the driver's efforts to get him to the banquet on time, it was obvious he was going much too fast for the conditions.

If this had been Maury, Gossens would have said "Whoa there, big hoss," and Maury would've grinned and slowed the car. But this guy didn't seem the joking sort.

Suddenly it occurred to Gossens that he didn't even know this driver's name. Who had failed to give him the usual briefing? And why would the Secret Service change drivers on him now? Come to think of it, just where in the hell were they, anyway? Privacy was one thing, but no escorts traveling behind at all? Lord have mercy, how in the hell could the President-elect of the United States, regardless of his preferences, possibly end up so utterly alone, not even knowing for sure where he was, or with whom?

He reached for his mobile phone in his right suit pocket, and the stranger who was driving suddenly spoke for the first time he could remember on this trip. "Hold on, sir. Don't worry. We're right on schedule, be coming into Bowling Green in half an hour."

The President-elect sighed, and desisted. Where's Bowling Green? Why Bowling Green? Was that supposed to mean something? He reached down further and pulled out a book he'd been reading – a novel by an old-time genre writer he'd gotten addicted to during the campaign, Robert Ludlum, no doubt now long dead – and slumped down and read.

A minute or two later, the man, staring steadily ahead in darkened glasses, unaccountably and just perceptibly began to decelerate on a long curve and pulled the car off at a side road intersection. He drove onto the wide shoulder, stopped, set the brake, and without saying anything, got out of the car.

What in blue blazes was going on? Gossens glanced out the window and saw the man standing ramrod, relieving himself. His medium blond hair beneath his fedora fluttered in the wind. "Now I've seen everything," Gossens muttered.

The man got back into the car and said nothing.

In a minute, before they started up again, a blue sedan crested the hill opposite them and stopped beside them. It looked small and fuel-efficient, one of those European jobs. Its driver, a dark man almost as tall as Gossens, got out and walked toward the limo. Suddenly the driver came to life.

"Get out, sir," he said. "Right now."

Meanwhile the tall man, who looked Greek, or maybe Moroccan, motioned to him to climb into the blue car.

"What the...?" was all he could utter. He was wide-awake now, and getting chilled by the wind.

Inside the blue car, they sped off, wheels slinging snow in all directions, heading fast up over a series of hills. The driver wore velvet driving gloves. Gossens, in a state of shock, was struck with a kind of paralysis. He slumped in his seat. "How could this be happening in America? How could this be happening in America?" he repeated to himself, slowly shaking his head and sighing. And, what precisely *was* happening? He cast about for the stock rhetoric that normally bailed him out of any situation, and finding none to fit this one, closed his eyes and recited the alphabet, over and over.

After several minutes the angular giant of a driver abruptly braked and pulled off the road. He turned to the President-elect of the United States and wordlessly, almost gently reached across and blindfolded him before they continued on. It was enough to rouse him, at least partially. What was to keep him from struggling and taking over this car?

His opponent, for one thing. For all he knew, this new guy could be a highly trained martial artist. Or maybe he even had a gun. He really didn't want to get beaten up; he had a dozen more appearances with supporters to make in the days ahead, and it wouldn't do to show up with a shiner. Gossens realized he was at the mercy of this brute. Fear began to burn like a white-hot ingot (or was it a faggot?) in his chest, and his breath came in short gasps.

"How did this happen?" he kept asking himself. "How could it have?" He found he was close to sobbing aloud in his desperation and futility. He couldn't bear to even imagine where *they* – for surely this was one hell of a vast left-wing conspiracy – might be taking him, or what they were going to do to him. For now, there was nothing to do but wait. Really, there was nothing at all he could do.

After what seemed like another hour of rolling along down the snow-choked road, neither fast or slow, absorbing and feeling every bump, his balls shooting up into his stomach and rocketing back down like yo-yos, the car suddenly lurched sharply to the right and careened pell-mell down a very long and precipitate hill. Gossens half-imagined, half-knew he could feel the air flowing through the car becoming steadily, unendurably colder as they descended. Then, just as suddenly, the car pulled to a smooth stop and the driver shut off the engine. To Gossens's surprise, he reached over and removed the blindfold, revealing a still world that seemed to be just waking up.

They were, it readily developed, sited at the bottom of a deep cleft or "holler," apparently in some Appalachian outlier or range of hills. A creek gurgled freshly along near the car, and as they tread the ground together, he could more than imagine he heard the wind rush through the trees way atop the high ridge of limestone seen in shadow surrounding their whereabouts like a stone collar.

There appeared to be not a level inch anywhere on the floor of this holler, which was all brushy, broken and up-thrust like pictures he'd seen from earthquake sites. And then he saw, dead ahead, in deepest shadow, the merest outline of what appeared spectral through the mist to be an old house with perhaps one low-wattage bulb, or else the first reflected rays of a pale sunrise, reflecting forlorn on one pane. And for the first time, Gossens began to fear for his life, the fear squeezing his squishy entrails like a clamp.

Worn and tired and nearly sick with fear, he trudged with the driver up the indistinct path toward the house, which turned out to be a rather ordinary-looking bungalow. The driver conducted him inside and lit up a sulfur-smelling smoke. Just one room in the interior appeared to be lighted.

As he scanned the main inside room, Gossens beheld the spare furnishings of an old house of 1950s-vintage—a heavy oak table, wooden and leather-upholstered chairs, and on the wall above the fireplace, a picture that reminded him of one he had seen of a long-dead right-wing prophet, virtually canonized by some Christian or pseudo-Christian groups of his knowledge, Rousas J. Rushdoony, a writer of complex doctrine, revived recently as an icon, a mere cipher representing Christian Identity ideas or sympathies. A rudimentary mock-chandelier with three low wattage bulbs swayed over the table. But no one was, at least yet, present there in what looked to be the house's matrix.

Instead, noticing activity down a corridor leading to a side doorway, he spied a burly man in a wool plaid shirt, whom he learned from news accounts much later to be named Rad Davis, awkwardly holding large turkeys neck-first down across a big, black-stained wooden table. They squawked loudly in terror, their long legs flying.

Hunched over that table was a decrepit-looking, blond-mopped, swarthy individual roaring in boisterous delight each time Davis brought his bloody meat-cleaver down with a resounding whack across an outstretched neck.

The air in that cold, half-darkened side room sparkled with the rain of non-stop flying heads, crimson spray, and flashing blade.

A minute or so later, the men, noticing his presence, stood. The butcher left through a side door and the other strode into the room and took a seat. He was presently joined by a second man. The President-elect faced the table in the main room like the bar of stern justice, facing two men now seated solemnly side by side awaiting him. He involuntarily lurched as he saw the hard-faced old scourge of turkeys he had witnessed in sheer horror a minute before, now improbably calm, with an indelible red spot or two still gleaming on his collar. Though obviously advanced in age, he sported a strikingly boyish, watery blue-eyed countenance framed by boyish straw locks that alone might have passed him for thirty-five.

The other man was, by contrast, ordinary looking, nondescript and middle-aged, with a sort of small-town business demeanor. Dressed in a conservative brown business coat, he reminded Gossens of a stuffy-looking clerk in the Ace Hardware he once frequented back in Wenona, Georgia, over twenty years before.

"Mr. Gossens," the odd older-young man chirped in a voice like a deeply-accented hinge. "We have been watching you."

He extended a leathery cold hand at the end of an arm that seemed too bony and long to be real, which Gossens accepted with no enthusiasm. There was a faint whiff in the room of long ago death leaving behind dry bones and exhaled air.

He accepted the more conventional-looking man's nod perfunctorily, his own eyes watering in the glare of the unshaded, too-dim light.

"Mr. Gossens," the high-pitched nasal voice started again, "do you know who we are?"

He nodded that he did, though he really didn't.

"We have brought you up here to remind you that you cannot even *pretend* to negotiate with us. You can, at most, be our spokesman to the public. That is it. Otherwise…." He produced the still gleaming, dripping death-instrument from his lap under the table, the same look of delight flashing like lightning coursing the sky. Then he sobered just as suddenly and held his eyes on the President-elect's in a sustained watery stare. "…Otherwise, you'll disappear, and always be a mystery for the ages."

Gossens, the faggot in his stomach ablaze, nodded with bleary eyes.

"Good," the ageless one said, seeming relieved. "Now, I have written down a message I want you to convey to your people waiting for you in… Cincinnati, I believe? Step outside and call, right now, the reception will be better. We have to think about that down here, you know. And don't waver. Or…"

Gossens, weakened by some pretty heady fumes coming from somewhere, all of a sudden barely able to stand, carried the scrawled scrap back out through the door into the near-dark, and under a yellow porch light thoughtfully turned on to assist him, dialed the number written on the paper. Once connected, he read the message as nonchalantly as he could muster: "Jake? This is the President-elect. Give me the VP-elect, Mr. Weck, please, if he is available." His stomach was churning now, and he felt almost ready to hurl. After a brief, anxious wait, Ben's voice came on the line.

"Ben? Yes, this is Pierre[BJH1]. We've been inconvenienced by the road conditions down here. I'm in Kentucky now, and tell everyone I'll be there, I'm running just about two hours behind schedule. I'm sure you can hold the guests until I arrive. Convey my apologies. And, please, let Sarah know I'm on my way…. No, no more than that, you fiend… Great! See you all soon. Good bye."

"Now," the timeless, possibly mindless one behind him intoned, louder than before, "deny *all* rumors. Nothing at all happened. Bad roads. Just bad roads. Not even to your wife Sarah. Ever."

* * *

No one in the Gossens camp had suspected that the Secret Service could be answering to higher authority. But alarms went off when President-elect Gossens failed to make his scheduled call-in on the road. Somehow, word of it leaked to the press, including NNN, the network flagship, which led with "breaking news" reports on the President-elect's "disappearance." Rumors and conspiracy theories began cropping up like dandelions, most of them claiming that the president-elect had been abducted. Aliens, the Chinese, the Russians, and the Democrats were all indicted as perpetrators. At one point, an unconfirmed report crossed the wire that an unidentified official had, for unknown reasons, actually blocked the dispatch order to regional responders and local law-enforcement officials to find and intercept the car. That report was later vehemently denied, though the lack of a timely response was never sufficiently explained to quash the rumors.

The Travel Team did the best it could to launch a counteroffensive, but alas, they were late to the game, as they were dispersed in different parts of the country when Gossens disappeared. Melinda "Beantown" Thalanis, Mackenzie Ward, and Lundy Bond were still fact-gathering in preparation for reporting from their home regions on the aftermath of the horrific snowstorm. Their angle was to focus on the upswing in winter recreational sports. Holly Bronson and Camilie Auden were assessing anecdotal reports of sizeable illegal boat people landings in scows and rafts from Africa on isolated stretches of the South Carolina coast, which they planned to spin as more cheap labor. Adonis Wong was busily investigating how Hollywood had been gearing up to reflect positively the abrupt changes in the country's governance and financial situation. His big scoop was landing an exclusive interview with Brady Ganderly, the star of the wildly popular "Hondo" predator drone military action-film franchise, now in its sixth annual iteration. Meanwhile, "Tex" Thorter was with the Gossens transition team ensconced at the Willard Hotel in Washington, and Webster Bootle had been posted to cover the President-elect's scheduled appearance and reception as a hero in Cincinnati. Once all members were rounded up, they met by conference call to determine how they could discourage all speculation and accentuate the positive. Just as they were about to hang up, Fuba "Tex" received word that Gossens had called in. It was Macko Ward's brilliant insight to explain the absence by saying that Gossens had made an unannounced detour in order to pick up Kentucky Derby souvenirs for his two sets of twins.

News coverage the next day carried stories of Gossens the charmingly absentminded husband and father, so intent on buying gifts for all his children that he forgot about government protocol. A few, of course, disregarded by more serious citizens, continued to hatch "conspiracy theories," insisting, to the angry disgust of those who wanted to just hear positive news, that there was at least an hour's worth of time in which the rising leader of the free world had gone literally "off the grid." It was more than enough time, they said, for some real changes to have been effected and real damage done.

Chapter Four – A Hundred-Headed Hydra Hindered

The more he thought about it, which was day and night lately, the more it pained the chronically melancholy ex-Vice President, Gole, that he had failed to even deliver a response opposing his opponent's deal to literally sell the country in exchange for liquidating its debt. A scant handful of the pundits (mostly right-wingers) postulated that he had lost the election largely due to perceived moral shortcomings, magnified to gargantuan scale by the Republican propaganda machine, but Gole knew that was only the nail in the coffin. True, *The Husband-Elect* had caused an enormous flap, and he was still trying to undo its damage. It didn't matter that Jewell, his sweet wife of twenty-nine years, had rejected out of hand the accusations of debauchery and infidelity, it didn't matter that at the behest of his friends, all the dollies he *didn't* bed had spoken out about his ironic utter lack of libido or sex appeal, and it didn't even matter that the book itself was 100% fiction. In the minds of 52% of Americans, most of whom didn't read, it made him a pervert. It was small consolation that the slim volume, heretofore consigned to the remainder shelves, had in the election year been reprinted and had rocketed to the top of the bestseller lists thanks to the Republicans. Gole had deposited his thus fattened royalty checks with a sense of chagrin, even a tinge of revenge.

Then there were the meetings with Senator "Drinker" Topel and a couple of others. The most salacious of the tabloids cast him as the ringleader in that crowd's bacchanalian blowouts, when in truth he'd only been to one (dry for him) meeting, where it was only Topel who had overindulged. Gole could only sigh. In fact, he had a lot to sigh about. He reckoned he would just have to be patient and let history reveal the truth: that these gatherings were brainstorming sessions and not soirees, meetings of minds of, in fact, eminent public figures urgently and solemnly seeking to protect and defend the Constitution. In the meantime, however, the persistent reports of sightings of himself, drunk and with a young lady hanging on each arm, only besmirched his reputation the more.

Ironically, none of this proverbial bone-breaking really hurt, though. What he really did find disappointing in himself – in hindsight – was his failure to say *something, anything* in the campaign. He kicked himself down the street, down the hall, under the table, a hundred times a day, every day, every time he thought about it, which was constantly. The "it" was virtually conceding the high ground in advance to the sleazy, clownish Gossens, never once rising to challenge his gambit of contracting for a corporate payoff of the strangulating national debt in exchange for the nation's cherished and precious sovereignty. It was such a preposterous bargain that he never even entertained it, either to embrace or to nix it. He didn't think the people would in a million years fall for a bargain so idiotic it would end their sovereignty and rip the Constitution to ribbons. But they did. And he had to face the fact that he had not found even the gumption to defend the nation's precious heritage of self-rule, even though that was already fictional and bygone and legendary in fact.

If he had only ventured to speak up against the sell-off and oppose the take-over by the monstrous forces of The Company, he would have been right and a patriot. Even if he hadn't prevailed. As long as he lived, he would *never* – and never deserve to – escape his guilt over that particular crass and unspeakable sin of omission. *If only he had just spoken up! If only...*

Finally Jewell had had enough.

"Abie!" she called him out of the fog of his reverie one afternoon. "You have *got* to stop this moping! What matters now is the *future.* You did not do anything to create this mess we're in – not in any way! But you *can* do something to get us out of it. So what will it be, Mr. Gole[BJH2]? What are you going to do to move us all forward out of this infernal snake pit? *Think, Mr. Gole!* No one is as virile and fertile, upstairs and down, as you are! Let me just remind you – first, I wouldn't give you the time of day, remember? Then you gave me eight kids in six years! And all of them wonderful kids! Now think of an *idea*, something new and bold that will change everything! You are capable of it, and we both know it! Now, *do it!*"

His wife was absolutely right. He had to get out of his armchair, lift his chin up, and get to work. Now that he had missed his slim-to-non-existent chance to prevent the notorious bargain outright, the only thing left to do was to find a role for himself that could somehow reverse it and restore the Constitution to the nation as the basis of governance. The handful of dissidents in Congress had their hearts in the right place, but he couldn't very well join them outright because his prominence could very well result in sinking, perhaps literally killing, them all. But there had to be *something* he could do. Whether the deal had really been his fault or not, he determined, right then and there, to do whatever he could to reverse it, pledging his "life, fortune, and sacred honor" toward achieving that end.

And so he put his fertile mind to work to come up with a way, *any* way, that would make all the difference and really change the world.

And over the course of one particular sleepless night, he got an idea that surely would fill the bill.

That idea he shared with nary a soul in America. Not even his wife.

*   *   *

Inauguration Day came and went remarkably peacefully. The weather in Washington was fine and clear, and – through Faustian efforts – the many thousands of angrily milling, ugly-mood protesters and would-be disrupters from around the country were blocked off half a mile from the White House and Capitol and kept almost exclusively off-camera.

At the swearing-in, the Chief Justice droned, hand raised, "…that I will faithfully execute the office of President of the United States…"

The president-elect, hand raised, intoned, "…that I will faithfully *exonerate* the office of President of the United States." The band played.

The new president, rambling and gawky, appeared rather shockingly unhinged and close to hysteria at times, yet automaton-like at other moments, in delivering his first Inaugural Address. In a word, he seemed more than a little buzzed. Very many who beheld the spectacle of the Address observed that, indeed, "something untoward must have happened." The conspiracy theorists crowed, calling the President's uneven performance proof that he had been drugged or brainwashed during his hour-long recent absence.

Passages of likely portent in his Address, from the expected to the outrageous and simply baffling, included the following: "Our national solvency, recently re-achieved, will permit us to move at last ahead once again. …And now is the time for all to admit, after centuries of largely fruitless internal struggle sapping our energies, what has finally become all but too obvious, that Capital is shown clearly to be prior to and independent in character from Labor. The result is that human Labor as an independent organized player in this nation no longer even exists as such, while American Capital has achieved its rightful, commanding position. Judging from its lack of competitive success, we must conclude that Labor, as a block, has, to the extent it has shown up at all, done so as a fruit and by-product of the progress of Capital, which it has rightfully served, of late at the latter's sufferance. Thus, Capital has thus shown itself naturally and beyond serious comparison superior to Labor and deserves, and hence must be accorded, much the higher consideration, to the end that Labor today can no longer take from the mouth of Capitol the sweet, commodious bread its virtue and utility have justly earned its providers."

The loser in the campaign, the outgoing Vice President, seated ceremonially to the right on stage next to outgoing President Folger B. Swansdown, could only listen with a redoubled sense of remorse at his reticence and failure to come to grips with such ideological brain-sludge during the campaign.

The new President continued, lamentably: "Now that Labor as a separate entity in national life has been vanquished for good and all, we can recall and quote with new understanding the defining themes of what we have always thought of as opposing fonts of abounding wisdom: 'Labor is the duty of all citizens of the Republic,' and 'Work will set you free.'"

In fact, Gole reflected sadly, he himself could not have stated the intent of his dreaded new administration more clearly, though most were not yet prepared to hear or acknowledge it, most seeing Gossens as a benign buffoon who had stumbled upon an ultimately useful tradeoff of the good for the better and necessary: of accustomed only loosely Constitutional order in exchange for efficiency and solvency.

"As our economic gurus know," President Gossens soldiered on, "the ping-pong of democracy is assuredly no way for us to pursue business. And so, let the people be patient and orderly. Because, only now, escaping at last the great expense to us of the thought-to-be eternal contradiction of freedom and effectiveness, and freshly invigorated as we are by the blessings of our restored solvency, we can now begin moving ahead steadily in this grudgingly respecting, but still envious, and violent world so full of blockheaded tendencies and the willful delusions of mythical self-governance for all the gullible and hapless nations. And so, my fellow Americans, ask not what your country can do for you. I repeat what I emphasized to you during the campaign we have all just recently won together: 'It's one way ahead!'" He was bellowing now. "There's only one future, there for the taking! My fellow Americans, *let's roll!"*

To Gossens' surprise, he found the applause in response to his remarks ominously lacking in enthusiasm in most quarters of the chamber. Why was it that the audience seemed to be at a bit of a loss? It was time, he accurately surmised, for his emergency punch-line quote, which he'd purloined especial for the occasion: "If 'some are chosen,'" he intoned solemnly, "then indeed some are quite obviously more chosen than are others, and such are not to be impeded by the same mundane guidelines, or what some call 'rules.' That, my dear friends, is the clear verdict of our national history. Lest we forget. And, that condition being obviously so, let us, or some among us, no longer amass our resources futilely and at great expense in opposition to it – nay! Let's make *the most* of it, *accepting* it as the verdict of God Himself on earth. For He surely, in His wisdom, has not, in all the time we have known Him, broken it down, has He? For, we can clearly see, and ourselves favor, those who He has favored right along!"

At the very last second he decided against adding "Amen!"

And so, the day ended with the nation's own verdict ratified, sanctified, and pronounced to an attendant nation suddenly having sprouted waxen ears, even to that which it had itself, albeit narrowly, decided.

* * *

At its first meeting, the new Congress, which Gossens had assumed would move forward with jubilation at resolving the country's painful and enervating financial conundrum, was thrown into an unprecedented uproar, easily its most acrimonious session since the start of the Civil War. In a sense, it hosted a showdown that had been building, with some brief respite, for almost 170 years.

Nearly all the contentiousness focused on two cardinal points: First, the matter of the American constitutional system and squaring that with the seismic change already set in motion. How could it be justified? And second, by far the most controversial and disconcerting subject for most of the members of Congress was the question as to their status and their august institution once their current terms came to an end.

The range of positions vociferously expressed to reporters on these two vital questions by members of the two houses ranged from mildly trusting and supportive of the top level functionaries involved on the two sides in the basic decision to, in one or two cases, incendiary threats and calls for revolution and overthrow.

One source of acrimony was the fact, which no member of Congress would venture to defend but none could undo, that the new President's very first act after issuing the Executive Order committing the United States to the pact with The Company was to classify as top-secret the text of that agreement. It was accessible, on jeopardy of prosecution for treason by executive order, to none but a tight circle of administration officials and their direct successors for fifty years. Hence, the only access anyone else would have to the terms of the agreement and the arrangement it spelled out was through carefully controlled statements and characterizations by top figures in the administration. Beyond this, Gossens had only promised a brief summary of the agreement, to be released "sometime."

The Travel Team had a devil of a time countering the fallout, but Luden Bond penned an article praising the President's "discretion," and the others followed suit.

* * *

Among the normal cascade of cabinet and other appointments by the new President, it had been pointedly noted by news pundits that no mention was made of an ambassador of the new administration to the United Nations. Then, on his second day in office, President Gossens, after a brief meeting with Edward Lambent, pulled the U.S. out of the U.N., gave that organization a deadline of the end of June to completely vacate the facility, and initiated arrangements to lease the space to commercial renters. To the stunned delegates and members of that august body, he abruptly characterized his message as, "Don't call us, we'll call you."

A predictable fraction celebrated the savings of grief and money.

* * *

The first official cabinet meeting, at 7:00 on Sunday night, January 25, behind closed doors, was inexplicably not conducted in the Cabinet Room, but in high-back chairs with the President behind his desk in the Oval Office at the White House. The Cabinet members were indignant.

The formalities of official welcoming weren't even completed before Val Rogers, the brand-new Secretary of State, a formidable, quintessentially handsome Hispanic woman, twice-elected Senator from Michigan, spoke up, softening her interruption with a little lightning-fast smile. "Mr. President, with all due respect…"

The President, until then mild and gracious, turned abruptly. "What do you think this is, Madam Secretary, *Law and Order? Hondo?* Please don't use that line! Due respect, indeed."

In his new whirled and swirled mind, he distinctly envisioned a gleaming, dripping blade appearing just at chair-level.

"I'm sorry, Mr. President, I won't say it again," Val Rogers said. "But Mr. President, are we going to be a government under the Constitution? Believe me, everyone in the country is wanting to know! Does the bargain mean that we – the whole country – will be treated as company property from now on, of, by, and for the benefit of The Company?"

Gossens leaned his angular elbows atop the executive desk. "No. Well, not exactly, no. Look, no one here is not patriotic. I mean, everyone is. We know that the Constitution, as a symbol, means a lot to the people. We will still continue to cite it, like the Bible, when it suits. Because of that, I mean, let us say, because of that… shall we say, fondness? Because of the fondness the people have for the Constitution, we will be transitional for awhile, and will fall back on it when appropriate."

"But, will we act in accordance with the procedures the Constitution lays out?" Rod Norman of Commerce asked.

"But, Rodney, *all* of you, you all know – you *must* know – *we* don't 'act,' not on our own, at least." He looked around to make sure they got it. "Let me put it this way: We are like the light bulb that is shining, that everyone sees, and sees by. But it's not we who *power* the light bulb, who, really, independently act. We'll be more like the image that people see on the screen, not the candle or candle-power behind it."

"You mean we're just the *show?*" Vice President Weck asked.

"Yeah, we're the show! And the people will love to see us, and believe in us and our magical virtue, and they'll follow and cling to whatever we say and do! So, watch yourself! But, remember, even Jesus couldn't act of his own accord. Remember? He said he only did what his Father told him to." The President stopped for effect and again looked around the room. "But, how they've loved him, or claimed to, ever since. They *still* claim to love him today! And, they will *us*."

(Secretly, his thoughts naturally descended to pondering quite a different dynasty, represented in his mind in an old house in a hole in Kentucky.)

Everyone nodded his or her head, a bit nervous because all of it was new, as something referred to, and all smiled in unison, having grown up, they knew, leaning on shadows.

"And, how will we always know the way expected of us? Well, there is one among us, who will be with us always, to the end of the age, who will know what to expect from us. Sort of our Paraclete, or *parakeet*, to form a new updated fig of speech."

The President snickered at his own joke. In his mind, he couldn't stop thinking of *turkeys*.

In a darkened corner of the Oval Office, unnoticed, Lambent blanched just a bit.

Theodore Kimon, Chief Presidential Strategist, wasn't to be deterred all that easily by so much loose talk of deity and dynasty. "But, sir, what if The Company – I take it you mean The Company as our source of power now, having the legal sovereignty to decide policy, and procedure. That's correct, then, isn't it? So, what if The Company wanted to *abolish* the Congress, for instance? Eventually, to just drop all pretense of directly responding to the nation of people? Or, to do anything but what *they* want to do for the country, or the world? Would we just go along with that?"

The President mocked being stunned by such a suggestion. "But of course!" he answered. "But, that will take a little while to get to that point, because they won't want to alarm everyone all at once, because then the people won't produce, will they, if they're disheartened? But don't worry, Kimmy, *the people will learn*."

"Sir," Val Rogers said, "I don't think that—"

"My, my, she's one hot tamale this morning, isn't she, folks? Let me finish. As I was saying, with the enormous benefit being that everyone will be on board, on the same team, everyone in the country will work together. Or be dropped off... And we won't have the contradictions and inner struggles anymore. Everyone will just have *more*, MORE! And that's what they all want, isn't it, so it will satisfy them once they learn that we're all permanently family, and all pulling the same way! And then, I don't think they'll care too much *how* we got there. Do you?" He grinned ridiculously, widely at everyone. "You know, though, I'm not sure why The Company would even *need* to get rid of Congress anytime soon, when they can control it so easily.." He laughed. "Hell, I think they've got it under control already!"

Kimon shrugged, smiling back uncomfortably.

The President, not yet convinced that they got it – and, feeling to the quick that his neck might be literally on the line if they didn't – glanced around the room, registering a fleeting instant of eye-contact with each of them and letting out a sort of mimic sigh, then continued.

"You may be asking yourself," he said, "why wouldn't The Company just content itself with exerting usually-decisive power in the system, over the makers of the laws and over the laws, especially as impacts its ability to operate and bring in profits? In other words, why would its directors move to acquire the country outright? What advantage could they possibly hope to gain, beyond the virtual stranglehold they already have had? Well, for one thing, you see, they're deeply patriotic. And, beyond that, how could they operate in and from a country, however gargantuan in potential, with a completely bound-up economy such as we've suffered?

"The answer is, *they* needed to free the government to operate on a liquidity basis as much as anyone! And, they tell me that by removing all the contradictions and impediments from the system, by, in fact, *owning* it outright to avoid any and all opposition, they figure they can *multiply* their profit levels by reducing the losses built-in otherwise in the process and cutting down the costs of business, legal and illegal, that sapped too much of available expenditure."

Gossens was longer-winded, for some reason, than any of them could remember.

"How could it be patriotic to buy the United States in order to cancel its Constitution, you may ask. Just remember: they, and *we*, don't look at matters the same way our adversaries – I almost said *enemies* – do! We don't see the people – *citizens*, they've been called – as legitimate voting members of a sort of club – a sort of *country* club – *heh, heh!* No! To The Company, and hence to us, the people are more like cattle in our fields. I know the people, by and large, would sometimes like to *kill*, to *annihilate*, the major owners and directors of The Company, if they could, out of resentment and jealousy and their own brand of greed, if you want to get right down to the truth. And the directors know that! And so, I ask you, how much regard can the directors and mega-shareholders of The Company be expected to hold in their hearts for *them*? Are they likely to regard them as their *equals*? As people with the same rights and interests, and consent to operate by the same picky little-people rules? HA! Fat chance! And, *we* have all cast our lots with The Company, am I right?" He looked around at each again. "We hold *all* the winning cards now, I remind you – but not for ourselves. So, let's play them and derive the benefits of the positions we've got ourselves in!"

Henry Herschel, now the Domestic Policy Advisor, and a Gossens political operative from the start of his venture into elective politics, took up the half-hearted cudgel – half-hearted because it all sounded so shocking, the way the President put it, but they *were* all basically on the same page or they *wouldn't be here*, true enough. This deal was going to require some major-league spin. "What will we call such a program?" he asked.

"Freedom!" Gossens said. "We'll call it *freedom!* People will have money in their pockets, that's freedom! Democracy is essentially just deciding which pair of pants to buy, which color car. And that's still up to *them*!"

"Excellent, sir," Hen Herschel continued. "But *how* is this show going to proceed? What are the rightful owners behind the scenes, in The Company, going to want to *show,* to keep the millions of people who only want decent care, and a little taste of riches, interested and contentedly producing? Have we reached the end of history, or something like that?"

"No! Hell, no, Henry! For one thing, we will still need an external threat! The East Asians fit that bill like a flint. They could have formally bought us themselves, don't forget, the country *and* The Company, too, for that matter, and would have if they'd thought of it! And where would we all be if that happened? Yessiree, they'll do just fine for an enormous, scary, and an almost too credible threat! Wouldn't you say? They're several times our population, and *inscrutable*, right? Everything you can imagine can just be blamed on their connivance. Of course, we might want to stop short of an all-out war with someone that big... Anyway, the people in this country will *have* to look up to us to protect them! And, we can pick our wars with smaller countries to keep our military in practice and try out new forms of deadly force. But even more importantly, the East Asian threat will keep our biggest export, the materials of violent death, continually flying and flowing out the door, to... *everywhere!* And we can *insist* on it, for hemispheric and global protection from those little yellow conspirators and terrorists!"

Gossens swooned at the image he'd painted and grasped the edge of the table to steady himself.

"Lotsa bangs! Lotsa good eagles to fill up our investors' kitties and line our pockets!"

All present shook their heads at that one. Maybe Gossens wasn't such a dope after all.

"Well, in light of that, how do we treat our allies?" Secretary of State Rogers asked. "The Europeans, for instance? The Russians?"

"Basically, we don't," President Gossens said. "Because other than being our buyers, we don't even *need* them!" The merry look of a rebellious 17-year-old splashed across his face. "The people like to think of us as independent and resolute. And, the Europeans are still copping democracy, right? As though they gave a rat's ass themselves what their lower orders think or want. Anyway, they're not ready to step out and free themselves from... from voter madness and sometimes indiscretion... yet! So, we're doing them a favor by pioneering the idea of jettisoning *the public* formally!"

Secretary of the Treasury C. T. Norman, formally a Democrat, who occasionally even now talked to Abe Gole, still had some reservations. "But—"

"But what, Collier? '*One Way Ahead,*' and that means everybody! As I told you!"

President Gossens' eyelids suddenly appeared to be fluttering ten dozen times a minute. His breath began coming in gulps and he started to turn a little red.

"Are you all right, Mr. President?" several asked in unison. It wasn't the first time this apparent bout of nerves had started to take over since Gossens had returned from his mysterious lost day in the snowdrifts stretching from Chattanooga to Cincinnati.

"Don't 'Mr. President' me," he railed, his tongue overshooting his mouth. "If you don't quit drilling me, or grilling me... I'm... I'm going to hold my breath until you all stop!"

Norman of Treasury had heard he could be like this.

Reynolds, the Secretary of Health and an MD, started to get up to examine President Gossens and found himself almost menacingly waved back. Gossens's color was rapidly coming back. It appeared Gossens would be okay, so it was time for the Cabinet members to think. They settled down in their high-backed chairs and turned inward to examine their own thoughts and motives. If they could pull this off there was a lot of money to be had. *If* they could pull it off.

* * *

Ensconced in its cramped quarters the very first day of the new administration by special arrangement with the NWO, the network Travel Team settled into its secret assigned "bunker" in a White House sub-basement, accessible only by tunnel from its undisclosed remote location.

This musty, dimly-lit space, had, White House experts suggested, originated as a second-line wine cellar, originally stocked by slaves, and frequented occasionally by certain eminent men in the past. Not surprisingly, the shadowy access route was said to be haunted.

Indeed, starting the first day of their tenure, the newest occupants were abuzz with tales of alleged encounters. William Howard Taft was mentioned, portly in his tailored suit, and a sketchy, transparent President Hayes was said to slink through, often casting furtive glances over his right shoulder to assure he wasn't being followed. J.Q. Adams was more clearly seen, proceeding more boldly. Adonis Wong reported once having found an old green bottle in a niche in the plaster, partially filled with a milky-looking substance, and that someone looking suspiciously like President Pierce had strode up to him briskly, lifted it out of his hand, and promptly vanished.

Web Bootle once tried to claim he had seen G.W. Bush skulking in the darkened hallway, but Fuba "Tex" Thorter, who had known more ghosts than most personally, called his bluff. "But he's still living, Webster! Old, yes, but he hasn't checked out."

In fact, the man they were talking about, seldom mentioned anymore, had become America's first expatriate ex-president, an all-but-forgotten figure who had for years mysteriously refused to leave his *estancio* in Paraguay, to the surprise of many. Not even to attend recognition ceremonies four years ago in remembrance of the twenty-fifth anniversary of his inauguration.

Chapter Five – Congress' Last Roundup?

The opening day of Congress was Tuesday, January 27. The day's session was highlighted by what had become an annual exercise, voting on rules that maintained the Internet as mainly the vehicle for ads and commercial announcements it had long since become. In the meantime, private communications between individuals, still given priority by a dwindling minority in Congress, were continued as required entrants in the stream of messages permitted by licensed servers, as authorized bandwidth space permitted, that is, seldom and sorely limited in extent. (This, while a predictable few members – the same handful every session – claimed something that surely must have been much exaggerated: that, still within living memory, anyone could simply email a greeting, *any* greeting, to any friend for any reason whatsoever at any time, without requesting anyone's or any system's permission). Their demand for public access as non-licensed, non-revenue-paying senders was simply unrealistic, so much so that no one in power admitted believing their unlikely claim, or could be bothered to check it out.

After that came the preliminary budget from the new White House, issued in light of the imminent payoff to zero of the nation's debt and the new administration's priorities. A large share of the projected expenditures, over a trillion Euros in all (technically, Ameros, a reserve, non-circulating currency in the U.S.), was earmarked for a strengthened military program. The objective, plainly put, was to thwart the highlighted ambitions of the East Asian powers and their supposed terrorist lackeys.

The "East Asian Axis" ("slant-eyed *nigga*s" to some, mainly off the airwaves) were especially to be feared now, it was stated rather crudely, since they would be freed from the longtime necessity of protecting the colossal sums they'd invested in their loan and assistance program with their unpredictable wholly-dependent client U S of A.

"Damn Asians," brayed Senator Henry Steele of Washington, a man best known for his bear-like snout, in open session on the first day of the new Congress. "We could have just re-interpreted the debt *out of existence* a long time ago, and it would have been in our interest to have done so, if it hadn't been for their dishonesty and lack of principles. Those ocher devils would've done most anything in retaliation! Why they've actually threatened as much, and been saying lately that *they* could buy us! I ask you this: was Pearl Harbor and all its aftermath too long ago for'm?"

Senator Topel of Vermont, though, perceived the real menace as coming from *within*, from, as he put it, "the combustible vacuums between some pairs of ears."

"The real menace is that this wonderful budget we're foisted with leaves the actual, day-to-day needs of the whole nation not a whit better met than they were when all of the government's income went to service the debt – in fact, even worse! The priority of the people's needs is actually being budgeted at less than zero. Practically speaking, the real purpose of governing is given a negative, *minus* priority."

"That's because the people's representative bodies, the houses of the Congress, are to be, practically-speaking, *abolished,* giving the people no voice, no stake, no recourse, not even a pretended one any more," lamented Senator Cable of Minnesota when his turn to speak came. "It's a devil's bargain, and it's a devil's government to come!"

"But, if we're attacked and we're dead," Steele sneered, "what's all yer big-spending notions add up to then?"

Remarkably, the argument died on that point. What else was there to say about it? And what recourse was open, once the essential deed had been done? So after a short break, during which Carbola surreptitiously made a call to Abe Gole, who intimated that he was preparing for "a long, hard journey" but wouldn't say more than that, the attentions of Congress turned to defense spending.

The largest and most problematic of the U.S. defense-related initiatives was the euphemistically named "Project Zap." Reportedly well-advanced in prototype prior to the rapid spiraling of the debt, its object was none other than to produce "the ultimate weapon," both maximally lethal and mobile. The principal was that of a single directed beam of highly-focused electrons so powerful as to completely vaporize, from a safe distance, of course, an airplane or armored vehicle, or even an installation or densely-occupied medium-sized city, cleanly, without radiation or any other contaminant being imposed. Its above-board, publicly admitted, funding portion was prominently included in the budget bill. As expected, the Democrats made themselves a general nuisance over this one.

Another initiative to be funded was the manipulation of existing light-bending technology to render invisible and radar-proof virtually all American planes and war vehicles as well as ground personnel. Even Senators Carbola and Topel had to agree with Steele that this one was "super cool," and voted accordingly.

Meanwhile, to the consternation of most of the Democrats, a paltry twenty-eight billion was budgeted for all non-military foreign assistance, while some four-hundred billion was to go for military aid, primarily to African and South Asian allies and Israel, mainly to finance purchases of munitions, planes, and military hardware as well as software, virtually all from American-based arms suppliers.

But, for a change, Congressional Democrats were even more outraged by something other than, in the idiom of the day, budget-gobbling "Hondo militarism." The problem for virtually everyone not consumed by conservative "flaming Hondo partisanship" was: What was going to become of the tattered remains of the social contract formally launched back in the primeval past by the ballyhooed Constitution of the United States? What the deuce was actually in the secret replacement contract that no one had been permitted to see? What was decided and set irrevocably, in a most unfair, if not illegal, maneuver imposed plainly to escape the rigors of debate and reversal, and what, if anything, remained yet to be determined? The questions were endless.

In the upper house, Senator Henry Steele, the Washington Republican, made an attempt to defend the shadowy new agreement based on long-term problems in governance that had knocked akimbo the essential checks-and-balances provisions implemented by the clearly overrated gaggle of Founders.

"The Constitution will always have its defenders and those who sing its praises and will never acknowledge its considerable practical defects," he said. "In fact, they *worship* it. But let's look at the results, my friends: Whenever the branches of the government have been controlled by different parties, we have had gridlock and inaction. And, whenever the same party has controlled all of the different branches, the intended oversight of the thereby puffed-up executive branch has become non-existent. So, just what's the God-almighty purpose? If it's mainly the Bill of Rights, that could just as well be tacked onto a different arrangement as it was onto the old model that's now so very clearly outdated."

It was Senator Joel Frankland of Pennsylvania, a moderate member of Steele's own party, who answered him: "But what are we replacing our Constitution with, Henry? That's the question of the day. If the Constitution achieved our Founders' best intentions imperfectly, then how do you propose to achieve them better? And do we even have the power to effect that change, whatever it may entail, under the new agreement, which has, anyway, already gone into irrevocable effect?"

Senator Steele, a reliable debater and partisan, could no more than shrug in answer. Because Frankland was right: the deal was already struck.

For his part, Senator Frankland took the floor again to declare that he would never have voted to abrogate the old and venerable document wholesale, regardless of its shortcomings, because at least it did serve to foster representation of the country's citizenry. "Who's to say that the new agreement we're now apparently stuck with will do the same?" he implored the Congress. "The worst feature of this new arrangement is that, whatever it amounts to, it's been forged with neither direct public participation nor consent as to its operative terms. Therefore, my friends, I have to doubt its basic legality, when it comes right down to it. So I ask you, are we so *sure* we're really tarred with it?"

Senator Roger "Drinker" Topel, Democrat of Vermont, jumped in rather indignantly at this point. "Representative? Did you say 'representative'? My friend, it's been decades since there's been any of *that*, except in name, in this government. We all know it's the big composite incorporation of everything investment-wise and the large, wealthy interests that get all the representation. Let's stop pretending. We needed to stop pretending, and start standing up and yelling our heads off a long time ago! And since the system has become anything but representative of the public will and interest, let's all pledge our solidarity to stand up and see that it gets changed to that basis, if that's what we all want. 'Our lives, our fortunes, and our sacred honor!' I hereby pledge mine!"

Senator Cable of Minnesota jumped up and called loudly for a comprehensive investigation of the entire matter of the hated initiative. Many others yelled "Hear, hear!" and shouted for a committee to appoint a committee to investigate.

But not all. The Majority Leader, Senator John Sokol of Ohio, big, raw-boned, and red-fleshed, rose to interject that an investigation of a President newly-inaugurated was the last thing the country needed to go through at this harried and much-divided point in its history.

Senator Gerry Fuller, a Democrat, at least in name, and a prim and proper lady, former State Superintendent of Education from South Carolina, took the floor solely to suggest that the body, and the country, "wait and see" what the conferees with The Company had come up with before condemning and trying to summarily replace it.

"The Spirit of the Constitution, and not its precise, perishable body, bears its Soul," she declaimed, provoking no small amount of head-scratching and head-shaking.

And so it went in the Senate, as the steam passed out of the objectors' considerable short-term fury there.

Meanwhile on the House side, the new President's audacious spending gambit was considered paramount.

Republican Congressman Richard Cory of Virginia opened the first day's debate with a mild critique, simply noting that, once again, an administration's own professed spending plans far outstripped its revenue estimates, a syndrome that dated back to the second Bush administration, if not before. None could dispute it.

Representative Calvin Jones, Democrat from California, averred that the situation was far worse even than that, lamenting that so-called social spending, on education, health-care initiatives, the pending retirement of tens of millions, food, housing, and fuel assistance to growing legions of structurally unemployed persons, were all being pushed aside. And for what? To make room for funding the latest "Ultimate Weapon" program and a few other pet projects of this administration, which could only add to world distrust, disgust with America and disillusionment over our always-benevolently-stated aims.

Jared Walkup, Republican from the Third District of Kansas, countered that the money was well worth it to create a non-nuclear "usable" deterrent to force our powerful adversaries in the "East Asian Axis" to rethink and scrap any plans for a military challenge now that they had been freed of their prior obligation to safeguard their massive sums of money loaned to us by avoiding an outright clash. And, by the way, who cared what the world may think?

Congressman Carl Fredericks of New Mexico retorted that what the world thought was the least of our problems, because under this administration, we were going to have a public-relations fiasco at home. He'd heard the rumor, and he was sure everyone else had, too, that whole sections of the country that didn't manage to "pay their way," instead constituting a heavy net burden for the rest, were to be cut loose or relegated to second-class standing at best. He couldn't verify the substance of the rumors himself, he said, but that was what he and some of his constituents had taken away from the President's remarks in the Inaugural.

Congressman Walkup objected to the introduction of "baseless innuendos" into Congressional debate, but raised a new line of fundamental questions just as "major and necessary for all present," which was the following: "When our terms are over, can we come back? Will the Congress still be selected in the tried-and-true traditional way or not? To say nothing of the now-unclear status of the courts. What basis, if any, will there be for them?"

The only immediate response from other congressmen was a crescendo of murmurings on both sides of the aisle and from every corner of the chamber. Because, indeed, no one knew the answer.

Then, from the very back of the chamber, the only man in Congress who, at 6'11," was actually taller than the gangling President, the newly-elected freshman Democratic congressman from North Dakota, Harry Carbola, rose to speak. His arresting baritone filled the chamber. "Mr. Speaker, I may be just one man in this body, but in truth, I am representing millions of my fellow citizens when I say that, if I can reverse the rejection of and reinstate the U.S. Constitution from this hallowed hall, I will do so. And if I cannot, along with others, prevail to do so here, then I will do so with masses of others on the outside!

"Mr. Speaker, I am told that to pursue this course—apart from deliberations here to forcefully oppose this craven administration and its treacherous agreement with Mammon and reinstate the Constitution I have taken an oath to protect and defend—is itself treason. My answer is that of old: If this be treason, my fellow members, then make the most of it!"

The House, America's body of representatives if it had one, suddenly arose into a singular uproarious erection, and even members who had been idly reading their newspapers up until then leaped to their feet as if prodded by shock.

Two other members, Nory "Noodles" Norton, Democrat from Arizona's Sixth District, and Tom "Sober" Topel, Independent from Vermont and Senator Roger Topel's brother, rushed up to stand with the towering North Dakotan, while others may, to put it charitably, have been simply too indecisive or timid, or camera-shy.

Carston Sanders, Republican of Missouri, managed to get himself recognized in the midst of the verbal melee. "Mr. Speaker!" he yelled, alarm in his rising voice. "Mr. Speaker, clear this House of miscreants!"

The gavel of the acerbic Speaker, Poague of Alabama, banged and banged down, and the floor was so cleared by the burly Sergeant of Arms.

* * *

The media-feeding Travel Team had continued to meet informally around a table in the brick-encased converted subterranean wine storage space they referred to as their "bunker," but rarely all together as they were now.

Fuba "Tex" Thorter, the leader, posed the day's question: "Ok, how will we dub this one?"

Web Bootle, now affectionately known as "Wide Bottom," interjected, "Is it true a power surge conveniently knocked C-Span blank when Congressman Carbola started to speak?"

"Yes," Fuba said, scowling, "but as we all know, there *are* unfortunate coincidences. But I know as well as you what it looks like."

"Actually, the blackout is good, in a way," said Sarah Dawson. "Now we're all free to construe it however we need to."

"Yeah," said Luden Bond. "So what do we owe our public, the American public? The important thing should not be what *we're* free to do or not to do."

Melinda Thalanis ("Beantown") shot back, "Yes, but even *that's* not the main question, however much we might wish it were. We saw what we saw. Sure, we care, probably as much as Carbola, or "Noodles" Norton, or Tom Topel. At least, I do. But really, that's not where it's at for us, ok? Remember, one false move and we can all be replaced tomorrow. In fact, they may well be listening to us right now, Rassole Corporation, The Company, whoever they are. If we want to be around for when we can maybe actually do something, I say we put a lid on it now."

"Do something?" Sarah Dawson asked.

"Sure," Melinda said. "Isn't it painfully obvious that something needs to be done?"

"Shhh!" Sarah Dawson hissed. "Don't even say it out loud, Beantown! You know good and well what our role is. We're hired to *help* the President, not undermine him."

"I'm with her," Mackenzie Ward said. "I signed a contract with the administration, not with the whole world. I know which side my bread's buttered on, and you'd better know that, too."

"Of course," Adonis Wong said, "we don't know when we can do something, or even if."

Melinda caught Adonis's quick warning glance. "That's right," she said. "I'm just, you know, blowing off steam."

"Hmph," added Sarah Dawson.

"Let's move on," Luden Bond said. "If we don't shut up now, there won't even be an us to do something or not."

Holly Bronson changed the subject. "So what's with the two Topels?" she asked. "They're brothers? And are their nicknames accurate?"

"Oh, yeah," Fuba said. "I saw Roger Topel, the older by a year or so, right on the Senate floor last year, when I was still working for 'The Hill,' drunker 'n a peach orchard boar."

"So," Luden Bond said, "just report on the part of the debate over the budget?"

"Yup," Fuba said. "You're learning."

"Good thing," said Mackenzie Ward.

Chapter Six – One Way Ahead

The members of the House who were united in their desire to restore the Constitution quietly organized themselves. The self-dubbed House of Representatives Dissident Caucus met late in the afternoon on Friday, January 30, around a solitary table appropriately tucked back in the recesses of the lower-level Rayburn Office Complex cafeteria farthest from the regular throng of diners and loungers. For the moment, at least, this most unusual and scorned congressional caucus was a gang of five, Gole being a member in spirit if not actually. Only one of the dissident five was a Republican, Howard Jellen, a moderate-to-liberal black man from Manhattan who had grabbed an open slot on the ballot after narrowly losing a Democratic primary against longtime incumbent Representative Norm Scott.

The group made no secret of its existence, but neither did it draw undue attention to itself, and quickly gained the reputation of a mysterious and notorious cabal. Its leader, either a marked man or a tolerated and hopeless Don Quixote, was Harry Carbola, the callow freshman congressman from North Dakota, already called "Tom Payne" by some, dismissed as "Bean-stock" by others, and ignored as a terminal back-bencher by the majority of those who were the just automatically go-alongs of both parties.

Carbola, hook-nosed and all sharp angles, sat holding his head in his hands, unwittingly resembling a prairie grasshopper in his moss-green fuzzed-up velveteen suit. "I'm already past frustration," he intoned in his breathy voice, information to no one, as he was a picture of advanced frustration. "Does anybody know what's really happening, or even what rules we're living under, or whether there *are* any rules now?"

Congressman Tom "Sober" Topel, also looking irritated, sighed deeply. "Gossens may be the only one in the government who knows anything. Although there are some who say that he doesn't even know himself, and only passes on what he hears from The Company, The Organization, or whatever their real name is, whoever they are. We've had *that* kind of president before, you know."

"Lord help us," said Nory "Noodles" Norton.

"It's an amazing thing, when you stop to think about it," Topel continued. "Our Constitution was laid out to represent the thinking and collective wisdom of the whole of our people in thoughtful, effective leadership, and all we get, far more often than not, are these strange constructs, part human, part corporate puppet, some of them partly divine as they see themselves – like the Roman emperor-gods – who can be, beyond merely swayed in their practical judgments, bought and paid for by some collection of wealthy interests or other. They ignore in so far as possible every manifest consensus of citizen opinion in this country on a whole raft of issues and widely-shared concerns. What is there about us that always plagues us with such?"

"Yes," Carbola concurred. "That is true and obvious. And I don't know the answer to your question. But what matters are *you* thinking of, precisely?"

"Well, the restoration of health care with universally-guaranteed coverage, for one," Topel said. "That issue goes back to, let's see... *way* before Obama... wasn't it Harry Truman? Over eighty years ago now! And this aggressive world-sheriff foreign policy aimed at shutting down or intimidating into submission one area of the world and then another...not to mention involving eighty to ninety percent of our national budget—when we have actual money to budget, that is. And, merchandising *lots* of arms even to countries too poor to feed their populations. Need I continue?"

"No, you're right," Carbola said. "Some things never seem to change, and I agree completely. But I don't think we *have* our Constitution any longer, whether it served as intended or not. The worst is that the people of America are numb and becalmed and just take it. *Just take it!* Also, I'm beginning to suspect that some of the worst rumors may actually be true, and we may not have our federal union, as we've known it, for very long. Back seventy-five years, as my dad tells me, at least, travel across country by bus used to be God-awful slow, because every bump-in-the-road jerkwater town had service. The bus would stop in all of them, as if it was their God-given right to have bus service. Why do you think that sort of universal service came to an end?"

"Because it didn't pay the companies to continue it," Topel answered.

"That's right," Carbola said. "And some parts of this country are about to be relegated to protectorate status, or something like that, if I have my guess. Those that cost the government more to maintain than they provide in revenue, that is. Net losers is how you'd put it. Just like they used to do with "failing" under-funded schools. And of course it doesn't pay The Company to bequeath health care service to everyone, either. Tom, you might be looking at the last congressman from North Dakota, *ever*. If such a place even exists in another five years..."

Topel nodded. "And you could be looking at the last congressman from Vermont."

"That's right. It could be. What galls me the most is that these are, for now, just rumors. Without knowing for sure, we can't really do much about it."

Representative Howard Jellen, another stand-in for Sancho Panza, chimed in. "Because we don't even know where the President is taking *his* directions from, is that what you're saying?"

"That bothers me a lot, too," Nory "Noodles" Norton said. "We don't know what, or whose, set of rules he's following, assuming there *is* a full blueprint. We don't know what the agenda is for the three hundred and sixty million people of this country! We in the government, the duly-elected representatives, aren't even allowed to know any of that."

"And that cat *changed*, too," Jellen said. "After that weird day when he got stuck and lost someplace off in Kentucky? I thought he just had some bad case of Republican disease before that. Now, even the hints that he does drop about what's going on sound... damn, like they're from the pit!"

"And he's so full of tics!" "Noodles" Norton said. "Did you notice how he blinks his left eye nine hundred times a minute? He didn't do *that* before, did he? I don't think so."

Barbara Cullen, black Democratic congresswoman from the twenty-fourth district of Texas, had been listening quietly and pondering. "Howard," she now said, "you're a Republican, on paper at least. Haven't you been in any closed-door, insider meetings with the President? Maybe he makes his own majority privy to something he's not telling us."

"Nope!" Jellen shot back. "In fact, neither we, nor the official cabinet members, those who've been confirmed up to now, have any more *real* access to the President or his counsel than the Democrats or anyone else."

"Ready for reading tea leaves, anyone?" "Noodles" Norton said.

"Actually, I might be," Tom Topel said. "At least possibly, I have a source who can read tea leaves, sort of."

All eyes turned, expectantly, toward the normally plain-spoken Vermonter.

"I didn't know whether to mention this or not..." he said.

"Just spit it on out, son!" Barbara Cullen said. "Our freedom is on the line!"

Topel, now sheepish, cleared his throat. "I know this sounds far-fetched, but, well, my brother Roger, the Senator, owns a sort of semi-rural place in Fairfax, not too far from here. And, you know his reputation for tippling..."

They all nodded. In fact, it was just what they were thinking when he mentioned Roger.

"Well, when he entertains there, which is fairly often on weekends, as you probably know, he orders frozen *caipirinhas*, his favorite drink, pre-made and delivered by a little company called *Sacanagem*. It's a Brazilian-owned and -run local outfit. It's quite good. Anyway, lately, at least when this one tall, slim fellow is the driver, there is always one bottle that has a message inside."

The consensus, across the board, was first a shared smile, then a little chuckle.

"No, really!" Topel said. "All of the bottles have green paper labels...with the exception of a single red-labeled bottle. And that one always has a message, very clearly printed in an elegant, unusual script, and very tiny, on a little tape wrapped around the cork, inside the bottle." He paused and took a sip of his own drink. "That message purports, always, to give a different bit of insight, a little part of the big, secret puzzle of what really is going on, who is really giving instructions and orders to President Gossens. Believe it or not, I think these little messages are giving an accurate portrayal of where the whole system's headed, and what can be expected to happen next."

Now realizing he was serious, they all stopped stock-still, not knowing what to make of it, their eyes staring and shining.

Finally Carbola broke the silence. "So you believe these... messages?"

"So far," said Topel. "I've known about them for a few weeks now but wanted to confirm their verity before I told the group about them. They're impossible to verify and they could come from anywhere, but so far, what they say seems surprisingly plausible."

"Any idea of the source?" "Noodles" Norton queried.

"No," Topel admitted. "Absolutely none. Except, the messages are always signed, um, 'Buzzy Wuzzy'."

Everyone laughed uproariously.

"So," Jellen said, grinning, "what does this 'Buzzy the Wuzzy' have to *say?*"

Topel stood, obviously hurt. "I'll fill you all in, just as soon as there's more of a reasonable pattern. You'll see," he said. "It won't be long. I believe that pattern is already emerging."

* * *

Ex-Vice President Abe Gole was on the road, unexpectedly finding himself enjoying the freedom of the open air. He had embarked upon Phase I of his plan to restore power to the people: travel to the people and actually listen to what they had to say. So he embarked upon an unannounced, unpublicized tour of the United States as a guest of Fruitland Associated Growers, a blanket organization uniting many of the hundreds of thousands of new individually-owned 12- and 40-acre labor-intensive, low-tech, low-price farm units that now provided America its fruits and vegetables in resettlement zones stretching across the fruited (and vegetabled?) plains.

At each stop, he sat and listened to the thoughts of the resettled former urban workers and their new neighbors in the affiliated new commercial towns and zones. Supported and stocked by The Company on millions of acres of recently abandoned U.S. surplus farmland, these poor, mostly-reluctant pawns in the gigantic game had little interest in the loss of the nation's sovereignty, so preoccupied were they in frantically trying to come up with a possible course of action to enhance their economic status.

In his wanderings by motor coach from Jackson, Tennessee, out to Peoria, Illinois, Lost Nation, Iowa, Winner, South Dakota, and Olathe, Kansas, then to Driggs, Idaho, and Le Grande, Oregon, to Yerrington, Nevada, and Calaveras, California, Gole found that the ubiquitous Mexican-American farm workers who rarely could scrape together the funds, or for whatever other reason couldn't qualify for the requisite loans to become actual owners, were deeply worried about the hordes of new workers pouring in from Gambia and elsewhere in Africa who, according to widely-circulated rumor, were to work, phenomenally, for under $7.00 an hour. They remarked, to the last man and woman, that they couldn't begin to ever live on such a wage (though they were afraid it might come to that).

Abe Gole found the hard-working new small-farm owners who were trying to eke out a hard life in all of those places indignant as well at the prospect of being recruited for high-wage opportunities in depopulated Gambia to develop that land to supply low-cost tropical produce for the North American market. And they turned out to be even less interested, as a group, in the high-wage opportunities already promised to those who would assist in building barracks and bases under brutal conditions in Antarctica, alongside forced prison labor. They and their parents used to have the extras without having to go to such unfair and demanding extremes. Gole found a consensus almost to-the-man in the pubs and fields of the agrarian blocks about the rank unfairness of losing the much-better-paying industrial jobs people had under the old economy, and being forced to move way out to earn only a fraction as much. And now, it seemed, if they wanted to improve their condition, to get back to anywhere near where they had been 20 or more years before, they would have to leave their families behind and agree to go and work at the punishing ends of the earth!

The harried workers he sat down with invariably seemed surprised that such a reputedly sleazy, alcoholic pervert as Abe Gole would even care.

But he was beyond caring about his reputation. What did concern him was that the loss of representation in the government and the loss of Constitutional guarantees didn't register all that much with the workers, with the exception of the occasional misplaced oddball intellectual or malcontent. A few **times, he saw a member of an audience waving a copy of the semi-taboo counterculture book *Bright Pebbles*. When asked to comment on it, Gole demurred, suggesting he was not qualified**.

Finding himself incensed more than appalled by the workers' collective apathy, he vowed to make it his duty, wherever he went, and wherever he could attract an audience of a few men and women, to exhort them and explain to them, in passionate terms just what it was they had lost as citizens and the vital importance of working to somehow get it back. It was time for Phase II.

He set out on a speaking campaign to spread the gospel of self-rule. After he was repeatedly denied access to large indoor arenas, he staged large outdoor meetings, often speaking from the back of a pickup truck or flatbed. The local sheriff's cars, with uniformed officers standing at the edges of the crowds conspicuously reporting on cellular phones to some central matrix did not escape his attention.

* * *

On Monday, February 2, at precisely 5:00 a.m., Armageddon came abruptly to the sub-basement of the ATF Headquarters Building in Washington, and thus to the world, with an explosion loud enough to rattle dishes on shelves halfway to Richmond. The whole south half of the massive stone building was blown to smithereens and scattered in dime-sized pieces all over the original District of No-representation. The Capitol Police apprehended a man identified as Samuel Lin, an ATF janitor, sitting seat-belted and unhurt in the driver's seat of a red Fleet sedan double-parked across the street, and held him, ostensibly for insisting he had seen nothing.

The D.C. Police attributed the explosion to a faulty boiler, but the Gossens Administration was not satisfied with this too-simple and hasty explanation. A rumor circulated at once that someone had found a shoe-sized detonation device on the edge of the rubble (though others dismissed it as nothing more than a sort of vibrator used to scare away mice), which had been manufactured, most tellingly, in China. The White House insisted that Mr. Lin be held at least as a material witness, and publicly suspected the East Asian Axis of setting off the explosion to spread fear and "make a statement on Presidents' Day."

(President's Day, of course, would only fall on February 12, ten days later, which raised questions for those always suspicious of government statements. Presumably, the answer was that some White House insider had gotten her or his holidays mixed up in penning the press release but was unwilling to be tagged with making a mistake.)

Immediately, the White House ordered a precautionary lockdown and special surveillance of the East Asian countries' embassies, and President Gossens addressed the nation at 9:00 a.m. Eastern Time that day from the Oval Office, as follows:

"My fellow Americans, we must not give in to the merchants of fear and dreadful death who are lurking in the world. I must emphasize that, at this point, the FBI's investigation of the terrible incident that happened this morning has only begun, and we cannot, and should not, draw any final conclusions.

"True, the alleged detonation device recovered at the scene was of East Asian Axis origin, as, of course, was the lone material witness taken into custody, Mr. Lin. We must ask ourselves who would have a motive for again rattling our entire nation, and for making such a statement prior to the most preeminent and hallowed of our national days. The embassies of the Republic of China and Japan, Inc., and of United Korea have been quarantined. However, their personnel have been duly apprised, as I have reminded you all, that our findings and conclusions have not been finalized at this time, pending investigation. All installations and law-enforcement units throughout this country have been placed on special alert, to avert any repetitions, potentially involving levels of casualties unimaginable from further reprehensible acts of the kind that are considered possible explanations here.

"We are asking all citizens within the reach of this message to remain on alert and inform your local authorities of any suspicious movements or activities by any individuals potentially connected in your line of sight. And, in the meantime, we are asking you to resume, with due circumspection, your normal daily activities, your carpooling and buying mittens or mutton at Target-K or Super-6, with the assurance that your government is at work, doing your business.

"Particularly, we are at work involving the program your precious tax dollars are going to bring into reality, to include what has become known in ordinary parlance as 'Project Zap,' holding forth as it does the promise to banish such incidents as I am speaking to you of entirely from our soil in the near future. My fellow Americans, God bless, and God speed."

And with that, if they hadn't already, the nation went back to its daily round of routines.

Chapter Seven – Chronicle: First Quarter

It just so happened that the new President's first non-official State of the Union Address, before an assembled joint session of Congress, was scheduled for the evening of Tuesday, February 3, 2033, the very next day after the incendiary event that destroyed the headquarters of the Bureau of Alcohol, Tobacco, and Firearms.

An air of surrealism settled over the House chamber as the nation's forty-ninth and most-hulking president leaned over the majestic lectern, evoking all the menace of a tranquilized yellow-wigged cobra. To Congressman Harry Carbola, seated well back, the President appeared as an ominous, misty figure of allure drawn from a mad Wagnerian *volk* opera. The Congressman marveled in near-agony that, after everything that had taken place, and despite all the widespread agonizing, Gossens's public approval rating still stood at 62%.

Peter Gossens appeared before the assembled Congress and nation via C-TV. In his heavy makeup and his head alone illuminated by a mini-spotlight, he appeared a spectral, disembodied head. A bead of sweat conspicuously coursed down his blue-veined temple, destined to stain his starched, high-vaulting collar.

Prairie dog-like, shifting in his seat, Congressman Carbola strained to catch every word, to try to penetrate the thick, odd ethos engulfing that chamber.

"My fellow Americans," the President began, his radio evangelist's stentorian drawl swelling effortlessly to fill the space in the room and beyond, "our world is poised tonight on a knife-edge of danger and chance."

"Where did he come up with that phrase, this dullard, loose-tongue clod from south Georgia?" Carbola asked himself. Had Gossens taken the crass, amoral poet Horace Morgen on his staff to smooth out his piney-woods style of diction, as rumored? At the last possible moment, just before leaping up to protest, the Congressman reminded himself that what he most needed to do on this occasion was to discern the man's meaning rather than try to plumb his peculiar expression, because he did have a way with a segment of the public.

In the meantime, this murderer of platitudes continued headlong into his peculiar rendition of the nation's most-critical day in recent times: "Our palpable danger lurks in our uncertainties," Gossens intoned. (Ah! Carbola thought. At last, something we can agree on!) "Environs teeming with our enemies confront us, unfortunately, with daunting imperatives before which we dare not shrink." (Here we go, baby, Carbola thought. You are justifying *anything* because you just might *do* anything).

"The best thing we can do for our country and to protect our beloved way of life from the East Asian Axis that may have pierced our defenses in a small but signal way yesterday, in the incident that is still as I speak under official investigation, but bears all the earmarks of perfidy..." (Oh, brother!) "...is to completely put an end to all temptation they have to war against us, by fully operationalizing our promising Project Zap project, in order to perfect the ultimate laser-beam weapon that will permit us to utterly and cleanly vaporize entire armies, fleets in the air, fleets at sea, fortifications, or any other solid and liquid targets of our choosing, such as tanks, individual planes, patrolling soldiers, and up to entire cities of the enemy. Without in the least harming the surrounding chattels or countryside." He paused to smile reassuringly, as instructed by the teleprompter, prompted, probably, by Edward Lambent.

"The concept of repellant borders which we have long had under discussion, to be activated upon notice when and where we wish, may also, ultimately, depend on adapting the same 'Laser-Zap' technology to that purpose. Therefore, I am asking Congress for a bill to authorize that application as well." (Talk about perfidy! thought Carbola. He watched amazed as the President earnestly presented a list of tasks to the nation, each one more chilling than the last. If he didn't know better, Carbola could have sworn that Gossens was merely reading a list dictated by some unknown entity, so removed he seemed from what he was saying.) "An electric line, activated without warning, to fry anyone we don't want entering the country; an electrified field equipped to disable at discretion any plane within five-hundred miles of the country..."

And still, the often-repeated swelling of applause, hoots, and whistles rose each time from one side of the aisle, interrupting his earnest elocution for a moment or two. It never waned. It was like watching a cartoon.

"We ask Congress to pass very quickly new legislation repealing wholesale consumer protections in law and government, *including consumer education,* and to outlaw consumer movements, correctly declaring them, by nature, in restraint of trade. We cannot and will not abide impediments compromising our economic efficiency."

Gossens paused to pour himself a glass of the mineral water in a crystal pitcher at his elbow. "Another initiative we in the inner circle of the administration have been discussing," he continued, "is something I have not found prudent to mention publicly until now."

(At this, Harry Carbola strained forward to the utmost of his falcon-like frame, now even more angular than that of the President who had splayed himself over the large podium.)

President Gossens stopped for another sip of water and continued. "My fellow Americans," he said, a bit gargly from swallowing, "we are proposing and preparing, with your support, to colonize a new Southern continent, which beckons to us by the bounty of vital resources it holds for our future." (Dear God! This buffoon wasn't going to try to occupy Latin America, was he?) "Antarctica, my friends and fellow citizens! Antarctica, a pristine storehouse of minerals we so badly need to maintain our storied way of life, is becoming slowly but steadily revealed in its fullest actuality by the beneficial retreat of its previously-eternal shackles of frost!"

He stopped for effect, noting a frosty stillness as the surprised audience began to take it in.

"This has to do also with a genuine crisis which has arisen regarding our governing Republican Party's longtime favored private prisons program, notably effective, up until now, through three administrations." (Congressman Carbola couldn't even take in the Antarctica plan at the moment. It was just too huge. For now, he could hardly believe that Gossens was actually being candid and leveling with the forgotten regular citizenry about something.) "But now," he continued, "of a sudden, it seems, we have on our hands a related serious menace from those private outfits..." (*Outfits! What a choice of words!*) "...now in control of the largest dangerous incarcerated population in the world. In short, they are attempting *extortion,* on a massive scale!"

(Now this *was* news. It had been anticipated in some quarters for years, but Carbola couldn't believe it was actually happening).

"Denoting the sudden dramatic increase in the funds we now have available as a nation, from the wonderful arrangement my administration was able to work out, even in its very own inception, with The Company, these prison outfits are demanding fifteen per cent of the entire annual budget of this nation as a payoff, *or else...* or else they threaten to unleash the murderous population of inmates they control to wreak havoc, sent out on hellacious missions and at will.

"So, I am proposing to instead retake control of up to half of the worst prisoners and to join them with the ranks of those daily and hourly convicted of serious drug offenses nationwide, and, by executive order, re-locate them on the icy Antarctic shores. This nefarious group will become forced workers in Antarctic mining operations scheduled to open up soon, which will regularly supply a proportion of all of our industrial market demand for gold, copper, silver, iron, chromium, manganese, molybdenum, nickel, lead, titanium, uranium, and zinc, all of which are in abundant supply there. And this says nothing of the relatively bottomless supplies of oil that are now known to exist in that quarter!"

He flashed an enormous map of Antarctica on the giant overhead screen behind him to illustrate. Harry Carbola noticed even at a distance that his shambling frame and gaunt face had become a sort of insanely flashing scoreboard of rampant tics and jerks.

The assemblage of lawmakers in the place still remained utterly silent for another long moment, taking in both the earnestness and audacity of the at least superficially ingenious plan and the stranger who was President.

"Which way's north?" someone in the assemblage finally shouted.

Then, unaccountably, an intense wave of all-but deafening applause swept the chamber, both sides. Thus Gossens arrived at his finest hour in the new presidency to date, sweeping aside, at least for that brief moment, the unexpected leaden reception that had met his first official gambit of liquidating the debt by in effect *selling the country*. Not a single revealing word on that most brazen and apprehensive maneuver in the country's entire existence appeared in the speech. But, he had at least come through in giving a famished, placebo-addicted nation the *something* it needed so very badly to feel halfway positive about.

There were also a few more token flourishes of glazed icing yet to be dabbed on the metaphorical cake he was intent on prettying up before he left the dais. One was a request for the swift passage of his administration's "Freedom From Information Act," intended to relieve the average citizen's burden of having to wade through so many viewpoints and stimuli in forming an opinion on any subject. Again, such a concession would but codify what was already in effect, and in fact many were cheered to have their habitual inattention praised as a virtue and sanctioned in writing.

The speech was immediately adjudged a classic by the preponderance of an admiring public at home, who approved already of Gossens's looks and folksy charm – qualities the Travel Team frequently highlighted. There were, however, a few sticks-in-the-mud who weren't so enthusiastic, such as the sourpuss hack politicos ascendant in Washington, like those insufferable Topel brothers from stifled little Vermont, and least of all, that dissembling, hard-eyed demon of the prairies, Congressman Carbola. Because, many viewers at home were prompted to ask themselves, what did *they,* or *he,* know?

* * *

Not long after President Gossens was elected, an unexpected ally arose as his chief effective propagandist and apologist to the public at large. This curious character was a mere voice on the radio, a previously little-known talk show host with the almost unimaginable name of Ed Barge-Commerce. To his fans, E. B-C was something of a nostalgic throwback to the likes of Rush Limbaugh and Father Coughlin from earlier days, but with an added plus. He was, or so he claimed, the President's school chum from when they were sprouts and his co-worker in radio for decades (although it seemed that no one could verify that they were close now). As such, he knew more than anyone about the nation's leader and the background from which he sprang. Thus did he enthrall the faithful and the progressives alike.

From the beginning, Barge-Commerce, a burly, truck-driver type with an oddly high-pitched but thick-as-cream voice, supported and talked up and extolled all of the Gossens administration programs to the hilt and over the top. The Travel Team members were beside themselves wondering how to respond to this development: they merely had to tune into Barge-Commerce's daily broadcast for a positive spin on even the most troublesome of the President's initiatives, and so the program became practically compulsory fare for all of them, whether they liked its host's unique style or not.

The forceful dual action of withdrawing from and expelling the UN, Barge-Commerce declared, "was something we should have done a long time ago, because they wouldn't any of them lay down their measly, counterproductive desires to regularly follow our lead or to benefit us."

Relegating the old, tired Constitution and accepting "the bargain" only made sense, he affirmed, "if we really wished to compete in a cutthroat world filled with the malignant gambits of our enemies – and if we really wanted to finally shake loose from the shackles of the ungainly debt, so unseemly for the leading country of the world."

The Antarctica Initiative was "the last word in anti-crime psychology and deterrent," he said, "and Gossens was a gosh-darn genius for thinking it up." Who could argue with its merits? Barge-Commerce asked his listeners. Especially when it "provides us our own, unique pipeline of minerals as the retreating ice unveils them, just in time to rescue our way of life, and confounds the prison corporation pirates who plotted to commandeer the sudden revenue surge afforded by the President's brilliant bargain."

Transferring our country's ownership rights to our own investor-owned corporations in and of itself? Barge-Commerce explained that this was merely a preemptive measure to prevent a take-over of America by the East Asian Axis countries. "Everyone knows how clever those East Asians are," Barge-Commerce said, "and as the previous owners of our unjust debt, they're no doubt planning to perform a truly hostile takeover of our fair land, using the leverage accruing as interest. We can all breathe a sigh of relief that President Gossens had the foresight to prevent such a tragedy."

The "*minifundia* initiative" (in fact, so called first by Barge-Commerce on his radio program) was – according to this purposeful and persistent persuader and promoter – likewise pronounced brilliant, permitting as it did masses of former urban industrial workers, displaced mainly by East Asian industrial robots, to own and harvest the fruited plain, insofar as domestic market produce could be made economically available, with the enthusiastic help later on of the Gambians and, hopefully, other proud Africans farther in the future.

And so it went with every aspect of the Gossens initiatives, all in their turn as they surfaced. Barge Commerce's thinking was so in league with Gossens', in fact, that in the minds of many, the two childhood chums quickly became synonymous. A few in the Gossens camp objected, not wanting the savior confused with the beloved disciple, but in the end the point was moot. Gossens's approval ratings took another bump skyward.

Not everyone, of course, was enthralled with B-C, or as the faithful had come to call him, "the Blessed Conservative." When a rogue reporter at the New York *Times* questioned Barge-Commerce's "naively uncritical take" on the Gossens administration, Ed Barge-Commerce fired back that the exclusivity of good news could not but raise the morale of the triumphant American people. Wasn't there enough negativity and criticism in the world? It was time for a change, and he for one meant to follow his democratically elected President's lead and not be such a crybaby liberal, always finding fault.

The nation largely agreed. The Ed Barge-Commerce Program in the morning (and re-broadcast in many places again in the afternoon and again late at night) came onto the scene like gangbusters. In work places, homes, and shops, and blaring from loudspeakers in super-stores and public squares, boomed that trademark axle-cream voice spouting wafers of wisdom to the famished millions, who had had of late to abide punchless empty Democrat administrations and their inane socialistic policies slowly draining the country of muscle. Almost no one seemed to find it problematic that not a single soul had ever laid eyes on the object of their veneration. "No one can see God, either," became the defense of some. Still, when the same cranky *Times* reporter started to make a stink of it, a slightly out-of-focus picture of the Blessed Conservative was widely circulated. Ed Barge-Commerce was a chunky, big-shouldered man sporting a winsome, handsome smile. Some said they could detect a rebellious pony tail just barely visible over his right shoulder; others said the dark patch was a shadow, most likely of the Washington Monument or a light pole. The public was satisfied until an anonymous letter arrived at the *Times* claiming that the man pictured was a hairdresser from Schenectady. Who knew?

Some of Ed's more recent anecdotes had already caused some of the more observant among the faithful to question where he was really coming from, and what his real motivations for glorifying the President were. One in particular put their faith to the test.

"Good morning, folks!" Barge-Commerce boomed. "Boy do I have a treat for you today! This morning I have a very special *tidbit* from the earlier, misspent life of my boyhood friend and fellow broadcaster Peter Gossens, our beloved President. The American people deserve to know if their President is honest. Or, does this President cherish larceny in his heart? I think that's a fair question, don't you?

"So then, once, while we were moonlighting together at the station in Brunswick, Pete see, gets this sudden interest in cut gem stones from a magazine article he read, and he goes to someplace in Florida, on a whim, I think it was St. Petersburg, or maybe Miami, to study lapidary art for just a week or so on his vacation. And he comes back with some tools and supplies. And about a week after he gets back, see, he's running this ad in some southern Georgia papers to sell these gorgeous cut diamonds – I don't know how he did it exactly – at unheard-of reasonable prices.

"His very first customer happened to be this very tall blonde in Macon he halfway knew from high school connections who almost could have been his twin, named Sarah Beal. And Sarah, if you're from Georgia at the time, everybody knew her name, because she pretty much rewrote the girls' high school basketball record book in the state.

"Well, Pete drove up halfway to meet her with the stone, and they hit it off. But then, she went off and had it tested – beautiful stone and big as a June-bug – and she called back and wanted to meet him again. Well, he was pumped, and got all spit and polished, and they met at this restaurant on the Interstate halfway between where they lived. And she brought a Mr. Rod Finch, a kind of society lawyer who was a friend of her father, along.

"And she told him, not so sweet now, that she knew the stone was cut glass because she'd scratched it herself, and then had it tested to make sure. And the only way she wouldn't sue him and press charges was for him to marry her and give her that beautiful fake. With his already gigantic career and an offer to go network, he had no choice really. And, friends, I hate to break it to you, but that's really how it happened. He didn't do anything else like that, so far as I'm aware. I think she tamed him down pretty good, don't you?"

Then that same afternoon, listeners were shocked to hear a special breaking news report from Ed Barge-Commerce. "Folks, thank you for joining me at this unusual time for a special announcement. I want to talk to you about an issue that's been weighing heavy on my heart all these days. Your President is as honest a man as they come, and I believe he would want you to know the explicit truth about the early circumstances of his courtship with your First Lady, Sarah Lureen Beal Gossens. The truth is, Pete and I were rivals for that lovely lady back in south Georgia. I met her first! Me and Miss Sarah were gettin' along like pancakes and syrup before Pete showed up with his big ol' diamond. Doesn't matter if it was cut glass – Sarah always was one for jewelry. Well listen folks, the network has only given me a few minutes here – the Disciples of the late departed Brother Rushdoony – still with us in the spirit, and some say in the studio – have generously allowed me a slice of their on-air time – so I'll have to finish the story next Tuesday, Monday being a holiday. Afternoon, folks, and God bless!"

The First Lady, when questioned by reporters over the weekend, blushed profusely at the mere suggestion, and shot back that Ed must be mistaken, because she never did and never, ever would date such a person, end of story. And a certain segment of America held its breath all weekend waiting for more, while the Gambia mass-kidnap-for-labor story was just breaking, practically unnoticed by the populace.

In the meantime, a pair of right-wing gossip columnist sisters became intensely curious as to just who this Barge-Commerce, whom they'd never seen, who was just a voice on the radio really, actually was, and what he might be like.

Breaking into the downstate Georgia studio just before air-time that following Tuesday, they found in the sole studio chair, all wired up and ready to rumble, a homely and skinny-butt blond woman with enormous, ratted hair, who couldn't have been over five feet tall or weighed a hundred pounds. The signboard in the room as the topic of the day read: "Decapitate Dissidents."

"What's your name?" Dagmar, one of the deliberately outrageous sisters asked the woman, who obviously recognized her.

"Ed… Edna Barge-Commerce," came the answer in that inimical thick-as-cream bland Southern voice by now so familiar to all.

"Is that your real name?" the other sister, Delilah, had the presence to ask.

"No," the now-crestfallen girl at the mike cried, deflated to be found out. "Marge."

"Marge Barge-Commerce?" Dagmar asked her pointedly.

"No. Marge Smith," the imposter disclosed, forlorn and desperate, seeking now to take the world's two most notorious gossips into her confidence, like grasping at noodles in a giant soup. And then she learned, to her absolute bottomless dismay, that the airwaves had just been literally cut off, and she spoke only to herself for the first time since protecting her gawky little tow-headed friend called Petey back in kindergarten. "Petey, oh Petey, it was you and I, and you left for that big hairy-legged mannequin. I only wanted to help you!" she sobbed softly to herself. "*How could you?*"

* * *

Later on the night of the ersatz State of the Union speech, the Travel Team came together in the secret subterranean site to break it down and coordinate their coverage in accordance with the understood conditions of their mission. Such was not always easy to achieve, though to do so, they all knew, was vitally necessary. As mutually understood, their reportage was to be terse and constitute only a sterile rendition of bare, accurate facts, to serve their masters, which they had come to call the "Administration-Company Axis."

Camilie Auden, curiously enough, was not content on the occasion of this address. "He didn't include anything that anyone was waiting to hear," she said. "He didn't clarify the nature of the pact to run the country from here on or say what was in store for our institutions or democracy at all. Not a clue! All just gigantic pet projects."

Luden Bond answered her with uncharacteristic nervousness, speaking in a loud, hoarse whisper. "Lower your voice, Audie, did you just wake up? The reason he didn't address any of that is that he really doesn't have a clue, probably, any more than the rest of us. He can't pass on what he himself has not been given to know."

"You know, I think there really is a 'Mr. Rassole' somewhere," Adonis Wong said, "and I think he's taken firm hold – like a death grip – on President Gossens. But that's just my opinion."

"Which no one asked for," Mackenzie Ward reminded him, acid in her voice.

"Well, *something* has happened to him, that's obvious," Fuba "Tex" Thorter said. "But what about that Antarctica thing? That really could be historic – tackling that problem with what? A penal colony and a *productive* penal colony, solving in one swoop a big, looming extortion problem that never existed before! Who could possibly have come up with that?"

"It sounds pretty strange," Sarah "Blink" Dawson said. "And we don't even know if it will solve *that* particular problem."

"But it did manage to divert attention in a different direction," Holly Bronson said. "Is that what you were saying, Fuba?"

"You got that part right, at least," Adonis Wong said.

And they all set about compiling what they had, after the manner they were constrained to.

* * *

The next day, the members of the Travel Team, needing some R and R, met at the D.C. Quay in East Potomac Park to organize themselves into three canoe-racing squads to practice for the new mid-February municipal "Palms on the Potomac" festival celebrating certain aspects of accelerating climate change. What an amazingly sharp contrast to the increasingly rare spontaneous snow blanketing of a mere two months before! How wondrously-displayed the climate change befallen!

* * *

The associated member units of the PPA, the association of America's privately-owned prison companies, were among the few large-scale stock companies in the country not amalgamated under the Court-permitted broad umbrella aegis of The Company. Jack Hegartha, President of the PPA of America, headed up the effort of the organization of prisons to extract an astronomically higher contracting fee from the government, using the threat of gradual release of prisoners as a necessary bargaining ploy, given the prison companies' stratospheric and rising expenses. He was as surprised and shocked at the related tactic in the new national Chief Executive's address as anyone. Answering the reporters' questions during the media coverage following the State of the Union Address, Hegartha vowed to block in court any attempt by the federal government to transfer levies of prisoners out of PPA member facilities in violation of the government's contract, and, that route failing, to authorize a mass release of prisoners into society, five per cent a day, providing them with escape vehicles and perhaps even guns, until the PPA's cost-covering fee demands were met from the public trough.

The White House came out the following day with a pledge to dispatch the military to remove all of the prisoners, without exception, for mass transportation to Antarctica on June 15 unless the PPA agreed at once to observe and extend the contract for incarceration and care with its terms unaltered. The White House cited the need of the economy for the anticipated influx of Antarctic minerals as a secondary compelling factor, and vowed to move forward swiftly in re-sentencing serious violators of the nation's drug laws, some retroactively, to hard labor in the Antarctica Mines that were just coming on-line.

The remaining civil rights organizations almost immediately launched a coordinated press campaign condemning the government's bold new plan to move prisoners wholesale to Antarctica as a particularly flagrant example of "cruel and unusual punishment," threatening interminable lawsuits. But the clear majority of constitutional and civil rights authorities interviewed in a long, seemingly unending chain on C-SPAN and NNN opined that the administration was on firmest ground in that regard, predicting that any lawsuits against the government of that tenor would be summarily bounced out of court.

Within days, announcements came that the government had contracted with three constituent divisions of The Company – Haliburton, Bechtel, KBR, and Brown & Root – to quickly begin the business of constructing the massive dormitory in the deep, polar South, to service the same, and to transport platforms, and work and living facilities to place the convict populations in what was being called "Operation Freeze-Down." Their mission would be to prepare the first mining sites on the proverbial cold continent. Drug crime experts, highly mixed in their assessments of the program's likely effectiveness versus the traditional drying out and rehab, predicted that the sweeping measure, unprecedented in recent times, definitely would have a salutary deterrent effect on the commission of drug crimes going forward.

At the same time, a parade of members of Congress kept insisting that the program would have to go through them, and some even averred that the Gossens administration could not unilaterally brush aside long-standing international pacts governing operations on the Antarctic continent. Meanwhile, the planning and preliminary steps toward an effective occupation continued moving ahead, at lightning speed, citing national security.

Chapter Eight – Chronicle: First Quarter, Continued

The administration's astonishing tandem "Operation Freeze-Down" program for drug offenders and the new Antarctica Mining Initiative succeeded admirably in diverting public attention away from the still-shadowy but momentous constitutional changes that were already coming into effect. Just after dawn on Monday morning, March 16, three full months earlier than the schedule announced, U.S. military shock troops seized 112 private lockdown facilities from one end of the country to the other, holding all inmates and all staff inside under the technical classifications of "opponent accessories" and "pawns of enemy outfits," sealed off from all exogenous contacts and communication. Some members of the President's party in Congress hailed it, as soon as the announcement came, as a bold move and a breakthrough on a number of fronts, lauding the President's "Reaganesque," no-compromise attitude. Surely, it was said, the country's "adversaries," the members of the East-Asian Axis (practically no one was as yet calling them "enemies," because the term carried legal implications) would be "put on notice" by his stunning action. President Gossens' approval rating in the polls, it was simultaneously announced, inched for the first time a notch above 60%.

* * *

Late in the afternoon of Tuesday, March 17, the informal House Dissident Caucus, with all of the five regular members, Representatives Harry Carbola, Tom "Sober" Topel, Howard Jellen, "Noodles" Norton, and Barbara Cullen, met in their usual sanctum in the far corner of the farthest-back side dining room of the basement cafeteria in the archaic and gently moldering Rayburn Building. A sixth House-member, Dan Foster, a conservative Democrat from Missouri, had asked to join their number, but they all agreed he was more than likely to simply spy on their proceedings.

Carbola, as usual, seemed to be high-strung and yet somehow relaxed and in his groove at the same time. Sitting backward and straddling a chair that was too small, his gangly frame leaning forward and knees bent almost up to his chest, he managed to resemble a lanky, hairy-legged kid with a baseball cap turned around backward, except without the baseball cap. As usual these days, he was fuming.

"Do you realize we still haven't received any word at all on the status of Congress, or even of next year's elections?" he said. "Party donors in my state are getting very anxious to know what's going on, I can tell you."

"I hear you," Barbara Cullen said. "But that's in every state, you know."

"And there's that rumor still persisting that they might not even all be represented anymore," Carbola said.

"*They* who?"

"The states."

"Well, I might be able to shed some light on those questions," Tom Topel answered.

All eyes turned toward him in rapt expectation, belying the individuals' professional outward sophistication. Something of a familial feeling had developed among the five, who risked much to meet regularly and exclusively on genuine principle. A certain distancing had become evident, as all other members generally gave them a wide berth in the corridors of the Capitol.

"I'm totally convinced now," Tom Topel said, "that this 'Buzzy Wuzzy,' whoever he or she is, is legit. He or she knows something about the inside and workings of a lot of things, that's for sure."

"So, what's the latest word, then?" Barbara Cullen asked.

"The latest cork-tape says there's now going to be a loyalty oath demanded for those who want to stand for Congress, that is, *if* there's to be any elections at all, meaning loyalty to the contract arrangements made with The Company – though we still don't even know what these are. Plus, a second thing: Only members from net-plus districts, those that over the past ten years paid in more to the treasury than they cost, will be permitted to run for election *or* re-election."

"Must have been a long tape," Barbara Cullen said.

"Well, Buzzy Wuzzy does write in a very small script," Topel said.

"Anyway," Barbara Cullen said, "sounds like no elections they can avoid."

"You got it, Bab," Topel said.

Carbola, snapping a pen in two, ink running down, interjected, "Great! Those s.o.b.'s!"

Howard Jellen did the mental math on whose seat would be endangered. "Sorry, Harry."

"It's not just me," Carbola said. "And our ranks of fervent opponents are likely to swell, if this becomes generally known."

"Noodles" Norton wasn't so sure. "Well, they'll come up with some kind of 'spin,' to use an old word. If you ask me, there will be elections, but only *they* will get to vote. And they'll plant this sour-ball in something real sweet, we can count on that."

"You might be right," Carbola said. "So what can we do?"

"I think we may have to resort to your Plan B, Harry," Howard Jellen offered dryly.

Congressman Carbola looked around at the others. "Are you with me, then?"

"Um-hmm," every one of them offered.

"That's why we're here," Congresswoman Norton added.

Carbola posed another rather obvious question. "But how can we know if this so-called cork-tape stuff means anything, Tom? Whoever it is could just be making it all up as a storyline to fit the facts as already known."

"You mean, like the 'Security' people do?" Barbara Cullen asked?

"Like with the old color codes?" probed Congresswoman Norton.

"Could be," Topel allowed. "But, I don't think this apparent insider is doing that. The sense of certainty the messages convey is really persuasive. True, the info could be just a series of good guesses, but you have to admit there is a certain way the messages are constructed, a certain logic to it. All of this would make a hell of a thriller, I'll tell you that."

"Wish it were," Barbara Cullen averred. "Maybe I need better makeup."

"Any clues, Tom?" Carbola asked. "I mean, who do you think it could be?"

Topel turned in fact sober. "Well, Roger's asked the tall black guy who makes the deliveries, and he claims he doesn't even know what Roger's talking about."

"Does he know any English?" Barbara Cullen asked.

"Yeah. He must have taken his driver's test."

Topel cocked his head to one side. "Right. Not quite like you or me, he doesn't. But, he's been here a long time – Brazilian. I'm sure he can read and write English. At least, he signs off on the invoices, and records the specs, I suppose in English, because they check those records from time to time."

"But how could we determine for sure who's sending the info?" Carbola asked.

"I'd say we can't, at least for now," Howard Jellen said.

Carbola wasn't ready to give up so easily. "You know what, though? The construction, storyline, whatever, in these tapes seems to make more sense than I, or I bet any of you, could make about these things, crazy as they are, right now. And, even if it is just made-up, there's something very seriously wrong when no one in the country knows what our fundamental document, or the rules of play, is."

"Are," Barbara Cullen corrected.

"Are. What the rules are," Carbola conceded. "Who's pulling the strings? Do we have any honkin' democracy left at all, or are we already into the Roman phase in our country, and we just aren't ready to deal with it yet? And, if we are being run over, how do we pick ourselves up, re-inflate, and huff and puff and take the whole thing back? Penal colony. Antarctica mine. Diversion! I'm almost sure this filthy sell-out Gossens doesn't like what's goin' on so well these days, either! Have you seen how pale and shaky he is, ever since he came back from his little few hours' disappearance?"

Jellen whistled. "What's he got to say about it? They're pullin' his strings, I'd lay money."

"Of course," Carbola said. "But maybe for someone with his political beliefs, it's not that far-fetched for him to just do the bidding of plutocrats, and not make unnecessary waves."

Barbara Cullen looked forward. "Well, I'd say that the time is coming, and fast, when if we're gonna do anything, any of us, we've got to get over being shell-shocked and start linkin' together for real and form a movement to demand a stop to this heavy horse-hockey, and re-commit this whole country back to a representative covenant. We need to get our Constitution back and no mistake!"

"Noodles" Norton liked the prospect. "And it might not even require violence if everybody, the ninety-plus percent that would want it, would stand up all at the same time and *require* it!"

"And literally not sit down until they got it," Barbara Cullen added.

"*If*," Howard Jellen said. "Only if—"

"Howard!" Barbara Cullen said. "You don't think that it could happen?"

"No, frankly. No. But, whatever… I'm with you. What's the saying?"

"These are the times that try men's souls?" Topel suggested.

"And women's," Barbara Cullen answered.

"We'll all hang together?" "Noodles" Norton tried.

"The first, hopefully," Jellen responded with a little laugh, feigning a shudder.

Carbola brought them back to the task at hand. "I'll see what I can do about getting regular information networks and an outreach organized, including, for a change, people like us with elected power, along with an online base. Any help any of you can give for this, please do. And Tom, I don't know how you can do it, but try to find out exactly who 'Buzzy Wuzzy' is."

"Yeah, I'll see what I can do."

"And see if you can figure out," Carbola added, "who we can compromise to get to leak to us the Administration-Company agreement."

"If there *is* such a contract or agreement on paper," Topel said.

"That's a thought," Carbola said. "But they must have a blueprint with some directions somewhere…"

"Well, let's wrack our brains," Topel said.

Barbara Cullen added, gruesomely, "…While we still have them, and access to them."

"That's a thought, too," Jellen conceded.

Cullen drew out a clean sheet of paper. "Let's divide up responsibilities and report next Tuesday, same time. Agreed?"

All agreed.

* * *

The Travel Team of the stellar young journalists were kept perpetually busy trying to compose strictly positive reports on everything that was assigned or going on, highly controversial and questionable though the majority of it inherently was, at the bidding of their new masters. Cracks had begun to form in their firm resolve to report nothing but positive news, as they weren't – as their contract required – strictly automatons. In fact, they found themselves forced again and again to push aside their critical journalistic judgments and even common sense. But they kept their opinions to themselves, save for an occasional surreptitious rolling of eyes or a weary sigh, because speaking out would surely have sent them home – at best. Fuba "Tex" Thorter, convinced that they'd be tried for treason, kept them all on the straight and narrow.

Which was getting more difficult, as well. There was much about which to be silent.

On the international side, there were the emotion-tinged pleas at the UN, now displaced to Geneva, for assistance from a jaded and tight-fisted world led by America for aid in protecting quickly-receding coastlines coming from the Lowlands Alliance countries, united in being the most gravely challenged by rising sea levels and tides. Included were the Bahamas, Bangladesh, Belize, Denmark, Holland, Maldives, Nauru, Uruguay, and one or two others. The truth turned out to be that people cared, but not nearly as much as was becoming obviously needed. Bangladesh had already lost 50% of its land mass, for instance, and the economic pressure of its population of two hundred million on the little scrap of fertile mud it had left was catastrophic.

On the culture beat, there were all of the new, strange sports spectacles that large segments of the public somehow couldn't seem to get their fill of. Which, of course, was the main intent of a system that was determined to go to great lengths to produce distractions, as well as shake loose hundreds of billions in spending with little or no cost in actual substance.

Example Number One was the "2-Car Racing Series," bankrolled by The Company, which was staged every weekend of the year except for Christmas week. The contest required a single driver to simultaneously operate *two* specially adapted stock-model cars, in necessarily close parallel, straddling the space between them, with a foot on each pair of pedals and a hand on each steering wheel. The public, at least a certain large segment of it, loved the spectacle of the drivers, faces contorted in rapt concentration, mightily struggling to keep their cars lurching ahead down the straight-aways and cranking around the curves, while carefully maintaining just the right, close distance between the two and avoiding the opposing lurching pairs of cars competing for the flag. In the unlikely event that a contestant wasn't maimed or killed, the public demanded their money back.

The attendant medical unit personnel had become lionized and much-interviewed special teams in their own right, and routinely made the morning talk show rounds to describe the carnage in grisly detail. Different commercial divisions of The Company sponsored not only racing teams but medical teams, and one particularly attractive EMT was "promoted" to driver after his popularity threatened to eclipse The Company's chosen media darling. He was dispatched with alacrity by a tricky curve in the second heat. The nation mourned. The ratings soared.

Celebrity runs were coveted by all branches of the famed and notorious, and – though of necessity generally far more timid in point of speed and daring – still resulted in enough spectacular crack-ups and blood to satisfy the viewing public. They also elicited much more concern than for the run-of-the-mill, working-class drivers, who viewed 2-Car Racing as their only viable ticket up. However daunting the prospect of racing, the occasional celebrity did decline the 2-Car Racing Association's invitation to participate. Though outwardly the public and media professed to understand—the Hollywood show must go on, after all—the celebrity in question was invariably branded with the stigma of cowardice, which led to merciless innuendo, which the enthralled public relished and thrived on.

There was, currently, an almost delirious pitch of anticipation in the air from coast to coast, border to border surrounding the semi-final and championship rounds of the second year coming up in Raleigh-Durham in April, following eleven riveting and grueling months of weekend elimination runs, beginning with 900 locally-based drivers from everywhere at the start.

Meanwhile, another popular new sporting and cultural event had recently come on line, designed explicitly to focus people's minds closer to home and appeal even to those who didn't participate in or follow conventional sports. In Challenge Ball, towns were encouraged to challenge their neighbors, up to 25 miles away, to a friendly match. The ball, an old-fashioned 60-pound medicine ball (once known as a "Hoover ball") was placed on the ground exactly halfway between the city limits of the contesting municipalities. All of the individual contestants from each of the two towns, adults, or, in some cases, by agreement, kids, would run for the ball at the signal of a siren or horn, loud enough to be clearly heard by both sides back on the starting lines.

The first player to reach the ball would lug it forward until someone from the opposing municipality succeeded in ripping it away and stagger with it back in the direction of their opponents' municipal limits.

In the course of the match, any number of players could lug the ball forward, together or separately, and any number could try to wrench it away and lug it back the opposite way. Any number of players of either gender could participate in scratching, clawing, and gouging the ball forward, with no weapons or motorized vehicles used. And no punches or blows could be exchanged. Reinforcements, all fresh and rested, could be run out onto the super-long field from behind either side's municipal limits at any time.

Regulation "Challenge Ball" matches could take up to two continuous days, but at the end of that time, the town whose municipal limits were farther from the location of the ball was declared the winner if both sides' captains agreed to stop at that point. If they did not, the game would continue either until the two captains agreed to stop play, or until the ball was lugged across one or the other locale's municipal limit.

Bets were placed between the two communities and a fortune in commercial prizes awaited the winning town and players.

The Challenge Ball match concurrent with the government's raid on the prisons involved Columbus, Georgia, and its challenger, Phenix City, Alabama, across the Chattahoochee River and a designated bridge. Phenix City bore the proud flag of Alabama to a victory before the entire nation, the meaning or magnitude of which few outside that stretch of the lower

South could even begin to fathom. The nation's attention was thereby held spellbound for three critical long days, complete with statements from the President, on camera donning alternate hats.

Luden Bond and Adonis Wong traveled to the "Battle of the Chattahoochee" to report and sum up the public mood and the spectacle, and took along files each had downloaded to draw personal-interest parallels to similar events fancied by some to have taken place in the provinces of the Roman Empire. "Resuscitated" in America, it became a good metaphor for… the meaning of life, or something.

Fuba "Tex" and Holly Bronson, meanwhile, drew the assignment of reporting the weekend's action from the site of the "All-Galactic 2-Car Championships" in North Carolina, from a strictly news standpoint.

Meanwhile, Mackenzie Ward was assigned to report developments on the new Project Antarctica front, with an assist from Melinda Thalanis. Fortunately, they were spared a trip to the actual site, at least for the time being. For the moment, they had only to cover the flurry of press conferences and briefings and proceedings of a relevant commission of top-level suppliers and investors.

On March 26, shortly after returning from a fairly long stay in Raleigh/Durham and points south, Fuba "Tex," the group's leader, with a degree of animation unusual for him, brought to the attention of selected team members a communication he had received. Two of the team members, Camilie Auden and Webster Bootle, had been invited to, in effect, go upstairs to conduct the first hour-long nationwide C-TV visit with the new President and the new First Lady in their White House living quarters, in prime-time on Friday, April 3. As soon as they accepted the assignment, unsigned memos and reams of exacting instructions started to arrive for the two, informing them precisely what they could and could not say and ask, what to wear, what their demeanor was to be for the interview, and the exact format prescribed to achieve the desired result of ingratiating the nation.

Speculation was, naturally, rife among the Travel Team as to whether Web and Audie's liaison had become known on the outside, despite everyone's efforts to keep it quiet, or if it was only their laid-back, photogenic charm (not quite unanimously acknowledged) that had resulted in their individual selection for the plumb assignment. How could one know? One couldn't, for sure, but it did seem strange.

Web and Audie arrived at the outer gates of the White House at 6:30 on the third, as instructed, and were escorted in. She wore a resplendent medium-blue gown she'd gotten at Gimbles' five years ago with a once-again newly-fashionable mid-riff, and he donned a moss-green, pink-flecked suit, some thought comedically overstuffed, and matching Southwest string-tie.

To say they were not nervous would be untrue – *Why,* they wondered, *were on-air professionals not doing this?* But each had performed well on important assignments before, although never as a team. Self-conscious, they did their best not to act "couple-like." Sarah Lureen Gossens, the President's wife, a strawberry-blond Southern belle emerged, all of 6'3" tall, the queen of Georgia girls' basketball twenty-five years before. Her well-remembered strawberry tresses were declared just as bright now as then, though now pulled back in a bun, making that style newly "in." She wore a broad-weave orange smock that also looked to some like ages past, although it was suitably demure.

She conducted Audie by the hand, and wide-bottomed Webster followed along. The President, his straw-colored mop in its patent so-so disarray, shambled in from the right, country-handsome and smiling with mock contentment. All four sat down in padded recliners, hardly elegant, truth be told, in front of the lighted fireplace in the Green Room, and the interview quickly began.

Web cleared his throat conspicuously and no more than opened his mouth to ask the first question when the Executive couple's four-year-old twins, tow-headed sons Tip and Tab, raced in like thunder, accosting each other as they scooted around with miniature "Zap guns" mounted on little carts, sporting real, super low-intensity laser beams. The little miniature "zaps" were actually visible in the dark and did no damage when the tiny mockups genuinely fired, Web had read, unless possibly in the unlikely event they severed a vein. This was the first time he'd seen the toy lasers for himself, and he swore he felt the mosquito-prick of one in his left calf now.

The presidential couple remained serene and smiled for the cameras. In fact, they appeared not to notice the twins in the slightest, though the boys were darting back and forth and even between the guests' legs, all the while firing their weapons. Web and Audie glanced at one another in disbelief and no little apprehension. Could this be an unimaginable set-up, Web wondered, or some sort of deliberate joke? He could swear he felt a little trickle of blood flowing down inside his pant-leg.

Another pinprick of pain erupted on his knee, and then Camilie uttered a little yelp of shock and pain. Meanwhile the President and First Lady smiled all the while for the cameras and made no effort whatsoever to call off their little savages. *What the hell?*

"Mr. President!" Web said, in a voice firm and steady enough to surprise himself and induce confidence, "when and under what conditions is the text of the pact between yourself, representing the government of the United States, and the doyens of The Company going to be de-classified and revealed in full to inform the American people?"

Out of the corner of his eye, he could perceive clearly that he was fixed in the steely, steady gray-eyed gaze of the formidable blond steel magnolia that was "Miss Lureen." The questions, they had been clearly warned, were to deal solely with matters of domestic life. Well, this one dealt with the domestic life of the country. Camilie Auden audibly sucked in her breath.

"Well, well now..." President Gossens said, unusually weak-voiced and sounding more than a little hoarse. "I have already told much of it. There are security requirements involved with treaties, as you know, and so my legal advisors say we're not ready to release those world-wide yet." He hesitated. "When we are, we'll give you the scoop."

Audie asked a few questions about the First Lady's different and interesting dress and her background as a small-town fashionable women's clothier, about how the family was settling into the White House, and gingerly about their teen-age daughters' momentarily-on-hold recording career.

And then, those very daughters, the older pair of twins, brunette, busty and largely identical, made a cameo appearance together in a doorway and giggled on cue. Then the President and First Lady were on their feet and thanking them for coming, it had sure been lovely. Thus it was over without Web Bootle getting to ask another single question. He felt as if he'd been zapped.

A valet showed them back out to a waiting car that took them straightaway to two different designated addresses within a block of each other.

Webster walked back to their shared address in the dark, and, entering, found a pair of FBI agents waiting, who took them away.

Chapter Nine – Gunnison Fever

On Saturday morning, April 4, the day after the much-celebrated, much-watched C-TV interview with the new President and First Lady, and the disappearance afterward of the debut duo of interviewers who had become an instant sensation, the other members of the Travel Team (except for Sarah "Blink" Dawson, who was still in Raleigh covering the hoopla surrounding the 2-Car Association Precision Duals Semi-Finals) met in their bunker to take stock.

"No, I haven't heard from them," Fuba "Tex" responded for the fourteenth time, looking as perplexed and worried as anyone had ever seen him. "At first I thought they must have been taken out on the town and given accommodations by the sponsors of the 'Periscope' series or the network, but then we didn't hear from them. I called right after to congratulate them and many times since, and there's never an answer. And the really ominous thing is that the media have barely even mentioned that they've gone missing. None of the heavy-hitters on C-TV have mentioned it at all, at least that I've heard."

"Let's face it," Adonis Wong said. "It was Web's question to Gossens. Those people aren't to be trifled with these days."

Fuba "Tex" gave a defeated nod. "Why do you think he did, especially as the very first question?"

"Because Peter Gossens is legendary for diverting attention away from what reporters want to know," Luden Bond said. "Web thought it would be his one and only chance to catch the President off-guard and address what everybody in the country really wants to know instead of dawdling over the style and origin of the White House drapes."

Adonis Wong said what they all suspected. "It might be his last question. Ever."

"Well, he must have forgotten just who he was dealing with," Fuba said. "Damn! He used to be a hell of a reporter, for such a young guy, a solid newspaper man for his age – the start of one, anyway – in the *Daily Arizonan* or *Phoenix Sun*, whichever it was."

"Isn't it a bit premature to be speaking of him in the past tense?" Holly Branson said.

Mackenzie Ward broke in, scowling. "I hope we've all learned a lesson from this! You don't bite the hand that feeds you, and we need to remember that, because we aren't ever likely to get another chance as good as this."

"What happened to confrontational journalism?" Adonis Wong said. "Can't the President handle a few serious questions?"

"Oh, don't be so naïve, Adonis," Mackenzie Ward said. "He doesn't like them because he might misspeak. You should know that, and give the man in charge the treatment he deserves. They were guests in his home, I remind you."

"Deserves?" Adonis said. "He deserves not to be called to account for selling the country and sealing up the deal before anyone had a chance to even look at it?"

"Well, he *is* the president," Mackenzie Ward said. "And he was elected specifically to set the country back on its feet and to restore our solvency."

"But what about our 'sovereignty'?" Holly Branson said, hands firmly on her hips. "He had no right to sell that."

"I just don't want to hear it!" Mackenzie Ward shouted. "What has happened to you people? Listen, Gossens was elected president, and you don't think he has any powers? How else could he have gotten the money flowing again? You like *that*, don't you? He's our *president.* Do I have to spell it out? And those two broke the rules!"

Holly Bronson's jaw dropped. "Audie 'broke the rules'? How? Webster's the one who asked the question."

"Well, there's more than one rule," Mackenzie said. "And *they* broke it. Fraternization is explicitly forbidden us, and they did it. Quietly, but they did."

The others just sat around the table looking at each other in shock and disapproval of what they were hearing.

* * *

Web and Camalie were blindfolded, bound, and gagged very tightly and sped away by car far out of the city. At least, that was a fair supposition on their part, since hours seemed to pass and the car was still traveling at speed, on and on and on and on into the endlessly bland and undifferentiated silence of the night. There was one stop for fueling, and Webster wished he could scream, because he had to go as badly as he ever had in his life, the pressure building, morphing into sheer pain. Now regretting the second large glass of iced tea he had accepted at the White House, he had no notion of how Audie might be getting along. Surely, the driver would think of that sometime, though then again he might not care.

His bladder throbbing and his eyelids simultaneously growing very heavy, Web found himself drifting off to sleep and even dreamed for a few seconds, and then for an infinite period, feeling for all the world like he was floating – which, in a sense, he was. The radio in the car came on once for a little while with some vaguely Latin-sounding music playing very indistinctly and static-y, with occasional garbled cut-ins from a talk radio show somewhere.

Once, Web uncomfortably felt Audie shift positions on the seat and lean more heavily against his back, and imagined he could feel her cramped restlessness, a reasonable inference, as the back-seat space in the car was small and seemed by turns first chilly, then oppressively warm. They were both sweaty-damp where their two backs touched. Then the chords binding them started to chafe and suddenly his arms and under his legs felt raw and rubbed red and lacerated. He wanted to scream. What was eternity to this? Presently, although his legs were cramped and went to tingly sleep, he himself could no longer doze off. How long he could maintain control of his bladder, he didn't know, although the act of doing so had become involuntary and every small undulation in the road felt like a punch to his spleen.

After hours and hours of fitful meditating on his mantra, "*NOTHING,*" Web sensed the car rolling to a stop and then, with almost dizzying abruptness, swing onto and jounce down a long side-road or drive, throwing Audie's warm, supple body weight against his back so that he could smell too distinctly her musty-grown socks.

And then, they did stop, and the left car doors were thrown open, admitting an inrush of impossibly chilled air. One of the men grabbed hold of Web Bootle's arm and pulled him out of the car, ripping the rough ropes away and setting him on his unfeeling feet.

Hurting as if he'd been doubled up by a fist-blow to the groin after all this time, unable to stand securely because his legs were cramped and asleep, feeling chilled in the sudden damp air, and with his sweetie, Audie, close beside him and never murmuring, Web was led away from the car the moment it had eased to a halt and his blindfold jerked away. He and Audie were led up a dirt path through the fog of dawn in a deep cleft somewhere, roosters, plural and at slightly different pitches, calling someplace far-off, through a yard and toward the open front door of a ramshackle farmhouse with one dim bulb faintly visible through a window.

They were pulled and shoved across the porch, its floor space filled with bags and barrels of old fetid garbage, and in through the big frame door of a rustic dining room featuring a heavy oak table atop a faded and frazzled oriental rug. On the wall above the fireplace hung a portrait Web recognized as the recently repopularized right wing prophet of the last century, Armenian immigrant Christian hero and super-patriot Rousas J. Rushdoony, whose significance in the larger scheme was his selection as an extremist icon largely owing to the utter irrelevance of his ideas to mainstream American life, and who was, coincidentally, the subject of a major paper on the Christian Identity phenomenon Web Bootle had written in college.

Rushdoony, Web recovered a memory fragment from an earlier, student, identity, was at the time of his young scholarly research a rediscovered and once again celebrated patriarch of the horrific persuasion of the authoritarian right wing that the prosperous and powerful (*at least if they were born-again Christians, hence legitimate*) are the obvious *chosen of God*, and as such, are fit to rule and manage others obviously not so divinely favored through laws and decrees designed only to control *them*. And those who dissent, especially disagreeing foreigners, are to be brought sharply to heel. To Webster, it was the old notion of *noblesse oblige* and the White Man's Burden, reincarnated by memorializing its apostle in America, and, feeling repressed himself just then, it made him burn red with almost embarrassing familiarity and loathing.

There were two men behind the table, one standing, one seated. The latter, wizened, puny, wiry, pallid, and very old, but with a strangely unlined face topped by a full head of straw-blond hair, seemed a sort of preternatural lad who had aged. The other looked ordinary by contrast, of medium height and with short brown hair, wearing a slightly-frayed baggy brown business suit, downcast a bit in demeanor.

In a tiny voice, which was now all he had left, Web asked the standing man if he and Audie could be shown to a bathroom. She went first, and then when she was brought back, he went and tried to re-compose himself from a pained sort of puckering up before being led back and bidden to sit down. Then, across the table, the old man (because that's what he was, forget the pretensions) started to speak in the pinched, totally self-assured voice of a dried-up bygone days Dixie aristocrat.

"Mr. Webster Bootle and Missy Auden," he addressed them, "I must tell you I loathed your demeanor on the TV with the President. You insolently disgraced both your own privileged position and your country."

OK, Webster thought with his mouth open, staring ahead empty-eyed, so you're a critic, one of countless millions watching. So what? He said nothing.

"You won't question *authority*," the old man commanded, with a dash of false mocking kindliness backed by just a hint of steel. He was suddenly sharp-eyed and, to Webster's hearing, his voice swelled to the equal of any barker's. "And you won't go back unless and until you have learned that. We will not have the people encouraged in self-assertion or in other such self-indulgent twaddle." His voice trailed off to a disgusted near-whisper at the end.

"Mr. Bootle and Missy Auden," the other, infinitely tired-looking man started in, evidently trying to parlay a mollifying voice of reason, "you see, you have disobeyed the essential instructions of your station. *If* you go back, you will *serve*. You *must* serve. And nothing more! If not, you'll be brought back here, where the consequences will be most unpleasant, we can assure you…even to the point that you will never return to your colleagues and your…*bunker*, I believe you call it?" Then he added, hesitatingly, "As it is, your fate has not yet been decided. You could *perhaps* go back, after you have learned to agree with us. We *do* have our ways of teaching you that, as you'll see. Furthermore, *if* you are allowed to go back, you must tell it about that someone slipped you knock-out drugs that kept you from communicating for a few days. Nothing more. We haven't yet reached a resolution about that, so be circumspect! *Nothing* is certain."

Unexpectedly, the two discordant figures stood up and disappeared wordlessly into a side-room.

Web and Camilie reflexively stood up, and drawn together despite all, embraced. Then, wordlessly, hand-in-hand, they walked over to a window at the north end of the long, deep-shadowed room and gazed as one out across the brushy, broken ground that was backed at a good distance, perhaps three-quarters of a mile, by a limestone cliff looming upward to freedom.

A stream's ripple could be heard through the big, screened window, along with heavy construction equipment off through the fog that still lingered in wisps. Directly below, they perceived presently, was an open-lidded, decrepit metal dumpster, filled almost to the brim with an oily gray substance that emitted a peculiar, unpleasantly-sour stench.

Camilie whispered in Web's ear that she thought she recognized the sickening odor from her girlhood in southern Ohio: it was hog guts or some such leftovers from butchering. Buzzing flies swarmed in the hundreds over this bubbly, churning porridge.

Web, suddenly almost overcome by a flash of his own genius, marched resolutely back over to the table and plucked two plastic drinking-straws from a dispenser at its center, and handed one to Audie. Without exchanging a word, they pushed out through the window screen together, pulled themselves precariously onto the sill, and dropped the six long feet to the ground, landing with a pair of thuds. Straws in hand, they clambered determinedly into the dumpster and, with a long, almost wailing *whoosh*, disappeared hand-in-hand, eyes closed, under the slippery, cold, nauseating muck.

Miserable hours passed, and they could hear the muffled voices of men and dogs moving around for a long time, sometimes very close. But no one was able to find them.

After all had been quiet for an eternity, Web popped up and discovered it was nighttime. All was quiet. In the moonlight, two rancid, brown-slimed bodies emerged, shivering and wet and gagging on chunks of offal stuck to their faces, but otherwise no less than alive. Dripping and unseen, they waddled toward the distant base of the outcrop, now visible only as a line.

In soaked, stinking clothes, they finally reached it, and puffing, pulled themselves up by grasping onto dangling tree-roots and loose ledge-rocks, slipping backward and landing in the dust, pulling themselves back up again, coated in muck and dirt, for what seemed like a mile of precipitous aching straight-up ascent, nostrils packed, tasting blood and bile, crawling with flies, dragging numbed legs with impossible aching arm-strength born of despair, scraped and bleeding. The remains of last-night's tattered formal wear clinging in tatters, they hauled up on top of the limestone collar and collapsed.

* * *

The House Dissident Caucus met in its usual hideaway location on the afternoon of Monday, April 13 to try to piece together what was known of recent events. There were rumors, still unconfirmed, that the pair of young interviewers from Friday night's controversial C-TV appearance with the President and First Lady had disappeared afterward and not been seen since. And although efforts to determine the identity of the mysterious informant, "Buzzy Wuzzy," had yielded nothing, a sobering new message from that entity had been received via another delivery of frozen *caipirinhas* to the Senator, Congressman Topel's brother, in Fairfax over the weekend.

In the new message, Buzzy Wuzzy revealed that the shadowy powerful corporate baron named, or at least known as, Mr. Rassole was real and lived in a rather palatial house in southern Virginia, while his father, the original shadowy magnate by that name, still the real potentate, who had started out a peddler well over eighty years before, stayed at a secluded site someplace in Kentucky and still exerted iron control to a degree scarcely imaginable. There was further intelligence that the President would be making a significant statement about a long-awaited matter of Constitutional import at mid-week.

Representative Carbola, already in such a nervous state that he had resorted to continuously teasing his hair and pulling long strands of it down to his chin, was beside himself at this news.

"This constant media emphasis on Antarctica this, Antarctica that is an outrage!" he fumed. "Who could possibly believe that our hope for gaining independence in strategic minerals, as well as freedom from the ticking time-bomb of the penal system, lies in Gossens' 'ingenious' escape from some looming extortion by the prison owners, our that our national salvation lies in mines under the receding ice of the Antarctic?! It's all such an obvious crock!"

"And if it's not exactly that, then it's bread and circuses," Topel added.

"Yeah," said "Noodles" Norton. "And you know, there weren't any daunting new crises every ten minutes until suddenly right now, since Gossens's election!"

"What about the *country* itself, our constitutional republic?" Carbola said. "And if we're going to *have* a country, and what we've probably given away already, perhaps permanently, in the idiotic bargaining of this dim-witted president with the inscrutable scamps of The Company, sacrificing all of the crying needs of this dysfunctional giant nation? Why are all of the overlords – miserable hoodlums in suits, all of them – basically invisible, not even real members of the regular community, like so many malevolent, all-powerful Greek gods? What did we ever do to deserve such a fate?" Congressman Carbola paused to think, then started again. "And what about the *disappearances?* The news media has reported *nothing* on that since the original DC Police report. Hasn't it occurred to anybody that it's so much like Gossen's strange disappearance? What has happened to those lovely, brave kids? What a sham!"

"And by the way," "Noodles" Norton said, "speaking of disappearance, has anyone heard from Abe Gole lately?"

"I get an occasional text mention," Carbola said. "He's doing some grassroots thing. I think he's out there trying to get the people fired up to take back the country."

"If we want to take back the country," Barbara Cullen said, "we'll have to simply take it back, you know. It won't just fall to us like some strange fruit back in the '40s. Antarctica and all the rest of that garbage is, really, mainly a distraction, as you said – although real enough, too, some of it. But, if the people really want their government to serve *them*, they are just going to have to *take* it and make it theirs, in a sense to *be* the government! Just like Mr. Jefferson is said to have told us! Otherwise, sorry, more of the same is the absolute level best we can ever expect."

"You really are a revolutionary, Barbara, my dear!" said Tom Topel. "So, let's see what we hear from the White House, maybe Wednesday. And plan according to that."

Congresswoman Cullen looked gratified at being understood.

But Harry Carbola, not near to being satisfied, intoned, as much to himself as anyone, "Always reacting... we're always reacting, never acting! I want to get ahead of the game. Otherwise," he said, looking at each of them, gravely, "we may not be here next week."

* * *

On the afternoon of Saturday, April 18, the President flew down to appear at the opening of a 2-Car double-header in Wilmington, North Carolina. Invisible in the crowd of sixty thousand was one Marge Smith (a.k.a. "Marge Barge-Commerce" once upon a time), of Waycross, GA, Pete Gossens's old jilted girlfriend, and she was hoppin' mad. Released abruptly from her lucrative nationwide radio contract, entered into disguised as a man, she had tried to help the cause of her lifetime hero by presenting a balanced radio commentary portrait of him, believing the truth she knew would result, on balance, in people favoring him and his efforts to lead the country. But how was she thanked for her efforts? She was coldly jilted again, shoved aside because she didn't make him out to be a saint, which he was not. And although she had as much gumption as he did, she was torn as to her best course of action now, between whether to try to greet him and kiss him, or shoot him. Literally! Her German D-9 handgun was loaded and in her handbag.

Her addled thinking at the moment she first glimpsed him leaning over the makeshift lectern, grasshopper-shaped but as big as an ant, far, far away while the cars revved their engines, was that the security was so tight that she would never make it up to him to say hello, so she would just try to shoot him. It was a terrible shame...she had practically raised him from the time she was little more than a toddler herself. But then, she chuckled, squirrel-hunting was her specialty. *No one* was better at it! She took a practice bead on him with her finger and clicked with her tongue, exclaiming in glee, "Heck, yeah!" in a fit of satisfaction. Then she nonchalantly rustled around in her bag, trying to secure the gun as the crowd, unknowing and craning as one for a view, pressed around.

Then, out of nowhere, a dark-haired man in a leather jacket swooped in, skillfully cutting through the crowd, and grasped her by the arms from behind. Firm enough to be authoritative, he encountered no resistance from her, once her little, startled *whoop* had subsided, and he walked her to an opening to confront her, his face but an inch from hers.

"Vat's ziss? You shoot President?" he asked in a thick accent, real or fake.

"I didn't," she said.

"But, you vood."

"How would you know about that? Seen a gun?"

"Ziss!" he proclaimed, producing a portable device from its leather case with a screen like an oscillator. "You zee, anyvun in crowd vith that thought, it registers from zee area of zer brain, und vee cun trok zem down!"

That is pretty astounding, she thought.

"But, look," he said, "don't you go try it, ok? Vee gonna try it, und not vant you mess up za chanz! Luk, vee do it for you, you don't hav to, ok my dear? Deal?"

By now, she was starting to hyperventilate, her heart leaping like a nervous frog. "Well yeah!" she readily agreed. "Yeah!"

"I tun you loos. But you leave za gun in za bag, ok?"

She nodded emphatically and rapidly, and he let go of her arms, practically sending her sprawling. Waiflike, she slipped back into the crowd. But then, after a few seconds, she started to sprint right through the midst of the assembled crowd, trying to make it up to the makeshift little stage to warn security, at least, and was swallowed up, perhaps lost to the futility of it, or met by security on the way.

For the President and his handlers, the event went off well.

* * *

Dead tired, the two escapees found themselves lying flat up on top of a windy moonlit plateau, crawling across a grassy opening on a wooded stretch above the mammoth sinkhole they had crawled out of.

"What are we going to do with these skunky clothes?" Web wondered aloud.

"When we come to a stream, we'll just have to hunker down and wash them," Audie answered, managing a smile, her eyes somehow shining in the near dark.

"And wait for them to dry?" Weary he was, but anxious to put miles behind them.

"And wait for them to dry. It won't take long, if this wind keeps up. And so, where do you plan for us to go, Mr. Bold Traveler?" They held each other close for a little while as they continued to stagger on.

"Well, we do have a choice!" Web said. "We can try to go back to DC, show up and use that story about the knockout drops… And really watch our backs."

"Or…?"

"Or, there's another alternative, but it's risky. One of the things I saw on a blog, one of the few halfway good ones that managed not to get jammed that day, is that there's going to be a meeting of dissident-minded people in scattered locations next week. The one I saw announced is out in Gunnison."

He answered her silent question. "Yeah. Colorado. We could try to head out that way, and at least try and cover the meeting for some news outlet. I'm sure somebody would pick it up."

"Then, let's try to go! I'll tell you one thing – I'm not interested in serving those kooks back there. Or being just anyone's mouthpiece, for that matter."

"Who do you think they were?" Web said.

"I think, I *sense*, that they're somehow right smack at the core of all of this rottenness! If we get out of here, pay close attention to where we just came from. Because I think this will make us just about the only outsiders who will know how to find them."

"*About* the only outsiders? What do you mean?"

"I mean, *almost* the only ones who will know! I have a pet theory that I'll tell you about once I've worked out all the kinks."

"So, is it Gunnison, then?"

"Hi-ho for Gunnison!"

Later on the next afternoon, after sleeping a little while in a stubble cornfield, Web and Audie were at a truck stop trying to find decals or markings, *something* to indicate a driver who might be sympathetic to dissidents, when a notably unsympathetic driver seemed to recognize them. He accelerated and careened almost sideways trying to run them down.

"*People were watching*!" Audie yelled as they jumped in unison, surprisingly gleeful and full of adrenalin after what was in fact an extremely close call. The driver sped away, cursing. They later fancied that expanse of concrete parking lot where they first avoided the fate of becoming road-kill as their Rubicon.

"And, *after* Gunnison?" Audie inquired.

"After Gunnison," Web said, "I think there will be plenty to do."

Chapter Ten – Great Expectations

On Wednesday evening, April 15 (the very "Dues Day" so justly stigmatized by the no-governmenters, as it happened), the informal House Dissident Caucus gathered around a table in the beverages bar in the lower level of the Rayburn Building to watch the President's announced address. If all unfolded as predicted, it would confirm and emphatically highlight Buzzy Wuzzy's latest tip.

"My fellow Americans," a slightly rakish big-haired, Li'l Abner-look-alike President Gossens began, sitting ramrod straight behind his desk and glistening under what incongruously appeared to be old-tech TV lighting. "Tonight, I want to speak to you in order to address some of the lingering concerns that I myself still have in this time of transition, and that I know many of you share."

"Maybe we'll finally get some intel about the status of the country constitutionally and, hopefully, about the Congress," Congressman Carbola whispered to Congressman Tom Topel. Topel nodded.

"You need to be aware," the President went on, "that our honor as a nation has been thrown at risk by a potential adversary. To preface my point, let me tell you this: Recently – and this is, understand, only in order to reinforce our position as the number-one trader in financial and other services and the leading destination for imported goods – I recently re-entered, accordingly, the heading of the files and postings pertaining to us at the World Trade Enforcement Agency and with the United Nations in Geneva, to conform to the slightly-modified new name, 'Aamerica.' – two A's, see, three, really – I did this so we would appear at the head of the list, and *all* lists, where our first place position clearly indicates we belong."

Carbola audibly gasped. "The bastard has changed the name of the country! For what? Vainglory. To leave his stamp on it!!"

"I'll be damned," Howard Jellen added.

"But now, get this," the President continued. "Just yesterday, Norba Hrzakshak, the President of Albania, just to spite us, there can be no other reason, re-entered the name of *his* country officially, in the same series of accounts, as 'Aabania,' an obvious attempt to upstage us, following up after last week scuttling his country's initial agreement to buy into the Lockheed Advanced Defense System program being required of all East-West Treaty nations. And in the past two days, he has openly declared a preference for associate membership instead in the East Asian Axis Defensive Alliance, as a follow-up to coming to terms for a new loan extended to his regime by the Sino-Japanese Economic and Strategic Partnership. In response to this latest slight clearly aimed at our good offices and name, I am ordering, beginning at noon tomorrow, a preliminary selective blockade, policed by vessels of our fleet in the Mediterranean, of that nation's one significant port, Tirana, pending Dr. Hrzakshak's verified reversal of the aforesaid provocation."

Congressman Topel looked puzzled and cocked his head to one side. "Is Tirana a seaport? I don't think so... And, what does this have to do with what he said he was going to talk about?"

The President continued: "Now, to some matters of concern to all of us closer to home. I am aware that many have expressed regret in recent months that an important constitutional milepost has been passed. I want to assure you now, as fully as I can, that every effort will be made by my administration, with no efforts spared, to continue to practice and apply the essential framework of our founders' Constitution, fully as amended, two-hundred and forty-six years ago this year, wherever it remains enforceable and appropriate to our day. And as circumstances shall warrant, as time passes, I intend to elaborate further as to what those unfolding circumstances are. Some of the old provisions, let there be no mistake, are no longer appropriate or befitting, while most are, and will accordingly continue to be observed when we can."

"My God!" Carbola and Barbara Cullen yelled simultaneously.

President Gossens continued. "Now, about the Congress, in particular..." (The five members of the above-named Caucus leaned forward in their chairs as one.) "Elections for the Congress, are, as we know, provisionally set, at least by long-standing tradition, for November of next year, for all members of the House, and for one-third of the Senate. Well, they will, I assure you, go ahead as planned. With the following minimal changes."

Again, all shifted even more forward.

"The representatives and states," the President resumed, "in the case of Senators, whose districts are in good, positive fiscal balance with the nation as a whole, regarding revenues received compared with services and monies provided them, will be eligible to be up for re-election or first-time election as has always been the case before, in November of next year, preceded by the primary elections to select candidates.

"Only in the cases of those districts that have not registered a positive balance in federal revenues versus regular non-military federal expenditures in their states and districts consistently over the past five years, their incumbent representatives or senators shall not be permitted to run for re-election, or their places be filled, until such time as they do once again register an annual surplus. In the meantime, the senators or representatives from those districts will enjoy observer status only, but no vote in the respective bodies. That is to give these failed states and failed districts the incentive and opportunity they need to succeed.

"Should they fail to succeed after an additional five years, their management will be assigned to more successful neighboring states, or assumed by appointments made by the president." He paused to think, then concluded in his usual progressively deepening drawl: "And, by the way, I want to thank the Senate for voting favorably on the Laser 'Zap' Security Program at the end of last week. I'm also expecting the House to come through for us on it before this week is over."

And so, he said not one word on Antarctica or that initiative, or about any specifics regarding the Constitution.

Carbola was on his feet before the last affected pause and had to be restrained by the others from breaking all glass in sight. But apparently the President still wasn't finished. He rose from his chair and sauntered around to the other side of his desk to directly address the dozen or so of a special pool of reporters admitted into his personal office for the occasion.

"Now, I can take a couple of questions at least," he offered casually. "Mr. Dennis… Please speak up!"

"Sam Dennis, *Savannah Journal*. Mr. President, Sir! What do you say to those reporters, and their readerships or audiences, who don't necessarily fully appreciate the enormous positive difference your proactive agreement with the consortium called in shorthand 'The Company' has made in this country's finances? And, I'd like to request a follow-up."

The President bent slightly and rested his chin atop his right fist, as was his habit. "Hmmm. I say, they haven't seen the books!" he answered. "How we could have continued on, with the bulk of our reasonably available revenues earmarked and headed for the East Asian Axis lenders and their dangerous regimes before we even saw it every year, I don't know!"

As his follow-up, Sam Dennis asked the obvious. "You said that some provisions in the old 1787 Constitution are no longer applicable today. Which ones would those be, Sir?"

The President took this perceptibly lightweight, perhaps planted, challenge in his stride. "Well, the provision for regulating the trade with Indian nations, for one. There is no trade with Indian nations like that now. That's what I mean by inoperable." He pointed next to a man in a plaid coat.

"Bob Weldon, NNN News."

"Yes, Mr. Bob," President Gossens said.

"How does the Bill of Rights shake out under your arrangement? With respect, that's what many people around the country are concerned about."

The President blinked a few times and tweaked the tip of his nose. "Well, we'll continue to observe it as best we can, where we find it to be operable."

"You mean 'operative'?" Weldon followed.

"Where it's operable, as I said. *Mizz Donovan?"*

"Sally Donovan, KNXO-News, Cleveland. Mr. President, can you tell us just what proportion of the financial consortium you made the arrangement with, 'The Company,' is American-financed and what proportion is foreign-owned?"

President Gossens frowned. "Well, I don't have the figures in front of me. But, the management, in this case, is all American. One hundred percent American, as is our administration, mostly," he added, with a wink.

"Now, I've got to meet the Ambassador from Belgium in an hour to discuss the Lockheed imperative and the Albanian blockade that they're helping with," President Gossens said. "We think they signed a deal for Chinese bases, as well," he added, dangling out the tidbit. "Thank you all for coming!"

The President left immediately.

On the screen, an NNN reporter interviewed a super-casual crowd gathered for the speech in a Kiwanis Club in Philadelphia for reaction.

At the Dissident Caucus table, Noodles Norton shook her head. "This town hasn't seen a president this good at candy-coating and schmoozing such a horrible blunder in… at least twenty-five years."

"And in this case," Congressman Tom Topel said, "the public are buying it. And, this is the *worst* case! We've *never* seen such an incredible, bone-headed thing done in this country as what he's done!"

Congressman Carbola was beside himself, nearly tongue-tied with rage. "I'm taking action!" he said. "Those who are with me, come along! They're going to *need* us out there in the… the *protectorates!*"

"Well, they don't need us *here*, that's for sure," Topel said. "He let us know *that* in no uncertain terms! At least he didn't say anything about any loyalty oaths."

"Give him time!" Carbola admonished.

"I'm with you, Carbola," Congressman Howard Jellen said. "I know what side of this my district will be on."

Barbara Cullen chimed in, "Count me in, too!" Then, she thought a minute. "Where are we going?"

* * *

In the meantime, Luden Bond and Adonis Wong were sitting down at chess in the Travel Team bunker, commiserating.

Luden Bond brought up what they both were thinking. "So, what do you think happened to Audie and Web?"

Adonis Wong frowned deeply and sighed. "I think they got them. I'm sorry, but I don't think there's any real question about that."

"Who's 'them'?" Luden asked.

"You know," Adonis said. "*Them.* The people who are doing all this, who are taking over."

Luden shook his head as if trying to remove water or sand from his ears. "But there have been sightings, you know."

"Yeah. And there are still sightings. Elvis, Mary Magdalene, Princess Diana."

Luden, giving up, shifted the subject. "Why do you think people, most people in the country, refuse to get excited or even alarmed by everything that appears to have been taken away from all of us? Why do they treat as traitors, for the most part, those who do see what's happening, and are repelled and appalled and want to do something about it?"

Adonis answered without hesitancy. "Because they so don't want it to be happening. They refuse to admit any evidence of it and turn in anger and disgust on those they feel are trying to force them to experience that *reality*. Those people – the ones whose tendency is to want to fight to reverse the final step of the takeover, which is what's happening now – are beginning to be demonized as traitors, terrorists, and even the enemy within, with the unreflecting hoi-polloi, from one end of the country to the other, going right along. They believe their leaders are at heart benign and good, because they can't face the awful, murderous alternative – *the truth* – about their leaders, who they think they've selected, and, by implication, about themselves."

"Do you think Web and Audie are dead?" Luden asked point blank.

Adonis relented a bit at this suggestion. "I didn't say that. I don't know. I just think there's a central control point that will keep everyone fearful and quiet and compliant. And people who disagree will jolly well keep their mouths shut."

"O.K., and what's their ideology?"

"I've thought this through," Adonis said. "Efficiency, a complete, thorough, unending shakedown. The system as a totally smooth-running engine, without any knocks, with all wealth produced flowing *straight to them!*"

“And so who do you think is really in control?” Luden asked.

“Mr. Rassole,” Adonis said.

“Do you really think he exists?”

“Maybe not someone with that name. But, could be, too…”

Luden Bond shook his head. “Why are we talking so low?” he asked.

“Because they might well know we’re here right now.”

Again, Luden shook his head. “That’s so scary it’s crazy.”

Adonis gave them both an out. “How are your investigations going, your reading?”

“Well, I’ve been meaning to tell you that I had concluded that it’s so stupid we’re still reflexively responding daily, after all these years, to 9-11, an attack that happened basically once, twelve thousand days ago now. By contrast, the ancient Romans lost 80,000 overseas Italians assassinated in a single day at the instigation of a hate-filled foreign usurper in 80 B.C. We needed to stand up to the bogey-man and laugh our heads off back when it happened to us, but instead, we turned out to be a nation of fraidy-cats who caved in to political exploitation and rolled right over year after year, refusing to see our leaders’ role in causing rage abroad, which they still can continue to exploit. By our misplaced trust, we’ve been the enablers of their continued abuse of us, as of others, as they strip us more and more away from all we once had. Or, imagined we had. That’s what I’ve been figuring out.”

“Wow,” Adonis said, impressed. “Were the Romans similarly turned into soft worms for generations by having lost 27 times as many of their loved ones as we did to terror on a single day?”

“Good question. I’ll need to look into that. But did you realize the Bush administration condemned about 50,000 people more to lingering deaths within just a couple of days after 9-11, by declaring the air at Ground Zero safe to breathe for the clean-up workers?

“About my other study, I’ve found that a group in Siberia in the 1920s was startlingly committed, all by themselves, to implanting *democracy.* But the culture that surrounded and engulfed them had no living underpinnings or traditions of what democracy actually was. That, I think, may be the dilemma faced by people we know in America who want to implant, or re-plant, democracy here now, by restoring our old Constitution. But now, *we* are the ones who don’t have a living tradition of underpinnings of actual democracy to build on, if we ever did. Because we’ve been under the control of a ruling oligarchy in control of our democratic institutions for decades! You can’t force democracy on a people, you know.”

Adonis Wong was perplexed. "So, you're not supportive of re-instating the Constitution?"

"I would be, yes, except, that it was conveniently ignored or circumvented or dominated in so many ways in practice for so long, anyway... They'd already really abolished it, long before now. Am I wrong?"

* * *

Web and Audie managed to hitchhike with a flatware salesman as far as Paducah, where they endured many stares from people who, at very minimum, thought they somehow looked familiar. They decided that hitchhiking on would be too risky, and that they were going to have to rent a car. But, when Webster proposed to pay for it with his IUC (imbedded universal chip), Audie reminded him that they could be easily traced. So, it was determined that she would have to, reluctantly, hock the classy diamond ring he had given her in order to obtain funds to continue on.

Within a couple of hours, she registered a maroon-metallic Lamsa coup they rented at a local dealership in her name from her first marriage, and they headed out of town west on Highway 60, bound for Gunnison.

They rolled across Missouri and Kansas under the blazing April sun, living on the proceeds of the rock and eating at diners where people stared, none too friendly, every one curious about their other-regional look. They pulled into Pueblo, within sight of the mountains, the next night and checked into the Eagle Ridge Hotel.

And within half an hour, there came a knock on the door.

Web opened it warily, and there in the hallway, nonchalant, stood a man who introduced himself as Mr. Albert Eldredge, a middle-aged westerner in blue jeans and a broad-rimmed Stetson. Audie came to the door then, too, and he told them, devil-may-care as all get out, that they had been traced by his group, "The Watchers," which happened to be one of the core groups of the dissident movement. And he suspected, he said, that they were going to Gunnison.

"I also imagine that the federal agents, who are taking orders from the Rassolites, or Rassoliums, or whatever they are, know where you are, too," he said. "The FBI is swarming over Gunnison already, and only some suckers and decoys will be picked up there. What I came to tell you is that the real meeting will be held at a way out-of-the-way place called 'Great Expectations' up in Wyoming. A car will be sent before noon the next day to pick you up and take you there, so you might as well turn yours in in Pueblo." He touched his hat in farewell like in a vintage John Wayne movie, turned his back, and was silently gone.

"I hope they didn't pawn my diamond," Audie muttered, closing the door.

Chapter Eleven – The Smoking Gun

On the afternoon of Tuesday, April 21, the House Dissident Caucus met in its accustomed Rayburn cafeteria dining room back corner. This time, a new weekend cork-tape report from Buzzy Wuzzy caused even more of a sensation among the five. In it, the mysterious informant undertook to fill in some of the Asia-sized blanks in the recipients' knowledge of the entities commanding all the disturbing changes that were taking place. The source again referred to the main protagonists as "Mr. Rassole" and "old Mr. Rassole," the father, sending the members scurrying to check their search engines to try to find out if there could possibly be known entrepreneurs or a single discernable extended family with anything remotely approaching controlling interest in the Amerocentric colossal global consortium now known as "The Company."

"Old Mr. Rassole" in particular, the informant went on to say, had been much disturbed for several days by the fact that a pair of guests brought at his bidding for instruction and admonishment had, in a manner unprecedented, utterly vanished, despite all the security measures effective in redundancy and the remoteness of the site.

Furthermore, this particular pair of delinquents had hardly been his most sophisticated or distinguished "guests," but more akin to *hoi polloi,* and thought unfit even for the third-order responsibilities with which they were charged in the new social ordering. He had turned his back for only a matter of minutes to take his obligatory daily constitutional, and came back to find them not overawed and transfixed, but *gone* – apparently *nowhere at all* in the thoroughly-combed wide radius surrounding the compound. He had considered even some form of *witchcraft* that their kind might be versed in as a possible explanation. *Vanished utterly!* He couldn't believe it, and he couldn't get over it, Buzzy Wuzzy remarked.

Currently, the Rassole dynasty, son and father, were concerned increasingly with countering and disrupting what were termed by them "coordinated dissident capers," operative under the guises of "restore democracy," and "restore the Constitution."

Such riffraff – nobodies and their handful of shameless marginal celebrities who were irrational and, therefore, had to be reigned in – were planning meetings to be held, according to intercepted postings, in remote sites throughout the country. Identified venues for their meetings included Bluefield, WV, Gunnison, CO, Katahdin, ME, Hiko, NV, and Hummock, FL. FBI units had been ordered to sweep all of these areas in coming days. Some foreign venues, according to the informant, were also under consideration and surveillance, especially in view of the possibility of East Asian participation and encouragement.

"Well, those two 'guests' who got away, most certainly, were that same pair that disappeared after the White House interview," Tom Topel said. "It's even more important now that we make it out to—"

"Shh!" Barbara Cullen said. "Don't say it out loud!"

"You're right," Tom Topel said. "Best not to. We could be bugged.""

Harry Carbola, deep in concentration, replied, "Well, we've got to *do* something, because if we do nothing, we know *nothing will happen*. And they will get away with the whole heist, and succeed in pre-emptorily terminating our career as a nation. Fortunately, the locale we're now preparing to visit wasn't on that list..." He paused. "You know, at some point, we're going to have to put together our own defense force, maybe even our own *storm troopers*. That's where it could get really sticky – and probably *nasty*."

"But not just yet, Harry," Howard Jellen interjected.

Carbola demurred a bit. "Not yet. Well, we'll see. As I said, if we don't do it, soon we'll be capable of doing *nothing*. Beyond the shadow of the event, there's nothing that can be done."

"Noodles" Norton spoke with assurance that was encouraging and touching for all of them. "You know, I'll be ready to go tonight as planned. Will the car come for us where we agreed upon?"

"Yep," Carbola answered. "We're all together."

Barbara Cullen assured likewise, "You know I'll be there."

* * *

Albert Eldredge himself showed up in his gray Mazda and wide-brimmed Stetson to drive the fugitives to Great Expectations, Wyoming. They started north up I-25 to Denver, then switched over to U.S. 287 and settled back for a seven-hour lonely trek across some of the most rugged and wildly-beautiful country in the West, affording plenty of time to talk and exchange views.

"Why do you think so many of the people in this part of the country, here in the vast heartland, cling to loyalty to this sort of administration in particular, tolerating even abandonment of the Constitution with all the accompanying secrecy and blatant diversions, and the end of representation for big parts of the country?" Web Bootle thoughtfully asked. "And why such hostility to opponents of these radical anarchistic moves, who simply want to bring back democracy?"

"Because," Eldredge answered, "these folks, most of them, don't trust power apart from some solid foundation they can see, buy, or hold in their hand – landed property or bank stock or ownership of production – even when some of them are brutally relegated to arduously raising market produce by hand on 12-acre plots.

"Control on their behalf by giant commercial interests they can own part of and therefore identify with makes a certain unlikely sense to them, since it's controlled by strong individuals like they want to think they are. They look at people who don't own anything, even when that means themselves, as sort of freeloaders, not-deserving to share in power. And, they know that the Constitution was really being shunted aside to a great extent, in many ways, anyway.

"Plus, they tend to admire a man of resolve who can solve the debt-strangulation problem that befuddled everyone else with just his signature and can defuse the prison extortion scheme with a bold plan to simultaneously end our minerals and fuels shortages and creatively punish the proverbial bad guys. And, they apprehend the lurking dangers of the East Asian Axis and appreciate the capabilities of the Laser Zap Weapon System undergoing testing…"

"Amazing!" Audie remarked. "You make it sound almost like you share those sentiments yourself!"

Albert Eldredge was quick to answer. "No. I'll take Constitutional order, representation, clarity as to what's going on, and civil guarantees and democratically-forged policies by law extended over, instead of by, the plutocratic corporations. I'll take that, instead of a sort of tin dictator on a horse, any day."

"Whoa," Webster Bootle said. "You could be a bang-up lawyer for either side."

Eldredge grinned. "Which I am! Adams State and Denver Law School, LLD, '24."

Audie, disarmed, smiled. "I've never heard anyone state either side of it as well. I'm relieved you're on our side, Mr. Eldredge."

"On America's side. I've heard that Mr. Gole, our former vice-president, has declared he is, too. Though, it didn't look like it before the election."

"Gole?" said Audie. I thought he'd pretty much become unglued after Gossens beat him. Snapped and took off West or something."

"Don't believe everything you read, Ms. Journalist," Eldredge said. "That's a sort of a cover-up Gole concocted – he's no dummy, you know. He did go West, to be sure. But not fly-fishing. He's going around rallying the people out here in the 'throw-away zone'. I've gone out and heard him speak several times, actually. Hell of a guy!"

"Gole? I thought he was a sleazy nerd," Web said.

"Well, that's what the Republican spin-machine said, wasn't it?" Eldredge winked. "Yep, the movement's gaining momentum, but we've still got our work cut out for us!"

Nobody thought of much of anything else to say for about the next three hours as they crossed into Wyoming and the treeless country opened up wide and sun-scorched already in late April.

Finally, as they saw the seeming oasis, or mirage, of the tiny high desert town of Lamont, halfway up across the state, come into the broad, panoramic foreground, each basically lost in his or her thoughts, Web began to wonder about something.

"What's your affiliation in the midst of all this, Mr. Eldredge?" he asked. "What's your motivation for getting out front on what seems to be more a dangerously unpopular issue-front with every passing day now?"

"Well, I'm the Rocky Mountain regional co-chairman of 'End the Take-over.' I'm a patriot in the genuine sense, as I perceive you are, too. And I think the two-hundred and forty-odd years of Constitutional history are a helluva lot more solid and promising than these shallow-minded bastards' tin-hat fundamentalist paranoia. We're just going to end up easy pickings for smarter folks overseas to dismember and appropriate our stuff if we don't get this turned around and these wretched frauds unmasked and probably locked down permanently!"

"*Ooooo*," Audie marveled. "You couldn't be more right about that. So, what's this 'Great Expectations' place like?"

Eldredge answered as best he could. "It's a big cave under a mountain. I've never been there, but I hear it's a very rugged and really *awesome* place… as they used to say."

"How did you know where to find us?" Audie asked.

"Oh, that was no great secret. You were tracked by sightings from somewhere in Missouri on. I don't know before that. We, and possibly others, had you under our surveillance. I couldn't have picked you up if we'd seen that the Feds were hanging around. Presumably, they intended to intercept you in Gunnison. I would be interested in knowing where you started out, though…"

Audie felt a check in her spirit for the first time. "Well…"

Web answered for both of them. “Well, we’re not quite clear ourselves on that. It will make a good story some day. I think we’d like to save it and think about it. Until we’re ready to tell it all.”

“Well, then, you’re no slouches, either!” Eldredge allowed. “I think that does make the most sense, from a number of angles.”

“Thank you,” Audie said. “Nothing against you. We’ve just got to keep it a single story, and keep it controlled for now.”

“I know what you’re saying.”

But Audie still felt a tinge of apprehension. “Do you think it’s possible they know where we are right now?”

“Possible, yes,” Eldredge answered. “We must always be awake to that possibility and be careful. But, if we let it paralyze us, then we can’t do anything.”

“Do you think they know about ‘Great Expectations’?” Web asked.

“They may. They may.”

“What’s going to happen there?” Audie asked, dark fear creeping into her voice.

“Well, I’ll tell you what I know,” Eldredge said. “What’s going to happen is a link-up, we hope, with other meeting sites, if our technical people can pull it off securely without being intercepted. It is a little scary. Everyone will want to hear from you two. We’ve got to try to come up with a plan to expose this thing that’s now gotten itself entrenched, non-violently if that’s possible, through some legal means or resistance in… Through strikes, or something.”

They took a local cut-off across a sagebrush flat to Riverton, then pulled onto U.S. 20 and continued north, the long curve of the Bighorn Range looming like a misty blue cloud building across the entire horizon dead ahead, harboring their precise destination in its nearest flank.

After passing through the sleepy little ranching town of Hyattville they arrived at the immediate approaches to the meeting site. Albert Eldredge’s Mazda eased to a near-stop on Forest Service path 17 and pulled into the rutted mud twin wheel tracks of a service road, still soft from recent rain, stopping dead alongside a number of other assorted vehicles that were parked willy-nilly at the edge of a grove of aspen. As they got out, they nearly swooned from a faint but unmistakable whiff of sulfur carried on the breeze. Web saw that it issued apparently from a gash in a wall of limestone rock that a good-sized nearby stream gurgled down into, abruptly vanishing. Audie saw it, too, and kept gazing over in that direction.

“That’s where we’re going, or so I’m told,” Albert Eldredge stated flatly, posing what seemed an unlikely or impossible scenario.

Unlikely as it was, they could see, walking closer on the path, what looked like the end of an open-top fire shoot sticking up out from the narrow fissure right next to where the gurgling little stream vanished.

* * *

A big, raw-boned, bald-headed man was standing by the opening into the earth, handing out warmly-lined rubber rainwear from a wooden crate. He thrust out his meaty right hand and introduced himself as Bob Pearson. It was obvious he knew Albert Eldredge fairly well. Others were coming behind now, and, donning the heavy cloaks provided on cue on a globally-warmed 85-degree day, they followed along bravely to they knew not where, sitting down in the big slide tube, and each in succession whizzed silently into the dark, steep tunnel, which was lighted somewhat by an apparently-unending string of seventy-watt bulbs. The reason for the heavy outerwear became obvious as the temperature in the sulfurous tunnel descended as they did. Paradoxically, the giant, runner-less cold luge descending in an enormous tight arc was a cinch to negotiate, leading Web to wonder how they could ever expect to get back out.

Finally, after what seemed like a full five-minute slide into the cold, and fortunately not oppressively-sulfurous depths, the tube leveled out and they coasted one at a time to a stop on top of a platform of planks, which, upon standing, they saw was next to a mirror-like pool. Following a partially-lit boardwalk ahead, now linked hand-in-hand, they entered a constricting natural tunnel of deeply-crinkled limestone, down to ten feet wide at the narrowest, to where the lowering ceiling forced them first to bow and bend and then kneel and crawl through the last hundred or so feet before emerging into the largest natural room any of them had ever seen.

Visible up into its farthest receding shadowed reaches, they found out later that the aptly-named “Great Hall” yawning unbelievably before them was all of two-thousand feet long, by one-hundred feet wide and one-hundred feet high. Its sheer size was totally daunting, striking everyone entering it for the first time as among of the greatest imaginable wonders in nature.

Voices were audible up ahead and, approaching, the trio up from Pueblo and others who had entered with them found a small throng of people arrayed beyond the midpoint of the Great Hall, where there stood a podium on a makeshift wooden stage, several empty rows of folding chairs, and a giant screen stretched on a sort of scaffolding, just perceptible in the dim light provided by overhead arc-lamps. This scene, Camilie Auden told herself, was a little how she imagined heaven. Or… what's the word? *Hell!"*

Startled, and held spellbound, Web thought he recognized some unlikely familiar faces glancing around excitedly in a group ahead. Yes! They looked like… he was all but sure there *were* some members of Congress standing there. Congressman Topel. There was that gaunt and gangly-looking Congressman Carbola from the Dakotas, taller and more ungainly even than the President. And, no! "Noodles" Norton? How did they ever get her in here? And a dapper black congressman and congresswoman, what were their names? A small man with an infectious smile and mop of brown hair fairly ran over to Mr. Eldredge and greeted him with a clap on the back.

"Camilie and Web," Albert said, "this is Roy Faison, from Cody, just down the road. He's my co-chairman. Roy, meet my new friends, Webster and Audie. Do you recognize them? Yep! They're the pair who interviewed Gossens! And now, we're going to hear from them what happened."

Webster felt just a bit put-upon, but didn't say anything, because their mere presence certainly made the statement that they were part of the rather intimate, if disparate, group.

But as he greeted the effusive Roy Faison, Web Bootle started to wonder seriously what he was going to say to such an assemblage. What *could* he say? And what *not?* How did he and Audie manage to end up here, in an even-weirder, if far friendlier, place than the house of hell they visited during their kidnapping? He almost wished they had left well enough alone. What a reward for asking a question!

The voice of the little man, Faison, presently came through the loudspeaker on the podium and everyone sat down on the wooden folding chairs, resembling cards shuffling into a deck. "Attention please, everyone. Welcome to Great-X! We all know we're here for serious business – *desperate* business, it so happens. So, let's get started!

"You all know that we are attempting a clandestine link-up with our other 'End the Take-over' meeting sites, at Katahdin, Bluefield, Hiko, and Hammock. We don't know if it's going to work; our technicians say it's programmed to abort if tapped, which seems a good possibility. We'll test in a minute and see if we can get any of the other sites onscreen.

"But we have plenty of things to do ourselves, and we are waiting to hear from our leaders about how we can become operational immediately and bring a quick end to the takeover and restore our full Constitutional government, which is the wellspring and blueprint for the popular form of governance favored by all of us."

After the applause, Albert Eldredge, looking like a red-faced range-hand in his Stetson and striped shirt under the heavy sweater-shawl, virtually repeated Roy Faison's words of welcome, and announced that Harry Carbola, representing the Congressional Dissident Caucus, would have a very important piece of news.

Carbola, like a progressive champion from days gone by, a true nemesis of the right – and already being caricatured and skewered in the press – exuded passion for the common cause of Constitutional restoration as he bent almost double over the podium.

"My good friends," he began in a new, reedy voice, "I want to greet and welcome our friends and fellows at Bluefield, Katahdin, and elsewhere, if you can hear us and see us. The fact that we are all here in Great Expectations, as dramatic a meeting site as we could possibly have found, can be taken as an omen of the great expectations we have of ultimately triumphing.

"Because of our government's long record of ignoring the wishes of an overwhelming and overwhelmed majority of the people, even back in the hopeful days of Obama, the people at large have become complacent and overly permissive toward safeguarding their rights, and scornful of any who would thwart the leader's designs, however subservient to the dictates issued by The Company.

"We must inform the people of the plutocratic tyranny we are now in fact under, and win them back to insist irresistibly on the full restoration of the real democracy under laws rooted in the Constitution that we once, not so terribly long ago, enjoyed. As the good regional co-chairman, Albert Eldredge, suggested, I do have what I think you'll agree is wonderful news to share.

"Thanks to the marvelous outpouring of over three million signatures by email for our petition to the Supreme Court to review the legality of the President's recent injunction to regard a list of Constitutional provisions as passé, the list will be ruled on by the full Court. Their decision will be announced in the next few days.

We believe that the full Supreme Court cannot, in all good conscience, favor the tyranny and the rollback of the very Constitution to which it owes its own existence. Our essential role for now, dear friends, is to spread information, to counter the spin of the 'national security' (or 'homeland' security) devils. We must inform everyone we can manage to contact of the probity of our cause, not only for ourselves but for everyone in the nation.

"If our efforts fail to turn the tide by weight of sheer numbers and sentiment, then we will call for revolution, and revolutionaries we shall be!

Please pledge as much now, everyone! Yes, *everyone*! Never stand by! And, triumph together we shall as one!"

The applause was long and loud, echoing and ringing off the walls even after it subsided. As the echoes of the raucous applause subsided into the far distance, Web and Camilie were called to the makeshift stage, their disappearance and re-appearance – here especially – considered a sequence of wonder and a special triumph, even while none as yet knew the whole story of it.

Web stood at the podium, Audie next to him, squinting out over the little throng seated there in rapt anticipation. Just as he opened his mouth to speak, a faint but distinct little *ding* ---- *ding* ---- *ding* ---- *ding* ---- *ding* was heard.

Immediately, the Committee of Safety – consisting of Albert Eldredge, Tom Topel, who had been a Deputy Sheriff of Windsor County, Vermont, before being elected to Congress, and three other individuals – sprang to their feet and flew back out of the Great Hall in the direction of the entrance/exit.

The rest of the gathered throng instantly formed into a line and hurried to a low-lying "basin" area farther in the gigantic natural hall. To Camilie Auden, shivering in her heavy outerwear garment in the 39-degree perpetual chill of the cave, the feeling of artificially brave solidarity of a little, despised group of dissidents virtually at the mercy of the callous general majority was more chilling than the air of the cavern, and somehow also evoked more warming in her inner soul than the sun whose searing rays she might never feel again.

As the huddled, standing group waited in silence, holding its collective breath, Albert Eldredge, Congressman Topel, and their fellows on the Committee of Safety, all strangers until that day, moved as fast as their legs could carry them, back up the open-top chute toward the entrance, arduously hand-over-hand up the suspended rope, desperately pulling their way forward.

At long last bursting back out into the sunlight at the cave's narrowed entrance, they stood breathless and gasping beside the bald-knobbed Bob Pearson, who, standing sentinel, had sounded the danger signal. Tongue-tied, he gestured strenuously in the direction of a dense stand of aspen some seventy-five feet up the trail from the parking area. Signaling caution with an upraised hand, still speechless, he reached down into his box and in turn thrust a ready and loaded 45-calibre pistol into the hand of each. In a huddle, they moved toward the aspens. Drawing closer, they could just detect patches of a distinctive blue-colored cloth inside the leafy little enclave that Tom Topel, as a member of the House Armed Services

Committee, tentatively recognized as the color of a particular military Special Forces unit uniform.

Meanwhile, the oddly mute Bob Pearson noted precisely the position of the ensconced figures, and that an uppermost limb of one of the aspen trees, suspended in the air, had grown conspicuously larger and leafier than any other part of any of the trees in the grove. As the others watched, he drew a bead with his pistol in his fully extended right hand and fired. The limb came crashing straight down on top of those half-hidden uniformed men. Immediately, the Committee of Safety members rushed forward as one and easily got the jump on the three startled officers of the elite unit, controlling them in a freeze position with their pistols.

Suddenly Tom Topel gasped audibly and blanched pale as a ghost. Following the Congressman's fixed stare, the senior officer of the thunderstruck unit grabbed the strange-looking object and hurled it into the gurgling waters of the little stream hurtling though its narrow cut toward the mouth of the Great Expectations cave.

The thing he had seen and recognized was a functional prototype of the devastating, hand-held experimental Laser-Zap Weapon that would have incinerated every living being in the cave.

Chapter Twelve – Grappling

A designated body of searchers was, fortunately, able to recover the spectacular prototype weapon unharmed from under the water in the little chasm in less than half an hour. So now Congressman Tom Topel had the controversial portable Laser-Zap gun in his possession and the leaders of the Rocky Mountain Chapter of "End the Take-over" held the captured trio of Special Forces agents as hostages. Congressman Topel took special care to assure that they didn't learn of the prototype's recovery.

Beyond that, the question became, what were they, the dissidents, to do to secure their own advantage and safety, with the stakes now raised to an unprecedented level? It was not lost on any of them that they were now in a situation of extreme peril, as a group, a movement, and as individuals. How would the Gossens administration, responding to the powers-that-be, react? The future of millions could ultimately depend on their actions and the response of the powerful.

Webster Bootle and Camilie Auden suggested that they might be able to offer at least a partial remedy to the hazardous, shared dilemma. They quickly put together a news article-length summary, as objective as possible, to be circulated electronically to 113 national and international outlets, of the Great Expectations meeting and what was known of its disruption. Congressman Tom Topel was interviewed for the story, but the captured Laser-Zap weapon and the government's foiled attack were not mentioned.

The dissident group's operational headquarters was quickly moved for the remaining days of the meeting to Roy Faison's isolated ranch in a lower canyon on the edge of the Absaroka Mountains outside of Cody, and the three agents were provisionally held in handcuffs someone had acquired, in a secret, stone-walled room under one of the barns. Congressman Topel quietly kept the hand-held Laser-Zap Prototype Weapon that had been recovered in his personal possession.

The five Congresspersons present meanwhile, jointly and very courageously, conveyed a message to the White House through an intermediary, admitting and defending their attendance, regretting it had to be a secret conclave, and announcing they had the three Special Forces agents firmly in custody. They offered to release them in exchange for a personal guarantee of amnesty from the President himself for all of the meeting participants. They also expressed shock and displeasure at the agents having been armed with the devastating Laser-Zap, and declared that it had been jettisoned by the agents, as the agents themselves could confirm.

The President, on learning of the message a full day after it was sent, rejected its demands at first, declaring that all present ought to be rounded up and tried for conspiracy to commit treason. Those present testified later that he denied strongly on that occasion, with a murderous oath, that the weapon in question could possibly have been the carefully-guarded prototype Laser-Zap, stating it was preposterous to suggest that such a weapon would ever be released into the field or authorized for such a piddling mission, or for any domestic purpose for that matter.

He stated his intention to dispatch to the area a force sufficient to achieve and arrest all meeting participants in the next several days or hours to protect the homeland. But the contrary urgings of some of his close advisors and petitions from a certain quarter of his base who remembered how similar expeditions in the past had gone badly awry resulted in a rare about-face by the President, who belatedly accepted the offer of exchange of the agents for amnesty and strictly particularized immunity. The article by Audie and Web covering the events ultimately appeared in a grand total of two second-tier cyber and print publications nationally and seventeen abroad.

Per agreement, the three disgraced Special Forces officers were released along I-80 outside of Wamsutter down in the Red Desert. The bulk of the business agenda undertaken in Great Expectations was carried out at Roy Faison's Upper Greybull River Ranch over the next three days. And then, the conferees from this largest dissident meeting, at least officially immunized from repercussions, warily went their separate ways.

* * *

More reports on the U.S. Antarctica Mines and Punitive Colony Program (AMPCP), as that program had come to be named, appeared in the media over the next few days. Plans were announced for the first levies of unfortunate prisoners to be sent into "freeze-down" to serve as free labor for the construction of the barracks and facilities. Their primary constraint would be the environment. One inmate in particular, whose interview appeared numerous times over several days, stated that he actually liked the idea because, at least as he understood it, the convicts would live more or less a free life, confined to base though it was. Penal guards were virtually unnecessary, because, as he put it, who was going to try to swim anywhere from Antarctica? The real danger was primarily to the other workmen – even though they were mostly convicts, too.

The Aabania issue surfaced again as well, with that small free-thinking southeastern European menace now being accused of having leased land for a naval base, in a very lucrative deal, to China, the largest and most dangerous of the East Asian Axis signatories, clearly in defiance of mandated international warnings and sanctions. Direct military intervention to shake up or remove the troublesome regime of Norba Hrzakshak was under intense consideration, according to State and Defense Department pronouncements.

The public's first inkling of the Great Expectations Meeting as well as the coordinated meetings at the other sites arrived in the form of a nationwide breaking newscast that interrupted coverage of the latest Celebrity 2-Car Racing match. Rioting broke out in no fewer than two dozen towns. The news brief recounted the details of the investigating federal agents taken hostage by members of a vicious left-wing fringe element. Fortunately the situation was resolved successfully through the skill and quick thinking of the Gossens Administration. The Travel Team dutifully issued follow-up articles on the President's popular "live and let live" attitude and his compassion for the agents and their families.

On Tuesday, April 28, the U.S. Supreme Court's decision was announced regarding the petition signed by more than three million persons, close to one per cent of the people in the country, alleging that President Gossens's selection of certain provisions of the recent Constitution to continue to enforce, while declaring others "inoperable" and passé, was arbitrary and arguably destructive of the government's separation of powers. The Court ruled 7 to 2 that there no longer existed an obligation to enforce provisions of a Constitution once it was supplanted, and that the so-called "balance of powers" was nothing more than a figment of that Constitution's relegated provisions. Thus, the President was not enjoined in any meaningful way from the complained-of selective acts of enforcement.

At the start of the next morning's session, Congressman Tom Topel returned to the House floor for the first time since being amnestied along with the rest of the attendees of the Great Expectations meetings. Recognized by the Speaker pro-tem during the body's debate of a resolution denouncing the provocative activities of the President of the nation of Aabania, Topel, the lone Representative of Vermont, came on unexpectedly feisty, brandishing an enlarged photo that he claimed to clearly show a portable hand-held operational prototype United States Armed Forces Laser-Zap Weapon with what he claimed to be the entrance to the Great Expectations Cave in the background. Those viewing the proceedings on C-Span at home said that the screen went blank for four minutes at that point, a condition C-Span denied causing, if, indeed, the hiatus actually even occurred. Recollections afterward were mixed, and no definitive pronouncement was made.

Those present in the Chamber, including reporters Adonis Wong and Luden Bond, seemed baffled by the proposition that military agents could have been dispatched to the shadowy meeting in the cave to test the devastating experimental "ultimate weapon" by incinerating the 168 dissenters who were assembled. Their first impulse was to flatly deny that their government would kill its own citizens.

Rep. Topel's unsuspecting Congressional colleagues, some asleep, responded with daunting silence. How much the tenor of the body had changed in the three months since opening day! One reporter filed a dispassionate chronicle of the odd presentation as news anonymously, and it appeared without attribution in the reports published in two domestic papers and at least twenty-nine papers abroad. Rumors of a roughly corresponding near-epic event, whether substantively correct or not, circulated far more widely out beyond the chambers and halls of the Capitol, across the country, during the upcoming days and seemed to cause what could be called a chilling effect generally, as people took stock of it, though most denied it, fitting the altered ambiance of the country.

Acting on the evidence he himself had presented so dramatically it had to be intercepted, Congressman Topel was arrested by Capitol Police in his office on May 1 and charged with possession of an illegal weapon somehow pilfered from the military in his capacity as a member of the House Armed Services Committee. The weapon itself remained beyond reach, location undisclosed by the alleged treasonous thief.

Discussing it in their subterranean bunker on the following day, April 30, Adonis Wong and Luden Bond confidentially interpreted the meaning of the event they had witnessed on the House floor, in the context of what they perceived to be happening in the country overall.

"I personally hope they don't do what I'm saying," Adonis said, "but I don't understand why it is that the administration and the Justice Department haven't arrested all of those members of Congress who attended the radical meetings and charged them with sedition. Why was it that the President, who has generally been so resolute, amnestied everyone there apparently without a qualm? He vowed he would run them all in, remember? Why would he have changed course on that one great thing, among all of the issues he's been confronted with and taken head-on?"

"That's easy," Luden Bond said. "Because he didn't want to raise sympathy for his enemies, but to belittle them by not taking their plea seriously. President Gossens' new Svengali is Henry Morgen, an old Rassole Company hand, as they're calling him, and he performed a masterstroke if it really was he, as most seem to think it was.

"The core issue for that small handful of dissidents seems to actually be dying out in the public mind – and ironically, since just about the time of those meetings, if you noticed. The dissidents really don't seem to pose much of a threat to them now, and the public's attention has been successfully diverted elsewhere – *for the time being*."

"Yes, but the dissidents are actually right," Adonis said, "and I'm surprised if you don't know it. I think the claim Topel tried to make in the House with that photo was not preposterous, but very likely true."

Fuba Thorter walked in at that moment. "Let's drop that talk right there, guy. If they overhear you saying something like that, we're likely to all be deep-sixed, and then we can't do anything at all."

But "Mister Woo" still demurred. "True. But we surely aren't the only people in the country thinking as we do, or, as I do, at least. I'm sure this struggle isn't over. You saw the flash. One reporter, I don't know who, even has a picture, if it comes out clear. At least, I don't think they saw him and confiscated it."

"That's enough!" Fuba said. "No more. Don't let's talk about it. Don't risk it for all of us, Adonis! Just do your job. They haven't asked you to report anything that didn't actually happen, have they?"

"No. Not *yet*," Adonis Wong allowed.

* * *

On the morning of Wednesday, May 6, an impromptu news conference conducted by rapidly-aging Democratic ex-President Warren Fletcher, who was rumored to be suffering from Parkinson's (and increasingly described as "demented" by ferocious right-wing attackers in the media), was inexplicably aired on C-Span 2. In it, the ostensibly-retired politician/elder statesman bitterly and brazenly denounced the Gossens Administration for selling away the nation's constitutional government in exchange for questionable economic security, and called for the Constitution to be immediately reinstated by a veto-proof majority declaration of Congress, on the grounds that the right of the people to possess their own government was, as he put it, rather quaintly, "inalienable."

Rumors began to circulate in the media at once that Fletcher, defeated in his bid for a second term four and a half years before, was trying to mount a comeback for '36, something he denied. Some in the print media used the occasion to point out that it was not absolutely certain that the four-year presidential election cycle would even be adhered to in view of the eclipse of the Constitution. The public paid little notice, though Abe Gole, in his meetings in what was now being called the "ag zone", sometimes suggested it as a possibility.

On the evening of that event-filled day, Ben Weck, the Vice President, a reliably drab, nearly-forgotten man who rarely had an opinion on anything, suddenly launched a scathing attack in a speech echoed in the media on Congressman Tom Topel, Congressman Harry Carbola, ex-President Fletcher, and "their ilk on the far left." In it, he openly impugned their patriotism and obviously selfish motives in seeking to divide the nation. Abe Gole, who was the recent candidate and ex-VP, was not mentioned by his normally low-profile successor, in deference to his delicate mental state. Word on the street was that the loss of the election had left him so scarred that he'd become disenchanted with politics and was spending an inordinate amount of time traveling the country, listening to people.

On Saturday night, May 9, as fortune would have it, President Gossens and Senator Roger "Drinker" Topel of Vermont, whom many had forgotten, if they ever knew, was a moderately successful novelist and regional historian before coming to the Senate, co-emceed a reception at the Kennedy Center for American Nobel Prize-winning author Stephen Karcher, originator of *The Garfingales*, a lyrical family adventure series set in the Alleghenies of Maryland back in the 1990s. As such, their paths crossed more than incidentally for the first time since the 2032 election, and they exchanged a few civil words as they sat together side-by-side behind the curtain waiting to speak

"Mr. President," Senator Topel said, "there are several matters I would like to touch base with you on, if you would accord me at least the courtesy of a meeting."

"That is a possibility," President Gossens allowed. "I'll have my Chief of Staff call you and arrange a time when y'all can come over."

Entering the Oval Office on Tuesday morning, May 19, Senator Topel's demeanor had changed. He refused to sit down, and remained standing bareheaded with his suit coat slung over his arm, glowering at the President, who remained seated behind his desk. Moving closer, Senator Topel glared across the desk. "Mr. President," he fairly hissed. "Let my brother go. You know that what he said was true."

The President was dumfounded by his menacing visitor's refusal to submit to the dictates of civility. This upstart hadn't even deigned to shake his hand! "I can't do that," he said, his voice rising. "I don't know how or where he got that Zap-gun. A whole city – perhaps *this* whole city – could be wiped out with one round from that thing! I was hoping you'd know where he put it."

"Well, I don't. But, you do know that those officers were sent on that mission with it."

"No, I—"

"And while we're at it, how can you just renounce the whole Constitution of the United States, the mightiest document in world history, at least next to the Bible and the Koran, and the rock of our national character and life, just for momentary convenience and to score some political points?"

The President was stunned. "You want to go back to our corrosive debt position subservient to the whims of the Asian Axis powers, with no resources to expend for this country, or much for its defense? And besides, *Drinker*, how could I possibly undo that arrangement and bring back to life that largely-superceded document, even if I wanted to? This country cannot – *will not* – abide a complete train-wreck presidency."

Topel watched in amazement as a look of confusion and then even defeat crossed the President's face. If he didn't know any better, he could swear that Gossens seemed for a moment to be pleading even with his adversary for understanding. Gossens sighed deeply and, for a brief instant, covered his face with his hands.

"Topel, this deal is all I've got."

Chapter Thirteen – The Medium and the Message

On Saturday afternoon, May 23, the House Dissident Caucus, minus Congressman Topel, re-assembled at the invitation of his brother, Senator Roger Topel, at his weekend home in a secluded quarter of Fairfax, Virginia. They were joined for their discussion by Senator Topel and his Vermont wife Evelyn Wadsworth, and Senator Jake Cable of Minnesota and his willowy and gorgeous dark-eyed Argentinian wife Hilda. Together, they examined a new Buzzy Wuzzy cork-tape message that arrived while they were all there.

Several present scrutinized the message with a magnifying glass. It was painstakingly-penned in indelible black ink in a fine-point hand, on an almost-impossibly-long, lavender-tinted, gossamer-thin tape. Their examination revealed plenty. Once again the author exhibited a certainty regarding situations and knowledge of the planning of events still to unfold that couldn't be found in any other source. The new message spoke of impatience and anxiety on the part of the two Rassoles, father and son, whom it identified as exercising ultimate sovereignty over the country, in terms of initiatives to re-order all aspects of American life and power – *change*, if you will.

Most chilling among the brand-new particulars was The Company's plan to acquire additional countries, followed by the shifting and trimming of populations to further The Company's objectives. In particular, in the short run, negotiations and an internal referendum were planned to commandeer the space and resources of a small African country and move its population of three million *en masse* to the U.S. southeast coast. Lucrative deals were anticipated for friendly affiliated companies for shipping this prodigious labor force to enter contract employment assisting the new micro-plot, labor-intensive fruit and vegetable growers. The optimal rate of pay would be $7.00 an hour, or twenty times the income those contracted wholesale could normally even hope to realize at home.

Then, as a follow-up, optimally-efficient agriculturalists were to be sent to the depopulated African land with massive equipment to grow and provide tropical produce in enormous amounts for the American market. Surplus African workers, beyond those needed as cut-rate farm workers, were to be employed at the same wage to inexpensively re-start in America itself the milling of textiles and sewing of garments for domestic sale.

Then, as the new textile operation expanded, another, larger (also unnamed) African country, with a population of nineteen million, would be appropriated and its working-age people put to work alongside the efficiency-remunerated workers already present.

Mention was also made of acquiring a fair-sized European country at some point, to harness resources and talented and educated workers to serve in tandem with those of the North American homeland that was already, indeed, starting to be known to insiders as the "United Station." The elder Mr. Rassole was particularly partial to the altered name and revised concept, devised to more effectively anchor and rationalize The Company's global reach.

The small cadre of Congress members present was truly and duly shocked by the cold audacity reflected in the new communication. But Hilda Cable, Senator Cable's consort, who was versed in graphology, seemed more intrigued by the tiny script and the medium.

"This, I can tell you for certain," she said, "was written by a particular sort of South American woman, and no one else. In fact, I might have written it down this way myself, if I had the kind of knowledge she does. And that by itself is a mystery.

"This kind of tape is something I recognize, without the slightest doubt. I can tell you that that tape was peeled from around the inner rim of the container of a common Latin American brand of cake decoration dye. Its lavender/pink-tan color is completely unique. I'd recognize it anywhere.

"And that much, my dears, suggests that the sender of the message must be someone who works domestically or professionally with that specific product. Except that this color is, I believe, only in the inventory of colors for home use, not the professional line, unless they have changed it recently.

"And as for that peculiar script, it is a characteristic Latin American one that was taught in elite elementary and secondary schools all over the South America until about twenty years ago, with the 7's *crossed*, for instance, as in the year, written two-thousand-and-thirty-*seven* for the expiration. See?

"And also, I cannot believe that any *man* would ever write in that way. And, obviously, this person is quite well-educated and must also have lived in this country for a long time to have mastered written English that well."

"But why would she have sent the messages like *that,* wrapped around a cork?" Barbara Cullen asked.

"Because she didn't want to be discovered!" Hilda Cable said. "She's obviously an insider. Would *you* want to risk it, in the present climate?"

"I think you've got a point there," Barbara Cullen said.

"She apparently has daily contact with this 'Rassole' family," Hilda Cable said, "and also with the workings of the concession company, what did you say it was? *Sacanagem*? They're not very well known. But it would seem she has access to them, too."

Barbara Cullen looked imploringly toward the two Senators and Congressmen Carbola and Jellen. “Are you hearing all this?” she said. “How many more clues do we need to blow this person’s identity wide open?” But then a concerned look crossed her face. “But on the other hand, how much can it really matter who sent it, if the information is so obviously good?”

The men looked at each other. “That’s right,” Congressman Carbola said, with an audible sigh. “We most certainly wouldn’t want to force this source to dry up.”

The *caipirinhas* went down well, as always.

* * *

The next day, Congressman Carbola contacted Web Bootle and Camilie Auden, the now rather-infamous journalists whom he had met at the Great Expectations meeting, and leaked the whole story about the anticipated African territorial acquisitions and wholesale population switching, without disclosing a specific source that he could not have named in any case. For the first time, the pair put out this story under their new, but once previously used and so recognizable pseudonym, ‘Cassio Harris,’ to twenty-nine publications. Three of the favored publications in the U.S. and seven abroad accepted and printed the story as “chatter” just on their say-so.

The administration didn’t refute it, precisely because they had not yet been briefed on it themselves. But there arose a certain amount of speculation a few days afterward about the identity of the country with the three million people and the country with the nineteen million.

Meanwhile, that Monday, not-yet-replaced Congressman Tom Topel, awaiting a preliminary hearing and arraignment not yet scheduled, received his first visitation by interrogators in his cell in the federal lock-up at Stafford, Arizona. He told them the simple truth, as far as he had decided he could go—that he had obtained the Laser-Zap Experimental Weapon from Special Forces agents who had quite obviously been dispatched to use it treacherously. Instead, they had ended up being captured with the awful weapon at Great-X Cave, just as he had recounted on the House floor. No, he wasn’t ready to say what had been done with the weapon, which he acknowledged was military property. Pressed to indicate some more nefarious way by which he had really gained possession of it, he stuck to his story even through some painful thumb-screw applications and reminders that he was going into “freeze-down” at the Antarctica mines unless he got a lot more forthcoming and soon.

But the government's strategy with him backfired. As C-Span had gone mysteriously blank during his heated presentation of the House floor and as the few members of the House who were awake and attendant apparently saw telling tales as not in their best interest, word of his allegations spread hardly at all. Strangely, however, after his first encounter with the government interrogators and his fresh re-telling of the potentially explosive story, it began to spread throughout the country.

Quickly thereafter it became obvious that the proliferating rumors were a source of chagrin to the Rassoles – father, son, or both. President Peter Gossens received a special message via the usual courier, the Lambent, impressing upon him the urgent need to come up with a way to put a lid on all the rumors, well-grounded or wild. This set the President to thinking harder than he ever had.

* * *

The Travel Team was abuzz in their bunker, having received a message exhorting all of them to stand firm and obey what their reportorial mandate from The Company required of them, until such time as their "inside" presence might become valuable and even merit the sacrifice of their position and possibly life and limb. It was signed "A & W." Audie and Web? Almost certainly!

Holly, Adonis, and Luden Bond were in the room when it came in on Wednesday, May 27, at 1:12 p.m. Fuba "Tex" Thorter walked in, read the message they were bandying about, and exclaimed with some sarcasm, "They finally get it! But don't answer that email!"

They all knew he was just being prudent, and they all envied the semi-fugitive pre-nups, who could on occasion lash out now, as most of them, with the exception of Mackenzie Ward, of course, wished they could do.

At the White House, President Gossens formulated a policy to ram through Congress making the publication of anything of national significance without citing at least one credible source a felony punishable by hard labor in Antarctica on the first offense.

At the younger Mr. Rassole's compound on the outskirts of Petersburg, south of Richmond, that elusive and very private gentleman was scrambling to determine how the earlier release of his brain-trust's plans as the substance of rumors would comport with the projection of those plans into reality. He was wracking his memory for clues as to how those secrets could possibly have been picked up and divulged, and at the same time, trying to deal with his father's screeching diatribe of red-faced fury just then flickering on his image-messenger over that insolent, freaky fornicating pair who had escaped his custody in some still-undetermined, preternatural way.

In the room next to the junior Mr. Rassole's study, a very petite woman with paper-white skin and shining auburn curls sat on a high stool at a counter. In late middle age, barely four-and-a-half feet tall, and wearing a green dress and a perpetual smile of kindness and reason, she was busy decorating a five-year-old Rassole grandson's birthday cake with boats, a sea, a moon, and gently swaying palms. Thoughts raced recklessly through her head.

Chapter Fourteen – Cold Air Warming

By June, President Gossens, a young man at 48, already had started to show signs of what appeared at first as haggardness, being bowed down, it seemed, by an endless dark vortex, or what some had styled a "snake-pit" full of trying and fateful events and enemies. The handful of relatively impartial observers left on the scene felt that his troubles had been occasioned by no one but himself. Some of the pundits, once fawning, were now describing him as a kind of political poltergeist – a Samson flailing around and bringing not just a temple, but a world down around his ears. Where were his legions of once-fervent supporters going?

An increasing number these days were again harkening back to the mysterious disappearance of his president-elect days of the past winter as the beginning of his descent from normalcy. Indeed, some began to contend, drawing from his deeds and actions, that he had become completely unglued.

Examples were rife. There was his reception at the White House of the madly-handsome and dashing German, Otto Snudt, the champion last remaining driver in the annual 2-Car race series. The President referred to the Teutons's driving victory as a "smashing *blitzkrieg*."

Then there was his increasing tendency to defer to research and pronouncements of tenured faculty at obscure Calvin College in all matters and fields politic and scientific, as if that small, sectarian institution represented the epitome of American scholarship, a sort of new, improved Harvard.

There were his odd, telling, often-repeated aphorisms, such as "we are not properly a nation-state, and no longer recognize nation-states as ultimately-proper forms of organization," and his habit of flippantly referring to The Company's armaments merchandising branch as "General Mortars." And, there were other curious habits, accompanied by lots of shudders and tics, to the extent that he was lampooned in some quarters as "President Twitch."

Simultaneously, the few genuinely un-spun news reports concerning the President and upcoming events that had made it into American news outlets were beginning to take a toll on the President's sky-high popularity; the numbers dipped for the first time since he took office. One example was the recent spate of economic reporting concerning the drastically revamped agricultural sector, touted positively and loudly by the administration as an outlet to balance plummeting urban employment opportunities, and the resulting plight of the ill-suited working class being shifted over as an under-compensated replacement for more expensive technology. At best, lots of people were simply starting not to know what to make of this president and his seemingly homespun ideas.

Worse, with the comparative proliferation of knowledgeable and disturbing reports that had hit the foreign papers, a vast wave of loathing, not directed to such an extent against an American president in nearly thirty years, actually tripping some nostalgia for the "bad old days", began to sweep Europe and several other foreign continents right on the eve of the upcoming annual conference of the G-9 heads of state, to be held in Padua, Italy in July.

The less-than-completely confirmed report about him sending the experimental Laser-Zap Weapon to clear out the meeting of dissidents also was as rife and reviled in Europe as it was missing in American reports. The arrest and incarceration of Congressman Tom Topel in connection was excoriated over there, and ignored over here, where the Topels were considered eccentric.

Anywhere other than the Homeland, in fact, Gossens was considered a nincompoop at best, a dangerous lunatic at worst. His bullying of President Hrzakshak of Aabania was deplored and lambasted by multitudes of sign-waving ordinary Europeans in the streets and plazas, as was his utter refusal to come substantively to the aid of the now-desperate Lowland Pact countries. His attitude toward the East-Asian Axis was considered blatant paranoia. His potential African policy of virtual rendition, and his bizarre Antarctica project, disregarding a wealth of long-standing treaties, were roundly denounced. And his alleged hijacking of the election, making it a Hobson's choice referendum in collusion with The Company, was viewed as an utterly disqualifying scandal.

Though his handlers ensured as little exposure to the world's opinions as possible, once in Europe for the top-level meeting of the inner G-9, the President began to sense the growing disdain for him abroad. The protestors in the streets as he whizzed by in closed, armored cars were hard to deny, but if he didn't know better, he could swear he sensed a whiff of contempt within the halls of the conference site itself. While the pith and spit of the mass demonstrations was largely lost on Americans at home, since it was shown fleetingly without sound, making the perpetrators look like members of the lunatic fringe, he himself felt the venomous disdain, and was baffled by it.

An ominous theme that began to mount inside the halls of the conference was the disinclination of the member states to deal with an enormous entity that no longer wanted to be regarded as an actual nation-state, a government representative of a people and their wishes. Instead, they charged, it now fancied itself as more of a business totalitarianism representing money and its self-serving intentions, the same as before really, but now without pretence or equivocation.

That same powerful country, it was widely noted, had, until recently, strenuously and – to at least some minor extent – credibly, preached democracy. This, even while actually operating the whole time as a self-absorbed giant autocrat – like a spoiled teenager – demanding its own way internationally, because it commanded a larger economy than the others, and despite the near-legendary goodness and honesty of very many of its so-called citizens. That latter point was always made in its defense. The other eight G-9 members, and the other however many countries in the larger world, let it be known that they would not deal with "the new mammon" (that was the in-phrase of the moment) until it had gone back to living by its once-revered Constitution.

Completely unprepared for such an unprecedented frosty reception – indeed, not shared in full even by all of the functionaries at the conference, since some tried to be cordial outside the sessions – the now-declared American head of *anti-state* sat in unaccustomed silence and, after three days, simply left. But not before urging once again agreement on purchases of conventional arms packages by the other members and prescribed limits on East Asian trade and cultural exchange.

Returning to bask as well as he could in the better atmosphere of at least lukewarm acceptance by the public at home, Gossens nonetheless felt what seemed like the beginnings of an ominous chill in the increasingly warm air at home, too. He, in fact, began to feel himself whip-sawed between the divergent public demands and the requisites of the new and immovable real and legal sovereigns, The Company. Gossens concluded quickly that he would have to mount a new public campaign of re-packaging and re-presenting his presidency and its initiatives, even if they were actually those of The Company.

* * *

Buzzy Wuzzy's latest message, shared by Senator Roger Topel with the remaining four members of the House Dissident Caucus on their June 13, now-weekly Saturday junket to his house in Fairfax, was full of cryptic news about the explosive reaction of the two Rassoles, father and son, to the events touching the President's negative progress in Europe and the deteriorating situation, from their point of view, at home.

Mr. Rassole the elder was, predictably, livid, holding that the President ought to have given at least as good as he got, ought to have excoriated the Europeans and Canadians for being so far behind the curve of what was modern, for lacking the courage to acknowledge that the nation-state had become a noxious, reeking dead letter, and that the new precise application of money absolutely without restraint or diversion was reordering the world as never before, and that to moderate its flow was harmful, reactionary and in a very real sense, blasphemous. That the twaddle about the have-nots without funds to invest being rightfully seated at the table in any fashion was just that – *twaddle*. That the auxiliary, piddling funds and gifts of the have-nots could be put to proper use only by their cooperating as good employees and consumers, and that they, too (meaning the Europeans, in particular) needed to formally reorder their governing arrangements to duly recognize the facts of the current world.

Instead, the pitiful American leader, Gossens, had waffled, and couldn't even be a front man any longer unless he straightened out in a hurry. And, people in America obviously needed to be more tightly managed to keep them on their proper leash. Their only conceivable value would be realized by their going along as workers and supporters. As for the mind of Mr. Rassole the younger, his thoughts were reliably the same as the elder's, except less sharply put. That much was not news to the gathering.

The members of the new, reconstituted Dissident Caucus were heartened in the extreme to find substantial agreement with their views among the general run of people in Europe, and they were quick to hale America's traditional allies as their own. Yet they were, at the moment, at a loss to know how to forge or even propose an effective trans-Atlantic link.

Nevertheless, over the next few days, European foreign ministers and parliamentarians, responding to public opinion in their countries, began to issue statements that in reality were cries of alarm and warning over the very existence of the hand-held Laser-Zap "dream weapon" the militaristic Americans had devised and alone now had. This, in addition to their loud protests of the new, authoritarian, anti-democratic regime.

The Europeans also expressed alarm concerning the cavalier-ness with which this prototype "ultimate weapon" had been inserted into a low-impact domestic situation, followed by the ease with which it had fallen into unauthorized hands and simply vanished. In an effort spearheaded by the French, foreign governments were actually beginning to demand that the Laser-Zap program itself be stopped and dismantled in front of European witnesses, and the existing prototypes destroyed.

Gossens declared a ban on Dijon mustard, éclairs, and French fries for all occupants and employees of the White House.

* * *

On the evening on June 16, after the closing gavel on the last full day of Congress before the summer recess, Adonis Wong sat down with Luden

Bond for a game of cribbage, their current choice of a competitive pastime, at the old cafeteria table in the underground alcove of their team bunker.

"What are you reading now, Lucien?" Adonis asked.

"The last couple of days, I've been studying the Peloponnesian Wars, from a book written about thirty years ago by an author named Donald Kagan. That time period seems to bear quite a bit of resemblance to ours."

"How so?"

"Well, the Athenians were the stronger power, see, and after the end of the deadly rivalry with Persia was long over, they forged a formal alliance with a lot of smaller states. Mainly a naval alliance, with the common treasury at first kept on the little island of Delos. Which is why it's always been called the 'Delian League.' But after awhile, the Athenians became so bossy and arrogant that they ended up just trying to exercise direct control over their allies, and the alliance of commonly-motivated like-minded friends changed into what came to be called ever since the 'Athenian Empire'."

"And then?" said Adonis.

"Well, then, the other, little states, pissed at being exploited and made subservient, got together with some of Athens's old enemies and ganged up against the bully in the Peloponnesian Wars. And that was the end of ancient Athens as an independent power."

"And you really think that has relevance for us?"

"Just *think*! This domineering stuff, economically and militarily, in the absence of a unified, actual, strategically capable enemy, has been going on for awhile. And now, the Europeans are beginning to find some genuine grievances, and ..." Lucien pulled his finger across his throat. "And they can use this sovereignty-democracy thing as, at least, an excuse to separate themselves, and restore their own significance."

"Well, you may have a point. But it's still a little too early to say. At least, until we see what they will *do*."

"True."

"So now we wait."

* * *

Before the President's scheduled prime-time address to the nation to report on his European trip and other recent events and revelations, Gossens uncharacteristically called up the Vice President, Ben Weck, at his residence, to go over a couple of things.

"Hello, Ben?"

“Yes, Mr. President.”

“Ben, can I count on you to keep on supporting my initiatives and policy directions? About keeping this corporate lock-in we have, for instance, smooth and on course?”

“You’ve got it, Mr. President. I’m with you all the way!”

“That’s great to know, Ben. And Ben, do you understand the thinking behind my statement at the G-9 that nation-states are now passé, museum pieces? Like they make such a big thing out of still having and maintaining that status, in principle, but they’re a thing of the past, and they might as well agree with us on that, and work on phasing all that old, outmoded functional machinery, that just makes them sort of bi-polar, completely out?”

“Of course, Mr. President! We’ve talked about this before. We both know that the organizations that run most efficiently and effectively are businesses and organizations on the business model. Not democracies, with machinery running in all directions! Not even our Founding Fathers actually signed on to a full democratic model, including dissent of the lower orders. A ship without a captain, run by a show of hands, is as good as rudderless, about as effective as an insane asylum, and a vessel sailing in a zigzag always ends up heading nowhere but onto the rocks, to absolutely no one’s benefit.”

“You’re damn right. Well-spoken! It’s precisely the reason that we floundered here for so many years. Ben, you’re a good man! Them that pays most of the bills, including salaries, and puts up the money for everything, can agree among themselves most of the time. But not the others, whose part it properly is to be active as consumers and functionaries and staunchly support those who are in a position to drive the car.”

“Thank you, Mr. President. I really couldn’t agree more.”

Literally a minute later, President Peter Gossens appeared on C-TV screens across the nation.

“Don’t believe all of the irresponsible rumors swirling around, outrageous conspiracy theories, my fellow Americans,” he said. “In fact, don’t even rely on what *we* say to you, because we never have an opportunity to say it all at the same time. That is, to tell you the *whole* truth all at once. Instead, look for and rely on what we *do*, for America and for you all.

“We will be bringing in more overseas workers, as speculated, yes we will. But they are for *you* – low-cost workers to help provide for your tables and to clothe your family without breaking up your bank. They won’t cost you or anyone much, and we don’t expect them to raise at all the price of your food or goods. And hey, they'll be getting far more income and benefit from living here than they ever could have gotten back home where they came from! It's a win-win, right? And the many of you who are hard-pressed producers will have the help you so desperately need, because of their presence, on a far more affordable basis than if they had to pay Americans.

"And, be assured that the rest of the world, too, will eventually come to see that America's business model of governance is best for all of them, also, and will come to agree with us. So, hold your heads high and be proud of what we are accomplishing together, and don't become discouraged by their slowness and reluctance to understand. We will show them by the surge of production and improvement in our way of life that we anticipate, with the new efficiencies we will begin to realize immediately. Their day of full understanding will come, too, I can assure you. My fellow Americans, stand tall and support those of us who are working for you! My fellow citizens and fellow travelers, good night, and may God bless and provide for us all, always."

President Gossens's numbers took a spike upward that very night among the millions who watched and listened to him and got the message. America's independence must be maintained, above all!

But, some in the land still didn't get it. They perversely continued to demand a return to the old days and the old Constitution. They continued with a vengeance to "kick against the pricks," to quote and honor the Bible.

Chapter Fifteen – Solutions Happen

A tanned, bearded, and much slimmer Abe Gole arrived at Senator Topel's Fairfax home that July 4th weekend and was met by a round of applause by the House Dissident Caucus. Fresh from the field, he gave a full report of what he'd learned. There was still a large segment of the population so concerned with making enough money to feed and clothe themselves that they couldn't be bothered to think about their right to self-rule and the abnegation of the Constitution. He deeply lamented their plight. But he was cheered to see that there was a growing movement to take the Constitution and thus the country back.

For those all-too-well-known politicos by now frequenting Senator Topel's weekend home in search of news and ways to participate in heretical activities devoted to restoring the invalidated Constitution, problems multiplied. First, the reason their physical presence was required, beginning with their arrival usually in less-traceable rented or borrowed vehicles or on public transportation, just as with the "Sons of Liberty" in the 1770s, instead of phoning or clicking it in online, was that they were all branded traitorous outlaws by the criminals running the show. Their electronic communications were usually intercepted these days, no matter how cleverly couched, on "national security" grounds.

In that weekend's rendezvous, there ensued much soul-searching and brainstorming directed at making headway against ill winds such as were blowing over the land, an analogy that seemed a little absurd on the beautiful, golden day of blue skies and gentle breezes that that bucolic early-summer holiday perversely provided. Gole was, needless to say, let in by unanimous concession on the secrets of Buzzy Wuzzy.

According to Buzzy Wuzzy, in an extra-special Saturday, July 4, cork-tape communication, the staffs of the two known Rassoles, son and father, were working feverishly on a new loyalty oath to be imposed on all public officials whose oaths of office had required them to "preserve, protect, and defend the Constitution of the United States." The secret informant disclosed that they were considering just redefining the phrase "Constitution of the United States" to mean whatever set of rules were currently in effect over the country. On the other hand, they were thinking that perhaps a totally new oath ought to be imposed to exact and enforce conformity and compliance. Political participation at any level, even just voting, could then be regulated and conditionally licensed, defining a new basis and body of citizens by design.

After some reflection and a round of key lime pie, Hilda Cable, Senator Cable's Argentine wife, made a stunning suggestion that had occurred fleetingly to Senator Roger Topel as well. "If we, or any of us, have access to that Laser-Zap Weapon that was captured, or if they have reason to believe our side does," she said, "why don't we threaten to *use* it on them if they try to disrupt us?"

Senator Topel answered this suggestion thoughtfully. "Well, assuming we do have access to it (and you don't want to know that, and I, for one, don't want anyone to know for sure), whenever we use it to actually detonate something, we will ourselves be the agents of mass devastation. Is that really what we want? On the other hand, if we use it in a more or less conspicuous but token way, say to vaporize a guardhouse or a mailbox somewhere – if it's even possible to limit it to that smaller extent – then they would just run it down and confiscate it, and we wouldn't have it anymore."

Congressman Carbola, growing agitated, commented, "And so, the question becomes, would we follow through on our threat if they were to tamper with our operations?"

"Right," Topel said. "It just becomes meaningless if we aren't really prepared to follow through. In which case, *might* – theirs – just naturally makes *right*, and they'll roll right over us and utterly destroy our cause to restore the Constitution and representative government for the country.

"So, I say we *go for it*, assuming we do have the capacity, and try to moderate our deadly response if it comes to that. It's the dilemma principled dissidents always encounter when possessing the capacity for violent means that would inevitably get them denounced as 'terrorists.' Just because the terrorism of the oppressors may operate more slowly and deliberately, it is no less oppressive, and no less terrorism itself.

"Those in power can inflict terror far more effectively because they are better funded, and thus, much better-equipped – meaning *their* terror is popularly-funded, often by its own victims. But being ground down or one's rights or plight disregarded and denied by their actions is certainly no less deadly. It's inhumanity and egoism that opposes us, and that is totally opposed as well to the long-abandoned founding principles of the very religions it loudly and clangingly invokes. So, use our weapons, judiciously, but I say we *must*."

Hilda Cable and Senator Jake Cable clapped loudly. "Our Fourth of July speech! Hooray!" both exclaimed, then looked at each other, delighted and surprised.

Abe Gole took a deep breath. He'd been thinking on this very scenario himself, and had been waiting for just such an opportunity to provide his counsel. "Well, I have to agree. If we don't threaten to use the weapon to gain concessions, we can't do anything. But we do need to maximize the impact and minimize the destructiveness of our threat.

"First, we need to sit down and agree on what would be an effective target to use it on, if it really does come to that. We don't want to end up killing half a million people in our one shot before being apprehended and deservedly prosecuted. Then, we need to nail down, if possible, a baffling sequence of frequencies and go on the air to educate people about the importance of our message to resist.

"The people are not completely ignorant about the Constitution and its protections, and certainly not hostile to it, I've found, despite the disinformation saying it's outmoded or parts of it are inapplicable.

"Then, we need to get the UN actively involved with a resolution, because depriving the people of the document protecting their voice and their basic rights, especially without due process, is illegal on the face of it. Why I didn't say that in the campaign, I'll never know and will never live down. I guess it's because I didn't think it would ever in a million years be approved. I thought it would seem such an absurd idea that I wouldn't need to speak out against it. But, I certainly have learned my lesson: *never* try to defeat *anything* without negating it."

"But wouldn't the Gossens administration be able to just veto a resolution opposing it at the UN?" Howard Jellen said. "We do still have a right to claim membership."

"I'm having that looked into," said Gole. "If the UN judges some way that this is an illegitimate regime, placed in power by what amounted to an illegitimate plebiscite, then maybe this country can temporarily be stripped of its very membership rights until its standing is rectified. So, will that matter? I'm not sure."

Congresswoman Barbara Cullen spoke up. "My staff and I have been doing some research, too, with an assist from 'Noodles' Norton's staff." She flashed a smile to her stout colleague.

"It occurred to the two of us in talking," she said, "that just puttin' things back the way they were in terms of governance, with the corporates buying everything, even if they didn't own it all quite, as now, wouldn't straighten everything out, because the system we had that got us to the bad place where we are, would still be in effect. So, we wondered how it actually got to be that way in the first place.

"Well, we discovered two senators, O'Mahoney and Borah, way back a hundred years ago, who almost succeeded in getting *federal* licensing required for corporations, giving government sanction over them.

"But even more to the point, we found at fault the outrageous claim sanctioned by the U.S. Supreme Court way back in 1886, that *corporations are persons* and hence have all the same inalienable human rights.

"So, they can't be prevented from exercising 'free speech' rights, and because 'money talks,' from contributing persuasively to candidates' campaigns, incurring big debts repayable to them by special favors. *That* imposed utter fiction – *that corporations are persons* – we discovered was the proverbial worm in the apple, the cause of adulteration of the American pie, dated precisely from 110 years into the American experiment.

"*That* malicious fiction most assuredly scuttled *the people's* government. And all of that spurious reasoning, we found, issued from the Supreme Court's twelve-sentence 1886 ruling, delivered by one Justice Harlan, in the case of Santa Clara County v. Southern Pacific Railroad Company. Now, all of us know that corporations and persons ain't the same thing, because, for one thing, a corporation can't self-motivate to register and vote. But that ruling alone elevated corporations to '*persons*' for perpetuity, meaning forever or, *until we wake up and rescind it!* So it occurred to me and 'Noodles' that if we could succeed in putting our Constitution back into place, we surely might be able to do *something* to get that idiotic, nonsensical finding knocked out, too, and give their marvelous Constitution back to the *people*, as in 'we, the people' and restore the original intent or content of that justly-famous phrase."

Senator Topel was delighted. "I think you make a really excellent case, ladies! Bravo."

"Yes, bravo!" said Abe Gole.

"I think we could find a way to do, or undo, that ridiculous *corporations are persons* statute. Let's all so vow," Topel said.

"Hear, hear!" they all said, and raised their glasses.

After each had spoken her or his piece and downed the last of the frozen *caipirinhas*, they adjourned, each pledging to go to work on at least one aspect of what had been discussed. Senator Topel, through channels, issued the not-too-veiled threat to the administration and powers-that-be not to shadow or disrupt any of their assemblings, or else. Then, they waited for reverberations.

That message from Senator Topel and the now-infamous caucus, perhaps through some negligence, also arrived in the hands of Holly Bronson and Mackenzie Ward of the Travel Team, who issued a laconic facts-only bulletin containing what little could be discerned from the clear threat, which then circulated all over the country under the screaming headline, "Dissidents Revive Terrorist Tactics." The "war for America" had finally begun.

Chapter Sixteen – A Day in the News

At 8:30 in the morning on Tuesday, July 6, Fuba "Tex" Thorter – watching the BBC News by international satellite in his plain, close-air apartment in Georgetown – learned that the rhetoric from European leaders had just escalated with the issuance of a new joint statement attacking the alleged illegitimacy of the regime in Washington. The outward basis of this attack was the perception of a mislabeled "democratic" sovereignty based not on a common citizenship but instead on autocratic decision-making by a privately held, many-tentacled holding company that had purchased the country's assets.

The leaders of what they were now calling the "G-8" (the G-9 *sans* the currently reviled Americans) announced that they were poised to go to the United Nations and offer a resolution declaring the American election of last November null and void because it made the repudiation of the formal Constitutionally-based government a ballot option, with a built-in powerful inducement to the voters to scrap it. This led to the extinguishment of the Constitution in exchange for an arbitrary government now refusing to reveal even the basic outlines of its own assumed powers and mode of operation. The statement demanded that said illegitimate regime be abolished and new elections held under the restored full Constitution, the results to be non-negotiable, with no further transaction to take place with the moribund, outlaw regime.

As for the additional question of restitution to The Company for its erroneous outlay pursuant to the agreement between itself and the incoming administration of the then-President-elect, the statement cleaved to the principle that the instigators of illegal transactions were not entitled to restitution for monies expended in pursuit thereof.

Fuba "Tex" and a couple of hundred thousand other Americans watching the BBC's international telecast by satellite were appalled by the abiding seriousness with which the Europeans were continuing to regard the change of the tone of leadership in America, which had been taken realistically in stride by Americans themselves by and large. After all, were the people ever really in charge of what was happening? Part of the reason for the Americans remaining so calm, it seemed to Fuba "Tex", was, ironically, the very scarcity of the aspects of forthcoming changes thus far announced. Americans tended to wait for the official word, it seemed, while others tended to take more stock of changed tone itself, and not trust authority as benevolent. The "Travel Team" leader was himself undergoing a metamorphosis on that.

In other news reported by the BBC, the leader of the Gambia confirmed that his government indeed had received an offer from the American government to buy out his country and transport its people wholesale to America to partake in a better-compensated life. He had rejected the offer outright.

At 9:29 a.m. that day, meanwhile, in their rundown kitchenette apartment unit in an undisclosed location, surviving on funds shuttled to them via the House Dissident Caucus, Webster Bootle and Camilie Auden were watching the *NNN News Daily* on the ancient boxy console-model C-TV they had picked up. They were shocked to hear that *they themselves* were the subjects of an APB issued by the Justice Department for arraignment on treason charges at the bequest of the President.

President Gossens was, the reporter said, "upset" by the apparent recent serial feeding of unfounded and uncleared "news" segments into the pipeline by the duo, under an assumed name. At 9:34, they also saw a segment of somewhat grainy footage, shot from an angle that suggested concealment, showing ex-Vice President Abe Gole clad in what looked for all the world like a trench-coat, sidling toward the front door of what was identified as the weekend home of a certain Senator Roger "Drinker" Topel (and the cognomen, they noted, was emphasized distinctly by the newscaster) on the outskirts of Fairfax, Virginia. The accompanying commentary was something about an organization on the "far-left fringe," which had very recently threatened extreme terrorist acts, holding periodic "cell-meetings" at the Fairfax location.

Next, a clear-enough view was shown of Senator Topel himself, the brother of the member of the House who had been arrested and arraigned on a related charge, talking with Congressman Nory "Noodles" Norton beside what looked like a dining table, apparently shot through a window or vent from a vertical angle. A trio of other prominent legislative-branch figures was shown approaching the door together. The segment hinted that more indictments could be coming for questionable actors in the public sector in coming days, although Web and Audie were still both a bit too taken aback by the announcement in the newscast involving them to pay very close attention.

At 1:45 p.m., Travel Team reporter Mackenzie Ward, lounging on her day off in the large northwest Washington, DC, apartment she shared with Holly Bronson, Melinda Thalanis and Sarah "Blinkenmissit" Dawson, heard an interview by host Raymond Cooley of *Pentacost News* on the Mount Carmel Network with Dr. James Etherington, Chairman of the Meteorology Department at Calvin College, about the present stage of global warming, which he declared anew to be a hoax. He described a study he had just completed that demonstrated that the statistical profiles used to document a global rise in temperature were based on selective data.

"Temperature time series from locations that seemed to confirm intensification over time were included in the averages, while those from places that recorded little or no change were left out," he said. In fact, he claimed that records he had collected from weather stations in states that had supported the Republican Gossens in the last election actually showed, on the average, a slight *decrease* in temperatures since 2000, while those from states Gole and the Democrats had carried recorded an increase.

When asked by Rev. Cooley to explain what was causing the marked sea-level rise most affecting the lands of the Low-Country Coalition, Etherington offered a stunningly original observation. He claimed that all of those low-lying predominantly coastal lands were, according to the field studies of Calvin College astrophysicist Arnie Eton, not really suffering from the effects of sea-level rise, but rather from *subsidence,* a measurable sinking of the land thought to be due to subterranean displacement caused by the extraction of large amounts of petroleum from sea-beds and undersea oilfields nearby. Mackenzie Ward noticed her own eyebrows rise to about the same extent as she saw journalist Cooley's at this statement.

Meanwhile, at 2:30 p.m., farm-workers and fuel-attendants in Libby, Montana, Windsor, Vermont, Baudette, Minnesota, and other locations near the country's northern border, receiving the feed from the CBC during their afternoon *siesta*, saw film-clips taken over the past holiday weekend in North Carolina, where President Gossens had made an encore appearance before some of his supposedly most-fervent supporters at the event marking the beginning of the 2033-34 "2-Car Racing Association Series." The footage and commentary showed that, contrary to the expectations of the reporters, the real attitude of most of the down-home-style attendees had been revealed not by overt protest but by politely sitting on their hands when he was announced to them. Some hooted.

The President's personal experience of this day at the races, from his perspective up on the dais, was quite different. Twenty yards ahead of him, in the front row of the mammoth crowd behind a barrier comprised of helmeted National Guardsmen, he espied Marge Smith – his early lifeblood companion, broadcast colleague, and would-be girlfriend – waving and struggling in vain to push past the guards and make her way up to greet him. He might have requested that they bring her up for a brief reunion, a pleasant moment perhaps, but knew instinctively it would only lead to another imbroglio, which he certainly did not need in this particular time of troubles, so chose to look away.

Marge Smith, from her perspective, saw her life destroyed once again by still another rejection by this man whose eyes she had held for an instant before he turned aside.

She turned now to slog the mile back to weep into her steering wheel, but then she saw something that nearly gave her a stroke. Almost right next to her, clad in National Guard riot gear and helmet, waving a riot stick, she saw the unforgettable face of the foreign-talking man from the other race day, who had stopped her then from killing Gossens and said he would do it himself. Their eyes met in mutual recognition and terror.

*   *   *

On the 5:00 p.m. "World Today" program on NNN, Luden Bond – in the townhouse he shared with Adonis Wong and another friend who was a Congressional aide – saw the President's weekend appearance at the North Carolina "2-Car Association Rally," showing a veritable sea of adoring, almost ghoulishly-grinning fans wildly applauding him. How at variance!

Later on the same newscast, footage and an interview recorded at the Antarctica penal colony site showed the construction of facilities at a surprisingly advanced stage, sustained in good part by medium- or low-security prison labor, encouraged by the promise of two years of furlough for every one year spent building and working at the colony. One man interviewed said he would consider continuing service work at the remote colony after serving out his sentence.

On the 11:00 p.m. late local news in Washington, Senator Roger Topel and his wife Evelyn Wadsworth watched a clip from a brief question-and-answer session President Gossens permitted that day following a summit at the White House with Pedro Almaya, the President of Mexico. Responding to a question, President Gossens said that he didn't take his recent opponent Abe Gole's apparent "campaign swing" through the West eight months after the election too seriously, and couldn't understand why candidate Gole hadn't taken the highly questionable positions he apparently did now during the campaign, which would have made him easier to beat, according to his campaign's polling at the time.

The President quipped that it was always easiest to criticize "from outside the barn." Asked about the reports of dissatisfaction with his administration still simmering in Europe and reflected in the new official statement issuing from there, he said that the State Department was studying the text of the communiqué, and opined that the Europeans had plenty of characteristics Americans didn't find particularly endearing, as well. And he was confident they would withdraw or moderate their opposition over time.

"Fair enough," Roger and Evelyn thought in knowing unison, "as far as the statement went." But what a bleepin' outrage that their compatriots, living in the cradle of modern democracy, could scarcely find out what was really going on. Often of late, the two found themselves self-consciously holding hands sitting together on the sofa watching the news, as though they were confronting together some overwhelming giant-screen spectacle or personal drama.

In a luxury apartment on a fourteenth floor in midtown Manhattan, Horton Candon – the Chairman of the New York Stock Exchange, watching that same interview clip on the hourly NNN newscast at midnight – turned to his personal secretary and paramour, George Ginflicks, and asked what the other's opinion now was of the President. Mr. Ginflicks, setting his New New Coke down, answered in his stentorian voice, "Well, he's, I'm afraid, ruined our business in Europe irretrievably by his boorishness. The severity of his crackdowns on his opposition is just beginning to sway public opinion decisively against him and, I fear, against the business-supremacist policies he and we have favored, which promised to tame the economic landscape for us. And, his apparent escapade of permitting that crazy, Wild West hand-held super-weapon to be unleashed in a cave full of his political opponents has, I surmise, zapped his own presidency. What more is there to say?"

Chapter Seventeen – Brainstorms and Fallouts

The Company's previously unknown ultra-secret Governance Council brain trust was approaching apocalyptic mode by the time of its weekly closed-circuit videoconference on Thursday afternoon, July 9. Each of the others flashed in a sequence of camera profiles, their visages uncannily resembling old-time death-row posters flickering and clustering on the giant wall-screen inside Japheth Rassole, "the Younger's," compound secluded among the poplars and oaks on outer Old Wythe Road in Petersburg.

His sire Joseph, called "The Elder" – age unknown, but past a hundred, held at that time by conventional wisdom to probably not exist (his son being equally unknown to the public at large) – checked in with a terrifying, flaming-red countenance a yard wide, filling Japheth's screen, sourced from his house down in the holler, farther out beyond the Cumberlands' west flank, somewhere on the edge of the broad shadow of Bridgeman Mountain.

Bob Fullmar, 48, heavy, sour-faced jowly lug, lovingly called "Bubba" by insiders because he originally haled from the South Bronx, appeared, jaunty enough at the moment (which should have been regarded as a warning to everyone), from his current digs far south on 63rd Street in Manhattan.

A cagey operator of more than legendary wealth, Sam Rickard, 57, a high-stakes oilman from Edmond, Oklahoma – representing a truly megalo-empire of Alberta tar sands investment and other strange and stray wildcatting that always seemed to pay off – was there as the member for the great Southwest.

And Edward Lambent, 52, that inner group's only living link to the daylight above-ground world, his first name known to only a small handful of marked insiders, was there in electronic guise as well. Smooth and savvy, his two roles were practical application and stabilization.

Japheth's waif-like, auburn-coifed Brazilian housekeeper slipped into his inner office sanctum briefly from an adjacent room to refill her man's plastic tumbler of New New Diet Coke and brandy from a pitcher clogged with ice. She was the only outsider permitted in, if briefly, during these meetings, because of her exceedingly limited ability in English, even though she'd been with the family over fifteen years.

In accord with protocol, Joseph "The Elder" spoke first, his sultry upland Southern boyish whisper all but inaudible, starting as usual with repeated clearings of his throat. "Greetin's to ya all! You know, things ain't lookin' so peachy for us. We've got to find out how to shut up all the opposition's messages that are so confusin' people, and keepin' 'em wonderin'. I thought by now they'd a seen the advantages of clear polities an' strong actions without all the hagglin' and unsartainties thrown in all the time, and we'd be able to slice our way straight through the world and do our enterprise and jus' make our country richer and more successful to ev'ryone's satisfaction.

"But, with these here doubts bein' sown and resistance even by our own kind abroad... Well... And they think they've got our hands tied to where we can't nab 'em and break up this reactionary opposition business. But, I'm tellin' you sumpthin', I don't think they have the guts to follow through on their threat to detonate that thang. It's jus' crowin', to throw their one an' only weapon an' themselves away on takin' out a city, or sumpin' like that. Which is all they could do, an' that once an' out! An' then, we would have 'em an' the people would all turn on 'em, too. I say, let's go ahead now an' round 'em up! I tell ya, I'm ready to give the order!"

Japheth tried to soothe him. "Pop, you're right, logically-speaking... as you always are. I don't really know what they could try to do in response..."

Bob Fuller chimed in, big, blunt nose close to the visual feed, making it appear mashed and half the size of his chunky face. "Well, that's their problem to figger out. I'm with you, Pop – I don't see how they can respond and do themselves a bit a good. If they *do* respond as they said they would, it will definitely be all over for them at that point. We have all the real guns on our side, so let's give the order an' send the posse."

"I'll go along with that, too," Sam Richard said. "I'd say it's a slam-dunk case. And, if we can get them to shut up, we know how to sell our plan, because we have all the best advertisers!"

Japheth Rassole, dropping his faint objections, joined in. "Agreed, then?"

All answered together. "Agreed."

Joseph Rassole, considered no fool, for all his seeming profligacy, injected an unexpected note of caution. "But, what about the international thing, and the other members of the inner G-9 going to the UN about us?"

"Are they going to follow through?" Japheth Rassole asked.

"I think the key there is Russia," Sam Rickard said. "If we can get Russia to stay with us, and I have some deals I think they'd like, I'm sure the others will have to come around. Without the Russians, they can't pass anything."

Bob Fullmar, visibly irked, tried to put Rickard on the spot. "You will work on that, then?"

"I will, yes, along with Japheth," Sam Rickard answered. "We've talked about it and we've got some diplomatic things already going. Japheth, if you can fill the President in on what to say and how to handle it…"

"Yes, I will do that," Japheth said. "And we can talk more about it this afternoon, and tomorrow when you come up."

"And I hope we can grab those young crazy reporters, the ones that was here," Old Joseph said. "They've turned out to be more'n half the problem!"

"The President assures me he's had the Attorney General and FBI make that a priority," Japheth said. "They're on it, and they'll catch up with them pretty soon."

"Not soon enough!" Old Joseph said. "Tell the President that his Attorney General's head is on the line. That one was *his* choice!"

Now it was Ed Lambent's turn to reassure. "They'll get them, Pop. I'll convey your exact words."

* * *

Buzzy Wuzzy's next cork-tape message reported the entire exchange to the Dissidents. Buzzy Wuzzy, ever faithful to herself, never told anyone from whom her intelligence came. Nor could she, ever.

She was a brilliant, lovely girl of Swiss expatriate ancestry, growing up in Novo Friburgo in the emerald tropical highlands northeast of Rio de Janeiro. She had heard throughout her younger years how her father had been jailed and crippled in his youth in the '70s, caught in opposition to the fascist military regime then in power, and she had, like her hero Jefferson, sworn "eternal opposition to every form of tyranny over the mind of man."

Later, at the University of São Paulo, adjudged an ingenious inquirer into the Helvetica printing script and the almost occult powers often ascribed to it, she learned to perfectly replicate it manually and gained an international recognition in the field of calligraphy. Her career prospects tumbled, however, after she exposed a faculty extortion ring and she was professionally blacklisted in Brazil. When she learned that her slightly older aunt's courtly American suitor was looking for a governess for his widowed children, she opted to emigrate to the U.S. and take the job. But it wasn't long before she learned that Mr. Japheth Rassole was seriously involved in the same sort of "darkness," which was her name for the fascist domination that had once gripped her country. Nevertheless she stayed on in order not to be deported, and taught herself to feign a sort of slow-mindedness, while absorbing all she could of the domination from the inside and devising her own way of exposing and fighting it by carefully disseminating information. A romantic, she eschewed liaisons to avoid compromises.

* * *

Congress came back into stormy session for a few weeks in mid-July. On July 13, members of the activist left wing of the minority party in the Senate – led by Topel and Cable, along with Harry Carbola in the House – demanded an investigation of President Gossens' failure to file the required paperwork when he chose to opt himself out of generally-binding pieces of legislation duly passed by Congress that he signed.

Word from the White House was that the president didn't need to file any of the said paperwork (informally known as "*Signing Statements*") in those instances, because he had used instead on each occasion the alternative executive privilege available since the Middle Ages, of the "King's-X" behind his back. He swore that he had so done in every instance, and that as a democratically elected official, his word must be accepted by the people on good faith. The litmus test wasn't a flimsy piece of paper, in other words, but the president's word.

The other important dispute that arose involved a Texas Congressman, Giles Fergusson, an ardent supporter of Gossens and all his programs. Indictment for tax-evasion of a more moderate Republican congressman from a district neighboring Fergusson's had resulted in calling a special election. Party officials in that district wanted to nominate Fergusson, a very popular and colorful congressman who had a house boat docked on a lake in their district and was registered to vote in school board and municipal elections there as well, to also serve *their* district and thus be allotted *two* votes in Congress (and, presumably, two staffs and two salaries). The Democrats, predictably, cried foul in no uncertain terms.

Before adjournment that day, resolutions were passed in both houses of Congress concerning both issues. They urged the Supreme Court to rule expeditiously to decide this unprecedented pair of questions, because they didn't want to deal with the can of worms.

Accordingly, by mid-morning the next day, the Supreme Court issued a statement that it would examine the two issues and announce its findings within days.

* * *

The administration's apologists launched an all-out blitz in the media concerning the nature of the rising opposition, insinuating that the public officials who stood against the serving government – including an ex-Vice

President and an ex-President, at least two current senators, and at least half a dozen House members – were all characterized as "irresponsible" and "reckless". The aforementioned were said by the administration and its apologists to be consorting with foreign agents and with at least one major active international terrorist cell operating inside this country. Its members had sought to instigate and link up with disaffected elements within the interior of the country in meetings and rallies with the intent of resisting necessary legal changes and actions already completed (i.e. the purchase of sovereignty by The Company).

And now they were terrorizing the nation with the clandestinely obtained prototype of the experimental hand-held Laser-Zap Weapon capable of vaporizing a city or stretch of countryside at these unauthorized possessors' option. They were suspected as well of providing the working link with agents of the East Asian Axis that had launched the assault on the ATF Building that resulted in the notorious bomb blast some months earlier.

The current Vice President, Mr. Weck, the Majority leader of the Senate, John Sokol of Ohio, the Attorney General, Mr. Montgomery, and Senator Henry Steele, Republican of Washington, all appeared on evening C-TV talk shows during the week and on the Sunday talk shows. All stated categorically that the shape and outlines of the radical new cabal's program of violence, threats, disinformation in the spreading of unfounded truisms through the press, and liaison with hostile foreign leaders posed a serious threat to the country's *de facto* independence. All of these spokesmen, and not a few editorialists in major papers, urged the administration to go ahead and round up the perpetrators and summarily bring them to justice.

On the international front, the new Secretary of State, ex-Senator John Diamond Tarn, after the first had been caught in a series of affairs, issued a communiqué on Thursday that got a lot of exposure in the world press, but less at home. In it, he warned the Chinese that if they were to go ahead with their reported agreement to construct a forward naval base in Aabania, the American military could justifiably find sufficient provocation to warrant a field test of the Laser-Zap weaponry at the site.

On Friday morning, the State Department announced that the President would be traveling to Charlotte Amalie in the Virgin Islands for a closed-door summit meeting with Grigory Gonchov, the Prime Minister of Russia. Subjects to be discussed were not disclosed.

* * *

In Fairfax on Saturday, July 18, the Expanded Dissident Caucus, with most of its members in attendance, weighed its options in light of the increasingly more obvious general assumption that the President was going to order a crackdown imminently resulting in their arrest, reversing his earlier acquiescence not do so, due to the perceived increased risk.

"If they break the implicit agreement and start coming after us on trumped-up charges," Congressman Carbola said, "I don't see how we can avoid following through, in some fashion, with our threatened action."

"But I don't see how we can do such a thing," Roger Topel said. "We're not terrorists. We can't kill a million people in a city."

"How about a compromise?" Howard Jellen said. "We could blow away *something*, something insignificant, like concentrate it on a guardhouse with no one there, or a group of trees, or something."

"But what good could that possibly do?" Congresswoman Norton said. "It would just show we *weren't* serious."

Howard Jellen sighed. "You're right."

"Hey, maybe we could do something else," Barbara Cullen said. "Like, maybe *kidnap* one of them."

"Maybe," Senator Cable said. "But I don't know how. We don't even know where any of *them* are."

"I might, actually," Senator Topel said. "I mean, I think I know someone who might know where one of them lives. I'll work on it. That's not a bad idea, actually, if we could do it."

"Who are you thinking of, Roger?" Abe Gole inquired.

Senator Topel played for time. "You'll see. I'll see what I can find out… And if I can even locate the person."

* * *

Web and Audie arranged to have themselves delivered from a borrowed blue Republic Express van in two large cartons at the Topels' Fairfax home late the next evening. They were desperately on the run, taking a huge risk in movement or circulation of any kind. Audie was pregnant, they had just learned two days before. And now they were called in by the highest coven of Constitutional-restoration dissidents in the country and asked to retrace in reverse the path of their escape from their abductors three developments-packed months before, and to describe the approaches to the place and circumstances under which they had been held.

* * *

At shortly before noon on July 21, during the President's absence at the summit meeting in the Virgin Islands, the Supreme Court reported its finding on the two matters Congress had jointly asked it to rule on.

The Court voted 6-3 that the President's claim of the validity of a "King's-X," opting out of his obligation to comply with selected legislation which he had signed, was valid, since the principle of selective executive non-compliance using "Signing Statements" had itself been set in cement nearly three decades ago. The previously required paper record was declared incidental. An analogy was stated in the opinion, written by Justice Alito, with the legally recognized institution of common-law marriage. It likewise didn't require a certificate to be considered valid in most jurisdictions.

As to whether Congressman Fergusson could stand in an election to also represent another district in which he had sufficiently established a residency to the satisfaction of that jurisdiction, the Court ruled 5-4 that he could, since it was clear he met the requirements, and since it was felt by the majority that his eligibility would increase the ambit of democratic choice for voters in the district choosing a congressman.

The President, informed of the two Supreme Court victories for his forces in Charlotte Amalie later in the day, was reported to be "exultant."

When the First lady, Sarah Lureen Gossens, spoke to her husband by phone later that night, she warned him not to exult quite so fast, at least not just yet.

Chapter Eighteen – Leaks in the Dike

At 4:07 in the rainy pre-dawn of Saturday, July 25, a terrific subterranean explosion blew the roof and the upper three stories off the block-long, five-story James M. Inhofe Education Building in southeast Washington, across the street diagonally from the ATF headquarters, destroyed by a blast months earlier. Seconds later, Capitol Police apprehended two men in the vicinity. The first was a dusky-skinned individual named Mustafa Balaya, a small, Oriental-looking man and an alien without a country, so far as anyone could readily ascertain. The second was the dapper-dressed Mr. Arthur Seldon, 6'5" and with cameo good looks, whom one police officer intimated unadvisedly was by profession a career customs agent assigned to the Department of Alcohol, Tobacco, and Firearms. He was caught strolling briskly and nervously down the sidewalk a block away from the destroyed facility just after the blast.

Within a few more minutes, the broadcast and telecast media were filled to capacity with the story, impossibly packed with details, fingering the dark Mustafa Balaya as a suspected agent of East Asian operations, with other fingers being already pointed straight in the direction of the Expanded Congressional Dissident Caucus. A few, but only a few, media outlets even mentioned Mr. Seldon. Only two, WRC in Pittsburgh and its affiliate KDN in Seattle, reported his possible ATF tag.

Very much later, interviews revealed that the arresting Capitol Police captain, identified only as "Mr. Blake," had been heavily-pressured to renounce his statement about the possible ATF involvement in the blast, or at least to state that it was considered unlikely that the man caught a block away had any actual involvement.

But he refused, even going so far as to claim that the chemical signature of the blast site was replicated on Mr. Seldon's swanky cufflinks and shoes. Meanwhile, the extremely scantily reported possibility of government involvement did make the rumor rounds, to the administration's palpable chagrin.

Right-wingers everywhere tended to liken this blast to the earlier ATF Building blast, and to lay it by association at the feet of the much-loathed "Congressional Dissident Six," increasingly referred to as "Namby's" for no known reason. For the next seven days, the leading C-TV network outlets ignored virtually everything else and focused on the blast and the alleged perpetrators and implications for the country, with frequent flashbacks to reportage of the associated February 2 ATF Building explosion.

In the meantime, the tie-in of the alleged ATF officer to the recent blast, although receiving absolutely no more on-air exposure after the first couple of hours, took on a spectral life of its own at the center of the informed segment of the public's awareness and belief system. This was an ominous sign for the government, which couldn't even properly deny what it couldn't bear to hear mentioned.

*   *   *

In the meantime, Abe Gole debriefed Web Bootle and Camilie Auden at Topel's Fairfax hideaway. "Who do you think it was that held the two of you?" he asked.

"We really think it was old Mr. Rassole," Webster Bootle answered. "He had us kidnapped because I dared to step beyond the bounds and really question Peter Gossens and the actual status of things in front of the whole nation. We were chosen, of course, because they thought we were safe, because our whole unit was recruited to report coldly and dryly, without questioning."

"So you think 'Mr. Rassole' does actually exist?" Gole asked, mock doubtfulness in his voice.

"I *know,* not just *think* that he does! Functionally, at least. Whether his real name is 'Rassole,' I don't know...although I think I saw an investment tycoon by that name interviewed on C-Span once. But he was younger, compared to this guy. It's a name that can stick with you."

"What was he like?" Topel asked.

"This one? He was... unbelievably old in appearance," Web said. "But there was a sort of youthful-seeming streak in his outwardly make-up, too. Like he's, I don't know, maybe on some sort of serum or something. It's hard to describe."

Abe Gole reflected. "Well, he may be. I think I saw that interview that you saw on C-Span, too. I sort of remember him. But, you know, those shadowy corporate types have that cult, really more like a religion-substitute. Cryonics, and things like that. Even those who claim to have super Christian faith."

Camilie Auden joined in the description. "Well, the results are really ... sort of ghoulish, I thought, if that's really who or what it, he is. ...Rassole, I mean. He probably is. We *know* he's somebody really rambunctious and audacious!"

"As I understand it," Senator Topel said, "the best they can do up to now is to have de-aging going on along with aging. They can't completely reverse the process. At least, not yet. So, you can have them going both ways at once, getting older *and* younger, in effect. And, you're very probably right about the identity."

Congressman Carbola, who was also present, spoke up. "Where was this place that he was, where they took you?" He was thinking how odd it was that they were just then, at that late date, locating the actual enemy, the true source of all the mischief and evil of these last rudderless days.

Roger Topel unfolded a large-scale highway map of the eastern half of the country on the dining room table, and all present surrounded it. Web and Audie, side by side, centered their attention on southern Kentucky. "Monroe County," Web said, pointing, "or maybe… Barren."

"South of Glasgow?" Senator Topel said.

"Right," Web said. "In a sort of a hidden cove, like a crater, in what we from out west would call a deep 'hole.' Must be in an Appalachian outlier. Maybe it is an impact crater of some kind, or karst; it sure seemed like that. We think we might be able to retrace our path out of there, if need be, though we were blindfolded when coming in, likely from the east."

Senator Topel commented aside to Congresswoman Cullen. "Well, if we can go in and kidnap that old Rassole or, if we could, possibly, surround and capture the site, and hold it for the world to take a good look at, and maybe threaten to expose their identity and activity and how feeble they really are…"

"True enough," Carbola said, "but if the feds are put onto us, they would come and grab *us*!"

"We'd have to be on guard, for sure," Topel said. "But we still have the Laser-Zap. Or at least, they think we have one. We may be able, using that threat and a loudspeaker, to actually get this 'Mr. Rassole' to come out with his hands up."

"And we may not even need to hold onto him," Congresswoman Norton said. "It could be enough if we could just *show* him and show how vulnerable they are, say through the international press."

"That was my thinking exactly," said Senator Topel. "In fact, we might be a lot better off not having to hang onto him at all. Turn him loose and we can see where he heads!"

"Good plan!" Abe Gole said. "Who's going to do the capturing?"

They all looked at each other across the table.

"Noodles" Norton spoke hesitantly. "I can contact some Arizona families I know who feel like we do about the Constitution and want to get it restored. I'm sure they would provide us some volunteers, since we have no access to regular military members or National Guard."

"Not if we plan to maintain an element of secrecy, anyway," Senator Topel said.

"I know a lot of so-called street toughs in south Bronx who would do just about anything to put a hurt on these clowns," Congressman Howard Jellen said.

Senator Topel spoke up. "I think we all can recruit a few, if we're careful so word doesn't get out to those who support our enemies."

"Right on," Senator Cable said. "I know a few young Minnesota farmers who are veterans who would like a shot at this crowd, for sure."

Congresswoman Cullen was starting to get restless. "Then get in touch with them, and let's roll, so to speak!"

"I'll get some better topographical maps," Senator Topel said, "and we'll pin-point this place."

Suddenly a piercingly bright light lit up the darkness outside the window and penetrated the dimly lit room where they were gathered. It remained on for more than a minute.

* * *

The heads of state and foreign ministers of the leading economic powers of Europe, whose rank-and-file citizens most despised the new-style unabashedly non-majoritarian American regime, pushed forward at the United Nations with their attempt to officially censure and impose global sanctions on the Gossens Administration and the new constitutional re-ordering in America, demanding that new elections be held to replace the government and restore its previous standing.

The sanctions connected could be taken as non-binding and likely survivable, political experts said. But the rebuke itself, especially if teeth were included, would certainly be damaging and deeply embarrassing to the American citizenry and business interests. Other member countries in the G-9, such as super-creditor Japan, which the Americans were in the habit of lumping with China and Korea and excoriating as part of the sinister and dangerous "Axis" of East Asia, and Canada, which now rued its longtime association as America's shadow, both pledged to cooperate with the majority decision of the members.

The final and, apparently, the decisive member was Russia, whose opportunistic reputation coupled with lucrative American partnerships on a number of major ventures rendered it enigmatic: a cipher. President Gossens's recent three-day consultation with Russia's top leader, it was surmised, had most likely helped his case. Still, the Russian administration, which had been at times critical, was giving no clues as to what its position would turn out to be, and there were reports circulating stating with certainty both ways.

This was one of several major recent developments that had glued tuned-in Americans to their short waves and foreign news sources for signals and credible knowledge the virtually monolithic American media were scarcely providing. As a result, a certain amount of nativist feeling and even, to an extent, paranoia of foreign news sources and foreign opinion was sweeping the more conservative segments of the American population. And, to the extent people mentally linked the disparate and disorganized American dissidence movement with foreign anti-Gossens and anti-American feeling, the Constitutional restoration impulse suffered.

Another current story that was pertinent was picked up and covered only by mainline foreign media sources, and it had to do with continued American activities vis-à-vis the small West African nation of Gambia. According to the reports that were being increasingly monitored by free-thinking Americans, despite the refusal of the Gambian government to entertain the American State Department's formal request that the nation consider ceding its territory and resources to American control in exchange for far more lucrative opportunities for nearly all Gambians as permanent guest workers, the State Department and the CIA were apparently undeterred. The latest reports confirmed that several hundred village headmen and chiefs in Gambia had been hired to spread the Americans' appeals and enticements to the people, and circulate petitions demanding a plebiscite to decide the matter.

Inducements offered to the petition circulators, it was said, ran up to five dollars – a normal week's salary in the Gambia – for every signature collected. And it was alleged on reliable testimony that petition signatures were simply being bought from destitute Gambians, including a great many who were basically illiterate and unaware of the petition's purpose. Reports had it that the petition drive was proceeding rapidly toward its goal of collecting signatures from 80% of the country's adult citizens, to secure the referendum leading to Gambia's lucrative sellout and rapid transoceanic transportation.

* * *

On August 2, the New York *Times*, in its Sunday edition, dared defy federal guidelines and wishes by publishing a section-long critical feature article, starting on page 1-A. The article detailed the disillusionment and simmering anger on the part of farmers in the interior states and the West – considered a crucial stronghold of the President's power – over the recent direction of the holding company of the country's imposed buying and supply policies.

It had developed that the rhetoric of the ruling clique about buying produce for human consumption and feed grains for livestock from the least-expensive source, whether domestic or foreign, regardless of quality within certain limits, was being followed verbatim. And the longtime corporatist rhetoric, both out of and now very much in power, about not subsidizing domestic production of commodities in demand that could be obtained more cheaply elsewhere, was also being strictly followed.

The upshot was that domestic producers of farm products of all kinds were losing domestic market contracts long thought to be securely theirs with the processing and manufacturing branches and components of The Company. They saw disappear as well their critical opportunities to obtain the production credit and loans they largely relied upon.

The article, by a team of *Times* reporters, noted that, by and large, residents of the interior states who depended on agriculture for their livelihoods may have found the issues raised earlier about the new regime and constitutional arrangements too abstract to concern themselves with. But related drastic changes of practice and policy directly impacting their pocketbooks and bank accounts were another matter. And these did concern them.

According to the *Times* article's assessment, support of the President, even in the staunchly-Republican breadbasket states, was now beginning to erode dangerously, especially going into the battles at the UN and given his increasingly sharp clash with "reactionary" forces in and outside Congress. A number of telling quotes from interviews with interior state politicians from both major parties, small business people, bankers, and farmers large and small, were included among the sources of the reporters' conclusions.

Segments of the *Times* article were picked up and republished by papers across the country, and also discussed to a certain extent in the broadcast media. The Gossens Administration, seared by the impropriety of the suddenly-circulated adverse press, although finding some defenders, suffered significantly. Accordingly, lamps burned late at the White House in the coming days and weeks.

In the meantime, the reach of arrests, planned arrests, and recriminations concerning the alleged terrorist blasts, now being referred to as the "twin blasts," and journalists being charged and politicians threatened with being charged under the current anti-terrorist act, all kept increasing. The trial of Samuel Lin, the building janitor charged with colluding with East Asian Axis agents and implicated in the earlier February bombing, was set to start on August 3.

* * *

Abe Gole's actual direction for a solution to the hated takeover came in a lucid dream. Drowsy in the afternoon on that Sunday (the Lord's Day), August 2, he had barely hit the sofa when he found himself conveyed in the spirit to the Oval Office, wherein he beheld ordinary citizens, the needy poor, medical patients, laborers dressed in mechanics' clothes, working mothers, farm workers, college-age students, parishioners, and low-rank, underpaid soldiers, all seated in the padded oversized cabinet chairs with the rising or setting sun design carved into their backs arrayed around the margins of the room. All of these were looking on gloomily and downcast, in respectful silence, while the President, seemingly unaware of them, was bent down on the plush carpet, brazenly sucking a lion's firm male member, while its tail kept switching rapidly from side to side to side. He could see the contented countenance of the lion, in the deepest throes of satisfaction, morph from the face of the reclusive tycoon he saw once, Japheth Rassole, into the irrepressible face of Rousas J. Rushdoony, Christian Identity near-recluse founder and icon, recalled vividly for some reason from a picture once seen in a book.

Out through the east window of the President's office, in the distance, humans lined the teeming shores of corrupt old Europe and debauched Africa; and out the west window, just visible in the farther distance, stood Orientals on the shores of the even more crowded countries of Asia, some of them straining to the utmost to see; and more humans from sunny tropic Latin shores to the south looked on, barely visible, concern marking their sun-browned faces; and a sparser line of humans warmly clad were standing, watching from the border of Canada out the north portal, not so far away, straining anxiously to see what went on there inside, in truth too low down in the room for them to really see.

But inside, Abe Gole knew in his heart that it was an abomination, a desecration, and was moved and wept bitterly.

And he saw that the secret contract, in the guise of a little scroll, was there on the floor next to the defilers, the whore President with the lion. And Gole was bidden by a voice to come and examine it. Not by reading it, which vexed him, but indeed by tasting of it. He found it tasted as sweet as honey in his mouth, but was so exceeding sour when he swallowed it that it soured his stomach. And then, he was given on a secret seal to know a remedy for the thing of his distress by the voice, which cured him at once in his unquiet mind. But he was therewith forbidden to reveal the contents of the seal until the fullness of time.

And then, all of a sudden, he was led up from his couch by two strangers into a disk-like craft. When he fully awoke on board and flying very fast, he asked these two where it was he was being taken. "Why, to

Croker Land!" came their reply, and it was explained that it was so that the inhabitants there might avail themselves of the benefit of his experience and counsel. And, supposing that it meant he was going away to croak there, he grew exceeding despondent.

But then, in only a minute, they landed with a *whoosh* in a snowy, gleaming blue, perfectly flat shadow land of that name, hidden up in the Arctic sea, near the pole. And, lo, the land was surrounded by open surging water for the first time in all the ages back to the early days of the earth.

And in the great hall of an enormous empty palace, infinitely far across the plain from the desolate landing spot on the shore, there were but huge-screen, blaring C-TV monitors up on tables, all surrounded by great, high-back empty chairs, each with the rising or setting sun engraved on its back. On each of the hundred redundant facing monitors that rose a hundred feet high, there were the spouting visages of lofty tycoons from boardrooms, the orgasmic face of the lion replaced alternately with the smug face of Rushdoony, of the serpent Rassole, and the horrid puppet President up to a hundred feet up, his mouth still agape and eyes glassy from the suck, all of them leering as one across the empty chasm, plotting in spirit to confound the world with shocking events. They hurled lightning bolts with their tails against the spirits of all men forevermore unto the ends of the earth, continuing their foul blasphemies against God, Love, Freedom, Goodness, and the Prince of Peace.

And then, the former Vice President Gole awoke with a start, and struggled mightily to his feet and strove to recall the substance of the seals and the remedies to the earth's waywardness that he knew so well, clear and vital the mere blink of an eye before.

Chapter Nineteen – Talking, Tossing, Training

Just after noon on Saturday, August 8, a squad of eighteen federal agents emerged from five unmarked cars and descended on Senator Roger Topel's semi-secluded weekend home on the edge of Fairfax. Observations had indicated that the members of the enlarged House Dissident Caucus gathered there by mid-morning every Saturday of late, and the newly resolved administration's agents were closing in. Approaching the flower-framed front door with measured caution, the leader of the special squad rang the doorbell and encountered no response. Repeated tries, and knocks on the door, followed by louder knocks, still brought neither answer nor appearance.

At length, the front rank of squad-men rifled the doorframe with a crowbar and pushed their way in, finding themselves alone and looking at each other in silence in the entryway and main parlor. Checking every room of the house, each was confirmed to be open and devoid of occupants. The government's quarry seemed to be elsewhere, having left only a haphazardly folded large, road map of the eastern United States on the kitchen table to remind of its earlier presence.

*   *   *

On Sunday, August 9, an open letter appeared in 119 metropolitan newspapers nationwide, but concentrated in the South and Midwest. Its author was a certain Dr. Arlen Coyle, Chancellor of Calvin and Mary Stoops Colleges, a man whose remarks the President had cited before in speeches. The piece was entitled "Democracy Can Deceive." In it, Dr. Coyle began by extolling President Gossens as a "man of God, and very apparently God's man to lead America at this hour." He listed Moses, Jesus, Washington, and Reagan as "great" men God had raised up earlier to lead their nations, and noted that, of that exalted company, only one, Reagan, had been raised to his position through popular election.

"Today," Dr. Coyle wrote, "the forces that hide behind the tissue of so-called 'democracy' are trying mightily to bring down this straightforward and resourceful man whom God has chosen to lead America. His opponents and detractors claim to represent the people's interests. Yet, they have adopted the tactics of terror threats and actions on the one hand, and prominent among them are craven foreigners claiming pure credentials of transparent democracy they by no means actually possess.

"They claim that we lost our rightful democratic representation when we lost our old, outmoded and inoperable Constitution, even though the good President who represents us at the head of our government was himself duly and transparently elected by the people barely nine months ago. That alone should insure that the manifest and steadfast will of the majority among us *is* being honored, by the program he ran on. And, even if we have had to exchange a small part of our 'democracy,' which is itself questionable, for economic security and the restoration of freedom of action for our nation, any thinking Christian man or woman who is the head of a family will realize that such was a very small price to pay for what we all gained as a consequence."

The writer proceeded to list two other facts that needed to be kept in mind. First, that there was no call for democracy whatsoever, and virtually no mention of it, in the Bible. And second, in God's Kingdom, neither democracy nor any other scheme of governance devised by man will be employed or known, but rather Jesus will be the King and He will likely do the governing. Thus, it would be good for us to train ourselves to partake in that perfect state that is coming.

"And so, do not be fooled, friend!" he wrote. "Those who are extolling 'democracy' and trying to thwart and overthrow the new system now in place maximizing heaven-sent efficiency, thrift, and thus civilization, are the enemies of God, and surely of the majority in this country, as well.

"Finally, let us remember that even the so-called 'apostle of Democracy,' Jefferson, called for the overthrow of and a new vote on the then-Constitution in every generation, something that has only happened, long-overdue, now in our own time.

"So don't be deceived by their false claims and cries. Join with me, my fellow citizens, in supporting our wonderful President and our mighty, richly endowed nation in opposing those, at home as well as overseas, who would thwart or limit the nation's great, divinely appointed purposes on this troubled earth. So help us God, even as the battle with our and God's enemies now rages around us! Virtue, the steadfast values of Christ's eternal rule, and solidarity forever!"

* * *

Uncharacteristically, Peter Gossens woke up feeling at least half-dead in the dark White House at 3:45 a.m. on August 10. Constipated and in a cold sweat, he sensed the first tingle of the now-daily tightness in his chest. Sarah Lureen and the two sets of twins had gone up to Turkey Creek, her aged parents' cooler-breezes, north Georgia, piney-woods retreat beside a granite-quarry lake.

A sharp cramp in Gossens's gut sat him straight up in bed. Hunched over in the dark, he made it wringing-wet to the lavatory to try to relieve himself.

"Sickly." The word formed, from where he knew not, on his lips as he squatted to the deed that proved excruciating. An eternity later, he toweled off the glistening of chilly sweat that washed over him, and trundled back to lay inert, utterly drained on the bed.

Sarah Lureen had given the chamber cook the night off, and poor, angular Peter kept thinking with bitterness of the makeshift meal (hash and eggs) he had heated up in a pan for himself. Too much salt, and now way too much bitter bile!

The Presidency! he ruminated. The summit of his dreams, of all public men's dreams, at 48! Was that how old he had become? Now, these days, hooted and unheeded even at the 2-Car rally in North Carolina, despised beyond the ocean and reviled in the very House of Representatives and he, *a Republican,* his name spat on the ground even by farmers in Kansas and mechanics in Utah!

And now he was finding himself hounded to suffer constipated, sweat-filled Pepto-Bismal nights alone in the White House, his semi-supportive family and detractors growing in virulence having pierced his hide. And most of his woes were, he knew, in recompense for the lamebrain, irreversible, world-class shenanigan that was sold to him of pawning away the Constitution! Even his very family had heard the talk of his unequaled stupidity. A goddamn piece of paper, the Constitution, but damn sacred to many who had no power, apparently. Squeezed and puny in the night for all his well-known lankiness, he was forced to recognize the pall of stigma that had begun to engulf him in the emanations that swam in front of his eyes as he clung to a big, rumpled, wringing-wet bed sheet all alone in the dark long pre-dawn.

At four a.m., he fetched himself up on the chair at the bedside table to write down a small thought to recall: "*Hounded to sleeplessness now with the hounds close behind me!*" And the Dissident Caucus was not even in easy reach in Fairfax anymore, they told him. And Sarah Lureen with the babies up Turkey Creek again without him! Leaving him with his scalp itchy, eyes welling red, *alone*, bile rising. These feelings had been building. "Damn it all," he wrote.

* * *

All of the Travel Team not out on assignment or on the lam gathered in their bunker on Monday, August 11, for a morning meeting called by Fuba "Tex" to square impressions of what had been taking place of late.

"Where do you think the UN thing's going?" he threw out invitingly, to no one in particular.

"I don't think that's really going anywhere," Sarah "Blinkenmissit" Dawson said. "They're not going to get Russia to go along with it, I don't think, do you?" She looked in turn to each of the others, seeking affirmation.

"I don't know," Adonis Wong responded. "If Russia can be bought off again with remote oil concessions, and maybe a partnership in the Antarctica minerals venture, they won't condemn the hand that strokes their bear-hair."

"I basically agree," Luden Bond said. "It's not much different from their own situation, the way things are with our administration, and the way with theirs. So, they have no moral standing with us. I think they can understand this President and his struggles. And I also think they know full well about commissars exerting power."

Mackenzie Ward took the cynicism further. "But I think the others, the Europeans, have their price, too. They're all just holding out."

"Holding out for a reshuffle. In this you're right!" Holly Branson said. "The others *do* have their price, of course! That's just the way of international business-slash-politics. It's always that way!"

Even Adonis Wong, an irksome liberal, had to face it. "I'm afraid that you're right, too. They talk like democratic purists, but only give the people their due after the bagmen's bags are full and overflowing. It's a shame the *people* can't actually start and have a government of their own, probably anywhere, because of them."

"That's where I think you're wrong," Melinda Thalanis said. "I've heard that civic-minded people in the towns and bigger farms of our interior and West have had quite enough of being abused, with the loss first of representation, and now of government price protection and credit, and are actually starting to circulate plans to re-activate the Constitution out there among themselves, in what they're starting to call the 'cut-off,' or 'cut-over' states, or whatever."

"You know we're having this talk to get our personal perceptions out *here*…" Fuba "Tex" Thorter cautioned.

"We know," Adonis Wong said. "So we won't put them in our articles."

"Right!" Fuba said. "I don't want to see any of you charged with anything, or disappeared. That is, any more of you…" Then, switching to a question of substance, he added, "Did you hear the rumor about the raid over the weekend on Topel's place over in Fairfax? And the feds coming up empty?"

They all nodded that they had, but nobody said a word.

"Why doesn't anyone want to talk about that?" Fuba asked.

"Too much like a bad movie?" Luden Bond ventured.

"I think that about sums it up for me," Adonis Wong affirmed. "That, and we don't have enough information available to really follow anything like that."

"All of these mysterious struggles are starting to resemble the 'Cultural Revolution'," Luden Bond said. "A lot of Chinese chess."

"I think so, too," Adonis Wong said. "The time for the *real* reporters, and not just storytellers and stenographers, is not here yet. I, for one, am hoping we will have a chance to *be* those reporters."

"Right!" Fuba said, with clear relief. "Not time yet. Keep thinking that way, at least until it *is* time!"

* * *

While the other members of the expanded House Dissident Caucus were safe elsewhere on Tuesday, August 11, Congressmen Jellen and Carbola, Senator Topel, Congresswoman Barbara Cullen, and former Vice President Abe Gole were ensconced in the Lookout Café, on a high bluff overlooking the Mississippi at the end of a back road through the walnut woods above the hamlet of Waterproof, Louisiana. This long-closed greasy-spoon was the designated rendezvous point for the thirteen hand-picked young and active members of the Greater Restoration Operations Corps activated in preparation for the kidnap mission projected by the Caucus.

Plus, Web Bootle, ever the journalist, was on the spot, observing and advising on approaches to the target location. Their meeting place and advance staging point, a dilapidated, long-abandoned, far-off-highway roadhouse, festooned by weeds and tall grass, had been suggested by Congressman Henry Evans, who was not a member of the Caucus, but a sympathizer who knew the owner of the plot of land, and in whose district it was.

The place, a little rusty and filled with cobwebs, was cleaned spic-and-span and up and running for the occasion, festooned with recruited servers and cooks. Beneath the lone, high eminence on which it stood stretched a mile-wide magnificently secluded cane-break merging into a mudflat, judged suitable and adequately secluded for unobtrusive mustering and training.

Present, in addition to the dignitaries named, were the designated commander, a Colonel Carrington, from where no one was sure, a large and stately man in his fifties reputedly with National Guard command experience, and twelve grunts. These latter included current and former Guard members David Meldsgar, 26, and Joe Klosterman, 23, of Owatonna and Windom, Minnesota; Arthur Fallam, 33, of Rochester, Vermont; Bradley Jeffords, 25, of King Hill, Vermont; Jamal Mapes, probably 22, from the Bronx; Jackson Gaar, 30, from Bisbee, Arizona; and Anthony Havelock, 26, from Frogmore, Louisiana – not far from the staging area. They were joined, at the insistence of Congresswoman Cullen, who had grown up in eastern Maryland, by a pair of nurses and "Janes-of-all-trades," Ellen Carbow and Janet Jones, both in their thirties, from that state.

In addition, Congressman Carbola said he had a group of Dakota veterans in clandestine training there, who could join the corps at half a day's notice if needed, or be deployed in the future. Carbola and Senator Topel both marveled at the almost-mystical shared resolve and common understanding that were palpably present, leading to instant comradeship among all those assembled, particularly notable arriving as they did from every point of the compass.

All had had at least some prior military training, and the mood was all-business and firm resolve. Their assurance of success, cheapened not in the least by there being no immediate opposition, seemed to fill and expand the hot Louisiana air.

After a rudimentary briefing, the recruits ate together and talked for a short time about their backgrounds and motivations, and then assembled and fell into formation as directed as if it were for their two-hundred and first, rather than for their first time ever together.

The patriotism of the occasion, above the sheer daunting and obvious idiocy of the greater task contemplated, was lost on no one at the site. Rifles were present: all were required to bring their own. Uniforms there were none, although all, by request, wore a resplendent Union blue, a spectrum of hues that at least seemed to blend together in most instances.

Of larger weapons, there was only the rumored Laser-Zap prototype hand held. It was just one, but commanding if it really existed and was in their possession. Rations, ad hoc, but availed, were paid for out of the semi-deep pockets of the sponsoring politicians, with no assumed link to any other funds. To avoid attention and detection, no guns were to be fired on site and no messages were to be sent or received by recruits. Colonel Carrington was in sole command, under advisement from the politicos. Four days of collective training here, and they were a go. Army surplus sleeping bags on the ground were their barracks. The die, to every appearance, was cast.

That very first night out, the sky welled a deep, bruised, swollen blue-brown-black and unleashed a deluge of four-and-a-half inches of rain on that sorry mud flat inside a thunderous, non-stop display of sheet-lightning brighter than glory, the start of a long monsoon season. Luck be a bitch!

* * *

President Gossens used the occasion of his planned address to the nationally-televised annual National Conference of Cities and Municipalities meeting in Denver, on the evening of Wednesday, August 12, 2032, to announce the general conclusions of his administration's Special Task Force on National Representation, which he had adopted as his own to recommend to Congress. He started out by declaring that, in the current divisive climate, it was hard for citizens to distinguish between genuine patriotism – support for the country's freely-chosen leaders and their mandated programs for the nation's future – and a patriotic-sounding adherence to modes of thinking and governance once appropriate, but now generally conceded to be outgrown and inoperable under prevailing conditions.

His mandate, he reminded, was to make and keep the country solvent and protect it from its overseas adversaries and detractors, who were even now trying to reverse that openly elected brave policy and bring its tenets into line with the wishes of other nations and governments, contrary to the desires expressed by the American people.

Under the present climate – where terrorists from within, with overseas support, had become the daily scourge and fear of millions – a new formula of national representation in government was called for, emphasizing loyalty to and support for the elected national administration and its program. For this reason, in accordance with the Special Task Force's freshly-minted report, he was recommending the following provisions: First, that a pledge of allegiance to the Republic as it was now duly constituted should be administered to every eligible citizen as a condition of national civic participation.

Second, qualified citizens' civic participation would be facilitated by organizing them into local wards or cells of at least fifty-thousand members each, but no more than two-hundred thousand, within every large municipality or fitting combination of smaller municipalities nationwide.

The first fifty-thousand citizens to step forward in each state to register their allegiance, he said, should be given automatic membership respectively in the political cells or wards of their own communities, with all later applicants to be admitted by vote of the charter members. These cells would then exercise the obligation and privilege of nominating from among their rolls candidates for seats in the House and the Senate as such became open. In that way, he concluded, a number of key objectives could be achieved.

First, all of the people of the Congressional districts and states would be represented fairly in the national legislature. Second, those opposed to the interests and preferences of the self-declared majority would be sifted out. Third, civic virtue would be encouraged and rewarded. And fourth, the national direction would be set forth clearly, eliminating further confusion and interference by anti-majority elements, who, while they might mean well in some cases, did not serve the expressed interests of the people as a whole, but only of splinter groups, and, thus, pointlessly wasted the people's precious resources and time.

If the President had expected thunderous acceptance of this new, altered plan of representation from this particular educationally superior audience mainly from the nation's urban centers, he was surely disappointed. Because, instead of an ovation, his remarks were met with an almost chastening, less-than-polite smattering of applause, as if to say, "thanks, but no thanks."

On NNN and the other major C-TV news outlets later on that night, explanations for this apparent lack of enthusiasm so far as it was discernable fell into two categories. First, about half of the commentators claimed that the President's plan was a little on the abstract side and would understandably require more exposure and study on the part of the delegates to the Conference. The other half of commentators held to the view that the President's advance coordination and planning team, most obviously Ed Ross and Henry Morgen and their staffs, had dropped the ball and needed to schedule his major announcements before more receptive audiences in the future.

Instant polling of C-TV viewers at home who had watched the speech likewise yielded mixed results, with just under half favoring adoption of the new plan. The commentators predicted with virtual unanimity, though, that the President's supporters in Congress would find sufficient numbers of votes, in both houses, to pass the plan, if only narrowly, into law by the end of the year.

* * *

At 9:00 a.m. on Monday, August 17, the dispirited and daily more scrawny and pale cudgeled former Congressman from Vermont, Tom Topel, not yet actually arraigned after nearly four months in solitary without benefit of counsel as an "enemy combatant against the state," was being conducted back down the corridor in the federal lockup at Stafford, Arizona, between his twice-weekly shower and his drab isolation cell. On the way, he overheard something on a radio down an adjoining side corridor that piqued his interest. It was something in a news report about a federal marshal's posse in Kentucky finding a nearly incoherent and scantily dressed old man with an odd glow of youth about him, according to an incredulous eye-witness, but shown according to routine age-testing to be 104 years old.

The old codger had been, the report said, abandoned alongside a rural road after being held for part of a weekend by an invading "dissident paramilitary cell" that had fled the area an hour earlier down a local highway toward the community of Flippin, reportedly in a decrepit school bus. The identity of the old man, who was unusually well dressed by the workaday standards of area residents, was not immediately known.

Paramilitary force? Topel wondered. In Kentucky. *Could it be...?*

Chapter Twenty – Gaining Traction & The Homeland Dynamic

On Sunday evening, August 18, the three Army Special Forces agents parked nearby Senator Topel's darkened weekend residence on Kitty Pozer Drive in Fairfax saw a beige delivery van pull up in front. They watched alertly as its tall, elegant black driver lugged a microwave-oven-sized carton to the front door, rang the bell in vain, and departed seemingly without a care, leaving the parcel on the doorstep.

Approaching circumspectly with a handheld detection device, three of the men in plain clothes tested the carton and then rifled it open with a box-cutter, finding it to contain the weekly delivery of two dozen quart bottles of specially frozen *caipirinhas* packed in insulation from the tiny, immigrant-owned company styling itself by the devil-may-care name *Sacanagem.* Well-prepared for all contingencies, the men uncorked all of the evidence and dutifully taste-tested it to the last drop with the help of the two agents waiting in the van, parked in a vacant, wooded lot nearby.

Up until then, it had been a humdrum weekend for the men, spent mostly cooped up inside the vehicle, and so the unchallenged and uninspired officers jumped at a chance of detecting possibly tainted evidence. Each of the bottles so obligingly and thoroughly tested sported bright emerald green labels except, curiously, for one, which was printed a bright, ruby red. Aha! Why? Could there perhaps be some *reason* for this? Leave no stone unturned was their motto (and no bottle untested)!

As it turned out, the different colored label *was* significant. That bottle was found to contain a very long, narrow white, with a hint of tan-lavender, tape wrapped tightly around its cork. And on that flimsy strip of tape, in tiny, elegant letters, was printed a curious message almost too miniscule to read with the naked eye.

That the anonymous writer either knew whereof he/she spoke, about matters highly secretive, or was high on something that was definitely not *caipirinhas,* was the consensus of each and every agent.

Interestingly, the message was addressed to the owner of the house, Senator Topel. It stated as a fact that all or some of the other members of the Congressional Dissident Caucus were holed up, under assumed names, at the Hampton Inn of Gaffney near Cowpens, South Carolina, preparatory to being spirited in disguise out of the country, to either the Bahamas or the British Cayman Islands. And, it noted in passing that they would be taking the hand-held weapon, already notorious and known even to the five agents, with them for international sale to provide money for the cause of dissidence, or to possibly detonate to destroy American government property in some as-yet-to-be-determined location.

Even more chilling, the message claimed that the dissidents were somehow in possession of at least *two* such weapons, and were actively training at very least fifty-thousand shock troops in secret locations for deployment and recruitment purposes across the interior of the country.

Most mysteriously, the strange message was signed "Buzzy Wuzzy." This curious "cork-tape" as they called it, with its unverifiable message, was speedily taken the few miles to the operational headquarters at the Pentagon for appropriate analysis and follow-up.

* * *

On the morning of Monday, August 19, Sam Rickard, the high-stakes oil tycoon and Rassole associate with holdings in the Alberta Tar Sands and elsewhere valued altogether at up to $750 billion, was in Moscow. Driving a Hertz rental car from his hotel, he met quietly with Russian Deputy Foreign-Minister Vasily Gudin, an old partner from his Uzbekistan glory days, in the dark recesses of a club called Stogie's just beyond the eastern shadow of the Kremlin.

"What inducement is it going to take, Vasily?" he inquired almost at once after sitting down with Gudin at a table beneath an umbrella on the edge of a garish outdoor patio.

"It's not about inducement this time, my friend," the dark pyramid-shaped Russian answered in his fetching almost-falsetto. "It is seen as about an opportunity for history, for deciding who will decide, if you will. This vote of the powers at United Nations is seen as an end to many years and many factors and a great watershed in the world. And *we* shall decide for all of the world."

The men's borsch and vodka arrived on a single tray, and Sam Rickard looked quizzical over his old friend's unclear remark, seizing the opportunity to lose himself for just a moment in his fare. He countered by asking another question in the form of a declaration. "What you're hinting at, then, is a grand, lasting alliance between our two peoples."

The Russian smiled at the suggestion. "A good alliance, yes, my friend." And they drank to it deeply, the lanky old Okie gratified that the ties he and so many other pioneers had forged through three generations in the Eurasian heartland were about to bear lasting diplomatic fruit to the benefit of nations. And so they toasted it again, and then again, Rickard ending up not knowing exactly what it was he was toasting. And the friend he didn't know now pledged his friendship with a contented smile. What was it these people *wanted?* Years of certainty seemed to be fading into unknowns. But the borsch was as good as he remembered.

* * *

The headlines that day were split between places experiencing opposite climates. The midsection of the country was enduring a scorching August heat wave, with temperatures east of the Mississippi soaring in some places as high as 110° F for the first time in years, and the sky had remained rainless and cloudless in the western Great Lakes states for more than a month. Meanwhile, part of the lower Mississippi valley had suffered a swift and relentless deluge in recent days.

At the same time, steady progress on construction of the Antarctic penal and work colony, despite blizzards and whiteouts, was headlined in numerous papers and newscasts, the four work installations being declared almost ready to receive the initial third of their full complement of felons from the country's major lockups. Part of the idea, of course, had been to dash the extortionate demands of the owners of those private facilities by emptying them and closing them all down at once, and it was urged by many, in and out of government, that those facilities be acquired and converted into schools for younger delinquents.

Other prominent items in the papers (in a growing few cases, now instead called "broadsheets") included endless stories from the 2-Car Racing Association circuit, including a spate of shockingly bloody, wildly popular celebrity runs, from events mostly in the South and Ohio Valley locations.

The new broadsheets were all the more popular because they were of late free, and filled with contests, prizes, and highly successful ads that were aimed at *everyone,* not just fickle and vanishing niche readerships.

Practically no mention was made of the European powers' attempt to sanction America for alleged detrimental changes in its overall reform and retooled basis of government. Such lean stories as did appear specifically noted that the President had expressed confidence in Russia's expected solidarity and extremely meaningful expression of friendship in siding with its great North American investment partner. The unanimous consensus was that America's Russian friends were most likely to break the suspenseful deadlock at the UN in the Gossens administration's favor.

The President's recently-presented new plan for democratic representation in Congress was widely lauded in major articles for fostering greater national unity in favor of the feelings toward the changes manifested by the clear majority of the voters in the recent election. And, predictions on the part of several prominent officials of success in the pursuit and capture of the "domestic terrorists" from the irresponsible fringe press and the loony-left fringes of Congress were reported and approvingly made.

Meanwhile, for the moment, only the growing small minority of Americans who were now regularly tuning into foreign news sources learned that President Norba Hrzakshak of Aabania was still defying the recent American threat against his country to stop the contracted joint construction of a naval base and port with the Chinese, with the tacit encouragement of major European elected leaders. He had, in fact, hinted, according to some insistent translations, that one of the hand-held "Zap" prototypes might be on its way to bolster *his* army.

The revived domestic retro-readership of the papers also learned that the concerted petition drive in Gambia sponsored by the State Department in Washington, to force that country to hold a referendum on self-liquidation and removal of its population to America, had surpassed its goal of 80% of all adults signing. Meanwhile, there was just occasionally a favorable reference made in the foreign press to a growing smattering of "End the Take-over" chapters in the states, ranging from local debating societies to something more like militias, arising in locales across the vast, blighted interior of North America.

But the real shocker of the day exclusively from the international outlets was a summary of an article by a noted French intellectual named Jantal Rancid proclaiming something that should have been obvious, namely that with its unbalanced emphasis on "collectivized" investment capital, the newly-imposed American-style democracy resembled nothing so much as the repudiated brand of "democracy" of the old USSR. Specifically, he made reference to the new American public leadership's ironic donning of the mantle of democracy and frequent obfuscation by claiming to embody the positive values they were, according to him and others, abandoning.

Thereby, they displayed a more-than-passing family resemblance between the newly-triumphant American ideology and that detested and reputed Russian "Communist" one of earlier decades. To be sure, Rancid's assessment, electrifying in its effect in Europe, never made it into the American media, or American consciousness, except at the very fringes of the commercially disposed Internet. Some would claim that his observations were too intellectual for Americans. Americans just wanted to *live*, they said, thoughtlessly. Meanwhile, the Europeans were ironically still stigmatized as the hedonists.

* * *

After driving through the night in a refurbished school bus from Louisiana to Kentucky on Friday, August 15, the still-rain-sodden Greater Dissident Operations Corps (GDOC), twelve staunch soldiers strong, plus their commissioned field commander, the mysterious Colonel Carrington (taken to citing Lao-tzu along the way), jounced through the southern

Kentucky town of Tompkinsville at 5:30 in the morning. The journey had been delayed a bit while everyone's rain-soaked clothes had gone load after load through a dryer.

With them were members of Congress Carbola, Jellen, and Cullen of the House and Topel of the Senate, former Vice President Gole, and two journalists, Bootle and Auden, pregnant, but refusing to "bail on the making of history." The hand-held Laser-Zap was said to rest in the arms box at the back of the "troop-carrier," though no one seemed to know for sure.

They arrived at the rim of the escarpment above the abrupt earth-cleft that Audie and Web managed auspiciously to find again. Minutes later, in the dim beginnings of a windless, rainless day, they parked in an overgrown field nearby and set out down the brushy incline in a little column, clad in shades of Union blue.

But upon reaching the deep floor of the cove, they were confronted at once by a problem no one could have anticipated. A roving pack of fifteen or twenty hostile German shepherds and Dobermans set upon them, tearing at their heels and legs. Surely more than just fortuitously, one of their number, David Meldsgar, was a graduate in veterinary medicine and proved to be a more-than-gifted dog-whisperer. Dr. Meldsgar soon had the beasts harkening to his commands, and, indeed, kissing his hand. Otherwise, the descent and approach, still in the near-dark, went remarkably smoothly, and they very soon stood side by side in the open no more than a hundred feet behind the old house, which they found was raised just a bit on a sort of earthen platform precisely centered on the floor of the strange, topsy-turvy natural crater.

The battery-powered loudspeaker they had lugged along was presently mounted on its stand and Colonel Carrington stood and addressed it in his booming voice. "Attention inside! We have come to arrest you, Mr. Rassole! We have brought with us a hand-held Laser-Zap weapon, and we are prepared to vaporize your house and all of its occupants, within a radius of ten feet, exactly one minute from now, unless you are seen coming forth at a walk on the north side of the house!" He repeated the message word-for-word.

There was no chance anyone inside would not have heard unless they were all deaf. Colonial Carrington started to count down slowly, from "one minute," to "fifty seconds… forty seconds… thirty seconds… Twenty-five seconds… twenty seconds, nineteen, eighteen, seventeen… ten, nine, eight…" At two seconds, a shadow appeared in the dawn light moving around the northwest corner of the house. A little, lengthening shadow, and then a pale spot of the sun's radiance lit on clothing, and they could see it was a man, small and somewhat bent, who came walking forward. He was expressionless, as far as they could tell, haggard looking, and scantily but well-dressed (as though they'd caught him in the act). They surrounded him and escorted him into their midst, and Camilie Auden in a blue jumpsuit continued to record footage with a small video camera.

Colonel Carrington asked the wizened, but still impressively straw-haired old man with the soft, pinkish cheeks of a youth his name. He answered, without hesitating, in the scratchiest remnant of a voice any of them had ever heard, "Dub Jenks." Carrington asked him to repeat. "Dub Jenks," he said. Colonel Carrington and a small cadre of specially trained operatives interrogated "Dub Jenks" for more than an hour, but the old man didn't offer even a word of usable information. He appeared to be merely the old retired farmer he was claiming to be.

When pressed to identify the old man now in their custody, Web Bootle and Camilie Auden positively affirmed him the same odd old-young synthesized person. But, as to his actual identity, they still had no clue. Was he a Mr. Rassole? Was he somehow at the core of hijacking the system of government and trashing the country? *That* they could not say, knowing only what he had said and done to them personally while on the premises.

Getting nothing out of him in the way of words, his abductors set off, bearing him along, on the fairly arduous climb straight back up the high, very steep bank to the general ground level before a tip-off to authorities should herald disaster or danger.

On the instructions of the ex-Vice President, after having had their fill of their man's refusal to acknowledge who they thought he was, they set him free a mile back along the graded gravel road going into Flippin. Many of the team argued desperately to detain him, most especially Web and Camilie, who, while not knowing his precise identity, still knew above all that was their man – their tormenter and the country's. But Senator Topel explained that they *had to* follow VP Gole's in effect *orders* now to maintain cohesion and reason, and that he in fact was in agreement. "We have no real purpose, no rationale, for holding him," he said. "In fact, the authorities probably know where we are now. And we don't want the struggle to be *against us*, but *for* recovery of the Constitution! Regardless of our feelings, we must content ourselves with showing the entire world how pathetic and weak the man at the core of the destructive matrix really is… in fact, the *complete opposite* of the all-powerful, unreachable monster they had reason to have thought he is!"

After he explained it thus, all concurred. *Psychological warfare was the game!*

Back in their bus, they started peacefully on their way to refuge and reformulation.

Chapter Twenty-One – Battles, Resolutions & The Gole Protocols

One hell of a dog-whisperer though he might have been, David Meldsgar of Owatonna, it turned out, was not much of a driver. Aiming the faded burnt-orange bus down the road between Rockbridge and Tompkinsville, destination Tennessee, he near to flipped it on a patch of loose gravel on the right shoulder and eased it down onto its side in the ditch. No one was hurt. But, there they were.

Reggie Gee, the Sheriff of Monroe, got a call from a rural resident notifying him and met them right there to find out who, what, why, where, and when. To Web and Audie, it came as a surprise, or even a shock, to hear Colonel Carrington, flanked by the Senator, the members of Congress, and the former Vice President of the United States, graciously and honestly explain exactly who they were, what they were doing there, and why that was.

Per instructions, the deputy stayed back in the car and kept his mouth shut. "I heard the alert go out on the radio this mornin'," Sheriff Gee announced evenly, "and they didn't know where you boys was then." As soon as he'd said it, he saw Congresswoman Barbara Cullen peering out from behind, and the two nurses sitting behind her, and politely touched the brim of his hat.

"Well, what you think I'm gonna do with y'all?" he asked.

"Well," Abe Gole answered, "you know now, at least generally speaking, what our business is here, don't you?"

"Yeah, I know. I follow all of that, thet I can. And I can't say I disagree. This Gossens been a devil, they's no denyin' it. But, I got a call… and they are the law!"

Senator Roger Topel spoke. "Well, you got a winch? You could set us back up on our wheels. That at least would be a response!"

Sheriff Reggie Gee answered, "Yes, it would. Yes, it would!"

"Do you know of a Mr. Rassole hereabouts, Sheriff?" Senator Topel asked him.

"That's the name of a company, ain't it?" Sheriff Gee said. "Never heard of an individual called that hereabouts. No, I'm afraid I don't."

He and the deputy had the ropes and pulleys and chains, stashed in the boot of their vehicle, out in no time, and they had the old bus back up on the road in a few minutes, almost as good as before. He wiped his brow on his muscular arm. "I don't know what *Mon*roe County, Kentucky, has got to do with y'all's business," he said. "But when you get this dad-blamed country back on track, you won't forget me, will you?" He handed Senator Topel, his card, and turned to climb right back in his utility vehicle and leave.

But suddenly ex-Vice President Abe Gole got an idea. "Oh hey, Sheriff," he said. "I'm not so sure we shouldn't have you take us in, if you would." Everybody looked at the top man on the totem pole among them, stunned.

"What I'm thinking is, that way, we could send out our footage of the attempted interview, and if he wasn't who we think he was, picking an old man up for an hour and leaving him off shouldn't get us into too much trouble by itself. Our objective is to get a message out, and if we're arrested, that at least gives us a chance, instead of trying to steal away and avoid capture. And if we are right, which I think we are, I don't think the administration will want to take us in and put us on trial. They have enough trouble now, without a whole team of well-known public figures as defendants speaking against them in a sensation trial."

"What makes you think they wouldn't just put us away, under a 'Domestic Enemy Combatant' category, without trial, or for kidnapping as they did Congressman Tom, for conversion of government equipment?!" Camilie Auden said.

"Well, it's because I think much of the country would join with the world and rise up against this administration for sure if they push that play any farther, with more and more well-known public figures," Abe Gole said. "If they do that – and, I still wouldn't quite put it past that crew of rub-a-dubs – it would play right into our hands and forward our cause even more. Wouldn't we all be ready to make that sacrifice, if it came to that?"

All spoke as one. "I would."

Abe Gole seemed ebullient at all this attentiveness, seemingly thinking in ways only he knew. "Ok then, Sheriff, go ahead then, please! Take us in! But have your deputy drive the bus, please. I hope *he* can drive!" (He was grinning at Meldsgar.) "Then, inform them, off in Washington there, that you have us. That should give us enough time to convey our footage and the new revelations we have to news outlets internationally. And maybe in the meantime we could take a peek in your Hall of Records about the property down below there while we await pick-up or whatever by the big boys and girls. Also, if possible, could you arrange a DNA match on the hair sample we took? And see what we can find about a Mr. Rassole, or Mr. Dub Jenks, or whoever he may actually be…"

Sheriff Gee looked admiring and patriotic in his uniform. "Yes, we can do that for you, Mr. Vice President. Be glad to."

Web and Audie had the start of a story already written up at a moment's notice, so ready were they. And they were able to preview and format the interview footage they had made of their brief captive and send it off with their portable equipment to media contacts in Paris, Toronto, London, and New York, almost before they arrived at the holding facility in Tompkinsville.

Curious now himself, Sheriff Gee immediately sent one of his deputies to rush part of the blond hair sample in to the multi-county branch state lab half an hour away in Glasgow for matching against the national universal DNA catalog. The sheriff conducted the senator and two of the congresspersons to the appropriate shelves in the county records hall, next to the lockup, as in a thousand other small counties, to look up "Jenks" and/or "Rassole" and check the status and ownership of the property in the crater-like hollow they found to be known locally as "True's Hollow" or just "the ditch," an area considered private, off-limits, and little-known to and even disregarded by its neighbors.

In thirty-eight minutes, Deputy Neal (whether his first name or last, the dissidents never learned) called back from the Glasgow Lab with the surprising news that the DNA produced a designation of "PDQ," which Sheriff Gee said he had seen only once before, in the case of an ex-Drug Control Agency officer, and that he'd been told that it meant "Private Designation, Quashed," or "classified." It, at least, would take more looking into. The land in the bottom of the hollow, it turned out, was registered to an entity designated as "Rancho Homesteads." Again, more digging was called for.

All twenty-one persons who had turned themselves over to Sheriff Reggie Gee were duly fingerprinted and registered on preliminary charges of assault, trespass, and false citizen's arrest, and ensconced on benches and folding chairs in the two ten-by-fourteen county cells. Word was relayed to the federal authorities, and around noon, instructions came back to continue holding all "persons of question" pending further instructions from the Justice Department.

And so they sat, for two days, sleeping on cots in the cells, and consuming sandwiches and beverages. The latter were graciously provided by the brave little Southern Kentucky chapter of "End the Take-Over" in Bowling Green, to avoid burdening the county and creating a case in itself with their keep, after the Sheriff's Office had put through a couple of phone calls.

Finally, the Sheriff, after consulting with the County Attorney, determined that he was not authorized to keep anyone in custody for more than seventy-two hours without formal charges, and so, hearing nothing further, simply released all of them on their own recognizance at the end of that time.

And so they gassed up the bus, with Sheriff Gee's blessing, at the county pump (he said he would cover it himself), and went on their way.

It turned out that all they were able to provide the world press and alternative Internet sites were the photo images they had taken – spectacular enough, and which might trigger useful identifications – and their stories of their brush with the super-reclusive suspected elder Mr. Rassole. Together, these tokens constituted scant, though not meaningless, evidence to show that he was, in fact, the most powerful and, by some accounts, most evil and dangerous, if pathetic, human individual on the planet.

Advance arrangements were made to receive and shelter the lot of them at the compound of a wealthy and prominent friend of Senator Topel's hidden away in an area of loess hills east of St. Louis, and they headed off toward there to await further developments. Though likely under surveillance, they were surprisingly and gloriously free, at least for the moment, just as former Vice President Gole, now their leader by dint of his prestige, newfound grit, and surviving leadership skills, had predicted they would be.

* * *

Meanwhile, a research specialist at the Golden State Stem-Cell Age Erasure Clinic in Sacramento, California, a chunky and excitable though brilliant man named Dr. Erico Fauntleroy, was sitting on his sofa at home with his wife when part of the footage Web Bootle had shot of the suspected Joseph Rassole flashed across his C-TV screen.

Turning to his dear wife, the good doctor exclaimed, "Hey, Florence, look! That's Raef Hanmer, that odd old mountain man from the Appalachians who underwent all those experimental reversal treatments that I told you about last year, remember? That's him, all right! What do they say his name is? I thought they said Jenks! But that *has* to be Raef Hanmer! See the little star-shaped birthmark over his right eye? I'd know that face anywhere!" He thought about it for a minute, then added, "And, I'm going to the authorities and contribute what I know!"

That particular sequence on the news was followed by the reported intelligence that the "domestic dissident terrorists" were thought to be holed up in or heading toward a location somewhere in South Carolina, and reported possibly planning an attempted escape from the country to the Caribbean, with at least one captured experimental prototype hand-held Laser-Zap weapon, intending either criminal mischief against an American installation, or perhaps sale of the ultra-top-secret hardware to foreigners.

The report stated that personnel in all potential target areas, foreign and domestic, were placed on high alert.

* * *

Though uncertainty reigned in the interim, there was the feeling in the air that something was about to change. Still, most people's personal lives continued as normal and mundanely as one could reasonably expect. A few, however, as always, insisting upon kicking against the goads, on "pushing the envelope," as used to be said a generation or so ago. Darrell Fauta, for instance, a smart man, 52, of Long Lane, MO, was an adjunct instructor of biology at Central Downlands Area Community College (CDACC). He earned almost sub-zero pay and he'd had no chance for advancement in, lo, these 12 lowly years because he'd started out as a sub, interim, and visiting professor at various universities on gigs that somehow never managed to turn into tenure-track jobs, and because he couldn't continue to snag the one- and two-semester temp jobs on that treadmill regularly anymore. So, he was stuck, and settled for the status of an academic serf.

His leading passion, like that of a great many of his ilk, was the deceptively simple yearning for a fairer and more concrete world economy that continued to sweep the country in the form of Eduard Chelsington's little 90-page book, *Bright Pebbles*. The bright-colored little pebbles, found ubiquitously, could serve as a new sort of gold, silver, or copper, but were available to anyone who would but look for them. It was, Darrell Fauta allowed, a rather crude idea, but was it cruder than the current principle of the economy, based primarily on debt, which produced only misery for the many and fabulous wealth beyond any need or practical value for a very few of the world's citizens? *No!* Further, Darrell Fauta figured that it was the principle of necessary debt always owed by others to the obscenely privileged few, the mainspring of the whole system, which was in fact the worm in the golden apple of America. In other words, it was debt, the very cortex of everything, that had finally brought the whole friggin' thing – the entire faulty tower of the economic system, into the immensely lucrative receivership of *precisely those few*. There *had* to be a way of reconnecting common human need to the enormous wealth of the earth that was there for everyone, and not just to benefit manipulators! Was it the formula of *Bright Pebbles?* Darrell started a local *Bright Pebbles* enthusiasts' chapter, whose inaugural meeting drew more than 100 attendees.

Darrell had been congratulated by phone for starting the group – which also functioned as an affiliated *End the Takeover* group – by the lady provost of the CDACC campus in Rolla, and invited to stage an event showing an informational film on that campus the following semester. Which he did, though inexplicably, without technical support. Barely a week later, upon picking up a copy of the next semester's class schedule, he'd learned that his two courses had been quietly re-assigned to a new instructor he'd never heard of. The provost went on a medical leave of absence.

Then, the past Saturday a week ago, his tragically-depressed gorgeous Latin wife Reva, who reviled his involvement in dissidence, telling him, "You don't mess with powerful people," overheard him conversing on the phone with a female member of his group about her bringing brownies to an upcoming Monday night meeting. The woman had refused to come early and make coffee for the meeting on gender grounds. "Then I won't see you till just before 7:00 Monday?" Darrell Fauta asked. Reva was convinced that he was setting up a date for Monday night. Accordingly, she'd stunned him by walking in and telling him to go ahead with the encounter with the woman on Monday, because her suspicions were now confirmed. And then she walked out.

Darrell, hapless, finding that his telephone recording device battery was dead, frantically tried to contact the telecom company to obtain a recording of the call, but was told, mysteriously, that there was no record of such a module, or that such a call had ever been made.

Later the same evening, in as calm a state of mind as could be expected, though irritated because he couldn't seem to get the Brazilian music module pushed into the player on his dashboard, he had headed off toward the campus at Lebanon, some distance away, to teach the course he had managed to pick up to partially replace the two he had lost at Rolla.

It was pitch-dark when he turned off I-44 onto highway 32 in his beloved cinnamon Kia Cheju to make the straight-shot run over to the rural campus. Getting up to speed at 60 or 70 on the lonely road, he was suddenly confronted by a single, dazzling and blinding light coming straight at him *in his lane*. He didn't know what he was seeing – was it a car with just one piercing-bright headlight? A motorcycle? And why *in his lane?* He thought it was farther away than it was, having no parallax to judge by.

Seconds later, he hit the vehicle head-on with a great bang. He spun several times and then stopped. His airbags, he found to his amazement, were inflated and out, but there was no sense of pain or, oddly, even of being shook up – it was all like watching a movie. Forcing his loudly scraping, door open, he squeezed out and discovered that he could move and stand normally. Miracle of miracles! Perhaps even more miraculously, there were three people standing out there in the darkness, supremely lucky not to have been hit and killed.

The light, appearing as bright in the utter darkness as the lone bright torch of a locomotive, turned out to be the right headlight of a big pickup, parked backward and tilted upward on the rim of the shoulder, inches from his lane, shining to assist the driver of a disabled car, whose two occupants were searching for something on the ground. The left headlight, he found, was blocked by the other vehicle. It struck him as something marvelous that he hadn't hit any of the three standing out at the scene.

Paramedics and the sheriff materialized almost spontaneously. Darrell's beloved Kia was totaled, the whole passenger side of the body ripped away. Equally amazingly, he emerged unhurt, but still missed his class.

A day later, Darrell's insurance agent called with a surprise for him. It was another Kia, the same model but two years newer. As Darrell drove it away, he found it even had the same Brazilian music module he had very much wanted to hear in its player. But it too wouldn't engage, just like the other one.

Upon examining it, Darrell found that there was another module already locked inside the mechanism. To his shock and amazement, the module contained the lost recording of his phone conversation with the female dissident! *But how?* Reality is indeed really sometimes more than strange!

Shortly after, Darrell and Reva were again walking hand-in-hand on a beach somewhere, smiling big. And life went on.

And the lives of the bulk of those whose complaints were now traceable to their inability to just accept the deliberate destruction of their mythic country with its mythic rights by corporate intent flowed and ebbed daily to about the same churning and punishing extent as always before, as they always found something to cause them angst and to fuel their endless complaints. And their eyes were all on God (*who else?)* so as not to miss whatever divine deliverance might mercifully happen to come their way. For, some in this country would not be content to accept as benefit *the stars, the moon, and the sun* in not the order precisely prescribed.

* * *

First thing Monday morning, August 24, Russia's UN Ambassador Dmitri Vostok announced in a speech in Geneva the Kremlin's much-anticipated decision as to its Security Council vote on the resolution and proposed sanctions against America (or Aamerica) under the Gossens administration. To the amazement of many, Russia's decision was to support the resolution. Moscow opposed the existence of one overwhelming superpower in the world championing ungoverned collectivization of financing as the old Soviet system had championed unfettered collectivized labor. Amazingly, all money sifted into a few hands was pitted against the freedom of billions of human beings in Vostok's odd formulation. His government's conclusion was, more simply, that there must be a balance maintained, with no source of power left effectively ungoverned or unaccountable on earth, especially in the world's strongest single country.

Ambassador Vostok's historic speech was received by a slow-building thunderous ovation at the UN. This was qualified by guarded praise from his European counterparts and, in still more careful tones, from the Ambassador from Canada. The American ambassador, in response, and echoed later by the evening news anchors, bandied the words duplicity, lackeys, ingrates, reactionary, and injustice.

President Gossens issued a statement strongly emphasizing the words, "We will weather this," and "We make our decisions for ourselves," and "If they want to bring world trade to a violent halt over the issue of our sovereignty as a nation, then we must simply tighten our belts."

"The Russians," the New York *Times* editorial writers noted in striking accord, "have never gotten over their humiliation of more than four decades ago from President Reagan's use of *realpolitik* to bring down their evil empire." The confrontation had been joined. The world braced for the colossal economic implosion it portended, if the sanctions were in fact imposed.

(Meanwhile, a companion binding resolution offered by France and Germany, which failed by a single vote – *Russia's* – would have required that any country that invaded or bombed another, without any exceptions, must give over its top leader for execution within sixty days. The penalty for refusal to comply was, again, an absolute trade embargo by all other members, violations punishable likewise by death and trade shunning, pending compliance.)

Unfortunately, what could not safely be announced in the current climate in America, was that the shockingly anti-war "Euro Protocol," as it was being both emphatically condemned and touted, should in reality have been hailed as the "*Gole Protocol,*" being, like its companion incisive measure, the brainchild of none other than the former Vice President, who had sold it to the leaders of three European powers and members of the G-9 at a secret meeting convened in Istanbul in early August. But the idea – which would have prevented the Iraq and probably earlier wars had it existed then – would come up again, as an absolute certainty. And the only reason the Russians had nixed it was, according to them, that the proposal had included no provision for dealing with genetic-specific, electronic, or resource-withholding means– that is, invasions without applied force.

* * *

So, then, did old Rassole, the most powerful and baddest man in the world, take the verdict of the European and Slavic "*wusses*" and their spawn's insolence lying down? *You bet he didn't!* Even though he had been in a reflective frame of mind of late, beginning to contemplate his own mortality for the first time ever, including how he would break the word about the family's secret Marrano roots to his son, and how to bequeath him, when it was time, the operative connection to his now-Middle Eastern source of intel and strategic partnership, which had secretly turned him into such a glorious winner over the years.

Still, he wasn't feeling at all serene about the events involving the vile Russians and the cretin president Gossens' contemptible weakness. To the contrary, within days, he personally, according to his betrayer Buzzy Wuzzy, set to work utterly determined to wreak exactly the sort of vengeance he had been itching to deliver for any number of months against the perceived enemies of the order he had striven so mightily for the past nigh on 90 years to establish, ever since fraudulently enlisting to fight the Krauts at 13 back in '44. In so doing, he took upon his own broad shoulders the mantle of vengeance for all of his more pathetic, wussy tycoon compatriots, who had not among them the slightest shred of a notion nor least expectation of either accountability or restraint or selflessness. They, he reflected, were *as bad as he was*, but lacking in the element of grit.

Confounded even more than piqued, he struck quickly and hard. He ordered thirty-five thousand units of fancy grade chocolate orange-gel candy from the confection plant managed by a lifetime family associate in Richmond delivered to his depot a few miles away in Flippin a.s.a.p. Then, he personally spent three intense days injecting each and every piece of the delectable confection, his favorite, with *botulism* culture from the two fifty-five gallon drums of rancid hog guts and swill retained from the last few years' butchering. As he worked like the demon-possessed old tycoon he was, a living, breathing caricature of himself, his personal aide, Rad Davis, packaged and addressed every single unit with a specially printed, signed note, as a "complimentary sample" from *Al-Venery Candy Company, Box 234, Dearborn, Michigan.*

Rad Davis, a bachelor living in nearby Akersville, was instructed carefully to load all of the small cartons on his truck, cover them with a tarp, and drive them up to Michigan to mail in bulk before the weekend. But, in the meantime, the poor hireling encountered *glitches* with both his current woman live-in and his truck. On Thursday at dawn, his current honey of three weeks, a certain Sally Dagget, suddenly moved out, scattering kitty litter and laundry soap through a succession of rooms leading out beyond the front porch door. Irked, Rad jammed his truck's transmission trying to get out himself, a full two hours behind schedule, to start for Michigan.

By four in the afternoon when he'd gotten it pieced back together, the gearshift was still loose and the forecast was for heavy rain. To make a long story short, he mailed the whole load it in Flippin[BJH3].

By the end of the second day, reports of emergency hospitalizations and excruciating deaths from *botulism* traced to the candy samples in the boxes began to appear and proliferate, coming eventually from forty-nine states and eight foreign countries.

The name of the fictitious candy company and its hypothesized Arabic derivation filled the nightly news reports. The Flippin, Kentucky, location had become famous, but was, on orders, never directly tied explicitly in the media with Mr. Rassole, from the earlier instance of the mysterious kidnapping and abandonment of the poor, probably confused old man found wandering on the road. The word came down to all of the national news affiliates not to mention either *Flippin* or *Kentucky* as pertaining to the postmarks of the unknown number of deliveries, leading eventually to at least twenty thousand deaths, though the final total was never announced. So, the evidence being linked neither legally nor information-wise, the public's attention refocused quickly and more happily elsewhere, and with fewer than normal viewer protests.

Secondly, Mr. J. Rassole, The Elder, picked up the phone in the midst of the initial reports of the dying and ordered every penny of the family's and the Rassole Corporation's $727.3 billions of investment in U.S.-based enterprise liquidated *immediately* and re-applied to dramatically expand Mr. R's personal already-active "Winged Duck Fund", for direct investment in military sectors of the economy of China.

This sudden maneuver started a battle-royal for its reversal and commitment of the old man to an asylum on the part of his two known sons, in Virginia and Texas. Reports of this royal feud, not his little-investigated onslaught by post, dominated the media after the first couple of days, by fifty mentions to one.

Old Rassole's motivation, as he wrote it down on his memo pad, was "retribution, justice to the cattle of the world and their herders," all of them out of control. "We'll just see how they like *that!*" he whispered, donning his knit-booty slippers.

And, almost simultaneously, the disgruntled old patriarch, inspired by a bit of intel he'd received from his Middle Eastern sources, got on the phone and, using a special-access number no one else knew and that he'd never before activated, wheedled and begged the family-installed Head of the Joint Chiefs of Staff, General David Morrow, to shoot down as an invading aircraft a helicopter which was very shortly expected to be approaching the White House by way of New York, carrying a number of meddling European heads of state. General Morrow, not quite sure what he might be referring to, cut him off with a brilliant, time-buying reply: "I'll think about it."

* * *

At the emergency meeting of his inner cabinet at the White House the day the outcome at the UN was announced, the President went volcanic.

"We put into effect what we believed in and what we on our side have been insisting on and fighting to bring about for *decades* – the reasonable recognition that progress cannot be made in this world while tying the hands of our financiers and thwarting the free expression of creative investment! And now, in response to our long-deserved victory, we reap instead this reactionary, anti-progress, whirlwind!

"Our own people here, most of them, didn't have too much trouble with our taking the stumbling blocks out of the way of creative investment capital, and a handful of *dissidents* who are bitter because they lost and are losers, and didn't even so much as speak out against us when we were posing the question, *now* find a voice and strong allies. Not here, but *overseas*, for Christ's sake, doing nothing but rendering aid and comfort to our most bitter and jealous enemies on this earth! First, we need to jail their asses – *all* of them! *Then we declare war!*"

The others in the room looked at him blankly.

Edward Lambent, The Company's liaison, parried back. "Mr. President, surely you don't want to risk revealing the identity of your secret brain-trust generally, do you? These rogue, dissident politicians, who have learned far more than they should have, must be handled very carefully in that regard, you know."

"Mr. President," Herschel Henry, the President's chief domestic advisor, cut in. "As I have warned you, I don't think the public will stand for any more criminalization at all of opponents who are familiar public figures… though I agree, a basic agreement, even if forced, on the rules on this side of the Atlantic would be better to deflect foreign criticism. But, I just think you'd be splitting the public more – more than we can bear."

Vice President Ben Weck interrupted with a sigh as big as Montana. "I don't think we will really have the domestic support now… We weren't going to even need it much longer."

Theodore Kimon, the administration's chief strategist and chief negotiator of the historic December, 2032, Final Operating Agreement with The Company spoke up. "Not entirely, we won't have it, Mr. President, for sure. We'll be looking at an estimated loss of $3.5 trillion a year now in international trade, or one-third of the total value of output of the economy, with practically no imports available. I have a letter here I received an hour ago from Thomas Flannigan, the current President of the National Association of Corporate CEOs under The Company.

"Here's what he says: 'President Gossens and members of the Administration – Representing a unanimous consensus of myself and my fellow Chief Executive Officers, we wish to remind you, especially today, that we have never asked for nor supported the abolition of the Constitution's checks and balances, or the enthronement of unchecked and completely unregulated corporate power in this country. While we strive to win, and have always done so, against foreign competition and among ourselves, we have never wanted the people's voice to be blunted, nor the aspirations of all citizens to be subservient or treated as subaltern to ours. On the contrary, we yearn to represent once again in the mind of the world and of our countrymen – and women – the voice of fairness and fair competition and the advancement of the rights of all to make an honest living, contributing their talents beneficially for all.

"'Therefore, viewing with alarm the extreme dangers the schemes of extreme ideologues have brought us to, we respectfully request, unanimously, that the Constitution of the United States be restored to its former place of honor and to full operation again in our national life, with any problems internal to it that may perhaps have prevented it from being truly the whole people's instrument of expression repaired. If it is deemed by Congress that a new presidential election or others must be held to achieve that end, then we resolve to fully support such a measure. Sincerely and hopefully yours, Thomas Flannigan, CEO, Weyerhauser Brands and President of the Association.'"

President Gossens, after taking in all of this in silence, slammed his right fist down on his desk with a splintering thud. "Ingrate bastards!" he shouted, then took stock of his obviously-broken and throbbing hand. Was there no recourse left?

Even if he sensed he might be wrong, trillions and a wrecked country were beyond forgiving, at least by man.

Chapter Twenty-Two – Denouement

The long-suffering Special Forces agents posted to watch Senator Topel's weekend home in Fairfax were cheered on Monday night to see the familiar beige van pull up, with the stately black driver at the wheel, even though it arrived a bit late. They watched eagerly as the dapper fellow left the much-anticipated carton containing the usual frozen *caipirinhas*, immaculately packaged, on the Senator's doorstep. And they pounced split seconds after he left, and, on inspection, found the anticipated cork-tape with the signature "Buzzy Wuzzy" wrapped inside the lone red-labeled bottle.

The message, in the usual tiny black *Helvetica*, flawless under a bit of magnification, stated that the mysterious feeble old man wandering along the roadway in Kentucky, left off by the notorious gang of militants, as reported world-wide, was in fact "Mr. Rassole, the Elder," the prodigiously-wealthy, low-profile tycoon, still deceptively cunning, who, with his son, likewise living in seclusion in Petersburg, Virginia, were the "de facto sovereigns of this country." Which, of course, was news to the Special Forces stakeout unit.

And Mr. Rassole, the de facto decider-in-chief, the note said, had seemed a bit scrambled since being returned home, and appeared to have lost some of his swagger. Since then, the message reported, he had spoken of little else but enhanced security – barbed-wire and electric fields redundantly ringing his compound, of re-training his unaccountably overly-friendly dogs to tear any intruders limb-from-limb, even of 24/7 surveillance by helicopter.

It had become a bit harder now to decipher what he was saying, as his speech was more agitated. But such seemed to be the gist. His son was consumed with worry and kept telling him they already had enough wealth and income and didn't need to nail down absolute control of everything to protect what they had, or to garner increasingly more.

None of which, of course, was the concern or province of the Special Forces agents. Their assignment was to deal with and pass along to their supervisors any evidence. And that, particularly on this occasion, they cheerfully did.

They swallowed the delicious *caipirinhas* quickly, passing around each and every long-necked bottle, the anticipated arrival of the weekly carton at least breaking the monotony of watching an empty house. And the details, a mere puzzling detail, were someone else's problem.

*   *   *

President Gossens sat in his private quarters in the White House late that Monday night with his black schnauzer Chester and a stashed bottle of Southern Comfort. Sarah Lureen was back up Turkey Creek again with the two sets of twins. "Old Fella," he soothed, and Chester sympathized and nuzzled his thigh and bandaged, wounded (martyred?) hand. "Fella, I was truly born a nullity, a nothing, and then I learned as a child about business and how important it was," he explained to his best faithful friend. "And so, I pushed everything else aside back home, runnin' our clothing store, and then together with Sarah Lureen, and in the talk radio I did from back there in south Georgia, and afterward, I went on to the big network, talkin' and listnin' and thinkin' about all that I heard and that was said.

"That the people who made and circulated the money was the pure lifeblood of just about everything, and how God's people was quite obviously favored, if you looked, and they always all lived on our side of the tracks. While down the other way, there was just the shiftless and no-accounts – they didn't have no account in my store, for shore! And, I got noticed and talked about more and more from all the radio and appearances. When you're 6'10" and can talk a south Georgia streak besides and please sarten people with what you keep on a-sayin', well, you *do* git noticed! And they let me know eggzacly what it was they *really* liked to hear. And then they set me in politics, and that opened up sarten doors for me real wide.

"And I jist walked right through and became an important Suthun Senator because of my reliable fiscal flosophy, one of the biggest, positively a hee-ro to some of our younger folks in the persuasion, and to some of the older!

"Then, a way sart of presented itself, when I was runnin' fer President, to pull this whole big country out of its deep debt pickle, and so I jist did it and become a hero for that, too, to just about *everybody*. That just turned ev'rything around. Course, I understood what the big money folks was wantin', and was entitled to, because I'd heard it all my life, and I was priv'leged to get just about all the people to agree and at last give it to 'em, for getting us out of that deep hole of debt.

"That was my greatest achievement, talking that through. Everybody seemed to think it was jist flat-out brilliant, and couldn't see a thing wrong with it! And, now, all of a sudden, look! Where are they all when I'm really needin' their support, the people and the moneyed, and all? Jist look what I've laid on the line for them! A little ripple abroad, some unkindly words from those that hate us over there and want what we got here, and they all jist abandon me!

"Well, Chester, my old friend, I sartenly know you won't abandon me, no sir, Chester boy, not for nothin'! You know, my parents same as abandoned me when I was little, and sometimes I feel like my own family's abandoned me now, I have to tell you, even though I know you like them, too, I have to say it. And, now, it seems like the whole dad blamed world's abandoned me. What in God's acre am I going to do, Chester? *What?"*

And the President sat there, eyes fixed on his bandaged hand, a tear of rage forming. And he called up another order of Sprite and Southern on his inner-calm.

* * *

Near morning, in the quiet awaiting the dawn, socked by another bout of nausea and all-night insomnia, the President heard a rustling sound in the hall and got up and eased open the door. There, framed by a barely-perceptible glow, he found, to his total amazement, a lithe black-shadow figure he knew unmistakably by a familiar dry scent wafting across the decades as Marge ("Barge-Commerce") Smith.

She slipped past him in the near-total dark and, when he sought refuge on the chair by the bureau, she approached him breathily and tearfully buried her supple belly in his groggy face, subtly drawing apart the folds of clothing just so that her warm flesh smothered him.

Pushing him off-guard, she held forth in a shrieking, unreasoning voice, "*You hurt me, Petey!* You left me and then you undid my success when I was trying to help you! *O-o-o-o-o!* And you, you ignored me and betrayed me! *W-a-a-a-a!"* She smote him a rain of sharp blows to the eyes, temple, and nose, and he was afraid she would leave welts. Stepping up her attack, she hitched up her skirts and straddled his hapless mouth and nose and sobbed loud and long.

"*Marge!"* he at last implored, catching his breath, in a desperate bellow exploding from somewhere deep down. *"What possesses you? And how in the hell did you get in here, girl? How did you? Oh, Marge, Marge! What is there I can do now?*" Wrapped in her skirts, he could barely even open his mouth.

She dismounted, as it were, her scent and warmth covering him like dew.

And then, slowly, painfully, he awakened fully from furtive sleep and dreaming, the first rays of sun coming as brilliant shafts across the rumpled bed sheets behind. "Marge! Marge! We all make decisions, sometimes even… we make… mistakes! *Mistakes even we make sometimes!"* He started to feel himself in command again, one scratched eyebrow he felt oozing a small trickle of blood. "You know how it was then, how it went – you, after all, told the *world* how my marriage came about! Was it the right thing for me to do? I don't know. But right now, we've got to get you out of here. You know how it would look, I'm sure!"

She looked at him with another, different look, of infinite sympathy, reminding him of years now long past. And then, her face abruptly transfused into a huge, watermelon-eating grin, and she tilted her head to one side. "*That's your problem, babe!*" she spat out loud enough to rattle the windows, and almost gave him a stroke. Then she laughed, still undeterred, as loud as if rum-soaked for real, though he noted no aroma of that.

He scurried down the hall and was gone for six seconds and returned with an apron and maid's hat, which, though they were four sizes too big, he made her put on. Oddly, it gave them one shared laugh at least, as she preened in the floppy outfit in front of the mirror next to the window. Then, promising he would call when he could in order to get rid of her, he shooed her straight through the open door, hearing her dash back down the spiraling stairs, back out toward Foggy Bottom.

Sad, sad Marge B-C, he thought, flummoxed by her again. She was like the inescapable integument of the Petey "Figaro" A. Gossens, it seemed, that he had hoped so very much to leave behind: cunning and ambitious, she and he, forever mired down in south Georgia marl and muck. He could no more shake her and the past that she knew he went clad in than he could shed his skin or the excess of his height. She had, thus, but accompanied him in his inevitable descent after rising far too high with her droll, exasperating tricks. He sensed ruefully now that he could no longer escape either her or his baser self. The homely cover he had worn was blown!

* * *

But, still, Pete Gossens, the piney woods wonder, wasn't completely finished as yet. Virtually sleepless for days, running in his mind like a scavenger, but steely-eyed for all that, he abruptly broke into programming on all licensed C-TV networks the next night, August 25, at 8:37, and read the following brief statement from the Oval Office in the White House:

"My fellow Americans, an impasse, as you know, has been reached, and our independence as a nation is severely vexed by foreign nationals who are jealous and hate us for our freedom and our way of life.

"I have it on good authority that the UN is about to mount an invasion by helicopter within the next two days – whether of the type of black helicopters so long spoken of, I'm not at liberty now to deny or affirm. But, they are, to my understanding, fixin' to penetrate our airspace, and to land in the heart of our nation's capital with the intent of enforcing their will on us all. Now is not the time for complacence.

"Accordingly, I your President am here to inform you that we have set a referendum by computer for tomorrow – *a Tuesday* – night, to register the emphatic rejection by the American public of this hostile takeover by foreigners and usurpation of our sovereignty. The details will be broadcast and telecast throughout the day tomorrow, and the web site to vote tomorrow, for all American citizens, beginning at 5:00 p.m., Eastern time, will be: www.STOPEUROS.com.

"Our plans, if you will stand with us now in this, will be as follows: First, we will, by the end of next week, send out blank checks to all American households and tax-payers listed on the Internal Revenue tax rolls. If you don't get one, you can let us know. You can fill in whatever amount you may need on the check to discharge your current personal bills and debts, and we will selectively investigate afterward to make sure you do not go beyond that guideline in determining the amount of your allocation. I got the entire country out of debt and purring along, and I will now do the same for you!

"In the aftermath of that, our unrivaled military power will provide sufficient backing – the dollar requires no securing, anyway, and the Amero will save us if necessary – for the amount of money that is needed to be printed at our government printing offices. And, believe me – there is *no* limit!

"Second, I'm calling on Congress to declare war against the meddling countries. Because, as we know, and they know it deep down, too, is that they can't stand up against us.

"And third, a full disclosure – *a full breach* – will be made over the next month of the extent and pattern long-rumored, of U.S. government involvement in twenty-first century PSYOPS, including the key to our most-recent third of a century of what we call glow-ball hist'ry, what *really* went down back on 9/11/01. Because, it's been long enough now, and the people are entitled to know. This is a concession to our long-suffering military forces. And, not to worry. Security and civilian personnel still living who may have been involved will be protected by a full blanket amnesty.

"And so, we ask you all for your continued support, to defuse the rationale for invasion and, by a show of solidarity to confront America's problems, whatever they may be. And, as Americans, *get it called off!*

"Again, details will be broadcast all day tomorrow, *Tuesday*, and the site to vote tomorrow night, at 5:00 p.m. Eastern, will be: www.STOPEUROS.com. Now, don't miss out on the benefits, hear? I'm calling for a full, clear supporting statement from the American people tomorrow night! Don't you all forget!

"Good night, my fellow citizens. Until *tomorrow!* God bless America!"

Though an unprecedented number watched and searched the next day, wanting to vote, just as corporations had been eager to serve and support their spawn before, the instructions did not appear, and the web site did not appear.

* * *

The following morning, Wednesday, August 26, a guest editorial appeared in the New York *Times*, Washington *Post*, and 154 other metropolitan newspapers around the country, penned jointly by Arlen J. Coyle, the Chancellor of Calvin and Mary Stoops Colleges, and Dr. James Etherington, Chairman of the newly-amalgamated Department of Meteorology and Politics at that same much-honored institution. In it, the authors blasted Russian UN Ambassador Dmitri Vostok, accusing him of essentially regenerating single-handedly the victoriously-vanquished Cold War, and outrageously re-instigating the long-dormant *communist* world view with his infamous speech at the UN and attempt to escort from office, on the basis of a pretended disgrace, God's Anointed, the first resolute and correct President in a long time, and "our second" (as they stated it) "*Lordly* witness presaging the upcoming Millennium, from the office of American President."

They charged that those Americans who prayed not for him, but for his *ouster*, on the pretense that he was destroying the outmoded *dead letter* that was the U.S. Constitution, were the *lackeys* of communist atheism and traitors to the advanced, sacred destiny of this country beyond its long-term nightmare of slavery to the majority.

"*...The most impressive, serious figure in a generation, now on the verge of being sacrificed, by American complicity with jackal foreign duplicity,*" the two authors from Calvin College pronounced it. They suggested that the world was, thus, instrumental in kindling its own funeral pyre, and that the God of the just would not be so mocked without smiting the earth with the consuming fire of His anger, that would assuredly devour the whole world, wicked and righteous alike, unless all should repent in the fleeting time left and come to the defense of the abominably sacrificed president – "*sacrificed to the lust of the unjust.*"

That morning around 10:30, most of the members of the Travel Team were sitting around their bunker waiting for their daily assignments to come in on the screen, which for some reason weren't showing up that day. Precisely at 10:36, the jerry-rigged buzzer that served as their doorbell, seldom used, sounded loud and rude. Adonis Wong got up to open the door and jerked it open, and there – *surprise!* – stood Webster "Wide-Bottom"

Bootle with a pregnant, tanned and smiling Camilie Auden on his arm, leaning, and over-towering him just a bit, in that well-remembered stance.

"Can we come in?" the two asked in perfect unison.

Fuba "Tex," in the habit as few were of believing in ghosts, stared and started turning ashen.

"We've got your story, enough live material for everybody for months!" Audie proclaimed. "All ready to write! And plenty more to research for as long as any of us want to! Believe me, this is all going to be a very big story for as long as any of us shall live!"

"Don't worry," Web tried to reassure them, "I don't think they'll come after us now." And I suspect we're all going to be needing *real* stories, on our own again. I think you'll be seeing that shortly!"

Everyone just stared, seemingly dazzled by the incoming light.

* * *

That afternoon and evening, there came the first-ever scheduled and expected full run across the Atlantic from La Havre to New York in six hours of the new no-fuel oceanic super-hydrofoil craft invented and owned by the European firm Transoceanic, a spin-off enterprise from Royal Dutch Shell. A huge, forward-looking speed-craft, with capacity for up to four hundred passengers, it ran on special cells from hydrogen drawn from the sea. It sped along above, deceptively silent and smooth.

Aboard, with neither formal announcement nor fanfare, were the Prime-Ministers of England (explicitly representing the now-independent Scotland for this occasion), France, Italy, Germany, and Japan. They all stood together along the rail, the wind of their magic progress whooshing overhead. Arriving in New York harbor at 4:00 local time, this quintet was whisked by waiting copter to Washington, where, accorded special clearance, they landed and disembarked on the White House lawn. News crews, alerted to intercept, showed up in droves immediately and reporters beamed their arrival live on national and world C-TV.

The arrivees were quickly escorted en masse inside the White House itself through the front door, and emerged a moment later, in company with the waiting, gangling, towering and blank-faced President, whom the English Prime Minister and the French seemed to be conducting along between them as though he were on rollers. The President's head was clearly bowed, a detail lost on no one who saw it, and no one seemed to be saying much of anything.

Off in some bushes a ways back and to the right of the White House, the sharpshooter, now in plain clothes, who had twice stalked the President from the crowd at events in North Carolina, had inexplicably somehow managed to get admitted inside the gate and into cover and now drew a bead on Mr. Gossens. A single apparent rifle shot rang out, distinct in replay footage, but muffled by a rising wind, which, however, somehow, inexplicably, seemed to miss its target, appearing in clear footage viewed a couple of times later to break out an East Wing window, although White House personnel denied it. (Wouldn't they have had bulletproof glass there, in any case? So, was it a light effect? *Endless questions!*) And then, the sharpshooter as inexplicably vanished. And, as crazy as it sounded, some viewers in parts of the Northeast swore later they saw the President go down on the live telecast. The mainstream news media reported the incident itself only once, never reporting *that* anomaly, to be sure. (So very much, some were saying who read their history, like the little-known attempt long ago on FDR).

Then, together, unruffled and seemingly unawares, the principals, including the President with small entourage were seen to disappear into a waiting sky-blue stretch utility vehicle that had pulled up, and the NNN commentator explained that there had been an announcement, not yet officially released, that the President was placing himself in his counterparts' custody and had agreed to comply with their wishes, ending the global standoff.

Off in their exile of some days in the middle of the country, the "Dissident Army," minus only Audie and Web, viewed the scene live all together in their benefactor's compound, and all raised their glasses in a triumphant and rousing great, heartfelt cheer.

Abe Gole was there among them, who, though he didn't get to be President, nevertheless exulted in secret in having led the way in bequeathing mankind a benefit so colossal that his partisan enemies would never in a hundred years be sufficiently large in spirit to credit or even fathom.

It wasn't quite *caipirinhas* they were drinking now. And yet, it was the bona fide beginning of a completely unprecedented national jubilee that came totally unexpected, celebrating anew a unique and mighty nation of nations and treasure of the world that truly knew no bounds.

And the country got it.

The End

TROUBLESOME COUNTRY

by James Hufferd — coming soon from Progressive Press

How well do we do at living up to our own values that we claim and market to the world? Addressing that question, *Troublesome Country* is a complete, nuanced, generation-by-generation history of the United States, from Columbus to Washington to 9/11 and beyond, held up to the light of our shared national creed. *Troublesome Country* measures our actions and tendencies against the values we believe make America a special nation.

The five creedal tenets listed below are propositions from our founding era, a living idea base that has united and defined our nation from its beginnings. How we apply them is documented by our history, revealing a distressing ongoing failure to realize our promise as a nation.

Examples examined include our abject failure to apply our laws uniformly for different economic and ethnic groups. Likewise evident is our governments' tendency to act separately from the public will in virtually every circumstance, flaunting the principle of democracy. A third crucial shortfall that's difficult to understand is the failure of Congress — at the expense of our independence and financial viability — to obey the Constitutional mandate (Article I, Section 8) for the government, not a private agency, to issue and substantiate our currency. Further glaring violations of our defining civic belief system are explained and documented.

This book is a measuring-stick that indicates the only likely cure for our now-conspicuous national failure to compete and thrive is for our citizens to deliberately live up to our magnificent common creed themselves, while holding to strict account our public servants and institutions to do the same.

The tenets of America's creed described and employed in the book are:

1) The people should control the government.

2) Freedom from government control.

3) All men (all people) are created equal: laws must be applied equally.

4) Liberty and Justice for all. (The mandate of due process.)

5) Personal and national independence. (Americans, richly advantaged by nature, should live largely independently.)

I.e., 1) Democracy, 2) Freedom, 3) Equality, 4) Justice, 5) Independence.

CPSIA information can be obtained at www.ICGtesting.com
Printed in the USA
LVOW051135150513

333884LV00002B/443/P

9 781615 778034